CONF
O
PROFESSIONAL
CONSPIRACY
THEORIST

CW01511257

Will Camden

A Note on the Nature of this Work:

This is a work of fiction. The title is a provocation. The events and characters portrayed within are the products of the author's imagination, together with various stories and anecdotes once told to him by unnamed persons. Any resemblance to actual events, locales, secret societies, government agencies, or persons, living, dead, or otherwise, is either entirely coincidental or deeply, profoundly questionable. Promise.

This particular story, unlike many of the narratives it describes, is protected by international copyright law, which, unlike a good conspiracy theory, is demonstrably real. Please respect it.

Published by Will Camden
www.willcamden.co.uk
hello@willcamden.co.uk

Cover Design by Ellie

ISBN: 978-1-0369-3432-3

First edition 2025.

*For Emma, who started this with me
all those years ago. How exciting!*

One never states the truth plainly. That is a vulgar and ineffective approach. One couches it in allegory, in myth. You give the public a grand story, and you allow the truth to be the quiet, hidden skeleton upon which that story is built.

A. Harrington

Contents

Part 3

The Return Home

Sometime in The Future

Part 1

The Ordinary World

Chapter One

An Introduction to Magic

THE ROOF OF WATERLOO International was a thing of beauty. This was back in '98, when the station was still a grand gateway to the continent, not just another stop on the line. It was a magnificent, sweeping curve of glass and steel that felt less like a place to catch a train and more like a proper, shiny, can-do vision of the future. This was the tail end of the Cool Britannia era. Tony Blair was the fresh-faced Prime Minister in Number 10, the whole country was arguing about who was better—Blur or Oasis—and there was a general, vague feeling that Britain was, for the first time in a long time, actually quite cool. It was a time when the nation was still coasting on a Britpop-fuelled wave of self-satisfaction, before the cynicism and the hangover had fully set back in. That roof was the architectural embodiment of it: sleek, modern, and rather pleased with itself.

I stood there for a moment, enjoying the splendour with the unique, smug satisfaction that comes from knowing you're travelling on the company's tab. A few complimentary First Class Eurostar tickets had been left rattling around the office from a launch campaign, and it seemed a waste not to use one. A nice little perk of the job.

I settled into a seat that was plusher than the sofa in my first flat—and far more comfortable—and I watched the grubby, unglamorous backside of South London slide away. The train hummed, a low, expensive sound, as it prepared to dive under the Channel. I was on my way to Stockholm for a two-day conference on the future—or more accurately, on how to sell the future to people without their written consent. It was the internet. Our shiny, exciting new toy.

The free croissants and corporate goodie bag were all well and good, and the conference itself sounded more interesting than these things usually are. But the main event, for me at least, was going to be seeing Jez again. It had been far too long, and it felt like a lifetime since we were just two young chancers, learning the ropes and having way too much fun for a paid job.

Thinking about Jez always took me back to the beginning. To our work placement at one of London's great temples of PR, a place where truth was treated like stage lighting—something you used selectively to highlight the best features and cast the unflattering parts into shadow. The office itself hummed with the low-grade anxiety of deadlines and the electric stink of hot computer monitors. I'd got my spot through a university scheme that promised 'real-world experience'. Jez got his because his dad was a member of the same gentlemen's club as the CEO.

He was effortless public-school polish; I was state school grit. He had the kind of floppy blond hair and casual charm that made you want to both trust him implicitly and count your fingers after you'd shaken his hand. He wore his privilege as lightly as his expensive cologne, while I wore my ambition like a new pair of shoes that hadn't been broken in yet. We were from different worlds. We hit it off instantly.

We were the office juniors, the dogsbodies. Our main job, besides learning to operate a fax machine that shrieked like a pterodactyl with a sore throat, was to 'build relationships' with the hacks on Fleet Street. This meant two lunchtimes a week were spent in some nicotine-stained pub just off the Strand, plying world-weary, cynical journalists with warm pints, and listening to their grievances about

editors, ex-wives, and deadlines. It was a grubby, transactional business, all so they might glance at our press releases before ceremoniously
filing them in the bin. But it was our other project that was the real
education.

Our firm held the contracts for both the *British Association of Tea
Importers*—and at the same time one of the nation's biggest coffee
brands. They weren't rivals in the traditional sense; they were two sides
of the same coin. Most Brits drank one or the other—tea or coffee. Our
job wasn't to create new customers, just to poach them. Each week,
Jez and I would be assigned a beverage. He'd get tea, I'd get coffee. The
next week, we'd swap. It was a game, and the sales figures were our high
score. We'd sit there, dreaming up horrors to inflict on the nation's
morning brew.

"Right," Jez would say, leaning back in his chair, feet on the desk,
looking like a junior minister about to privatise oxygen. "I'm on tea
this week. What have you got for me William? Frighten me."

"For you Jezza, I have... potential carcinogens," I'd reply, scanning a
scientific paper I'd pulled from the library. "Acrylamide. Formed when
coffee beans are roasted at high temperatures. Nasty stuff, apparently."

"Ooh, I like it. Very potent," he'd grin. "But I see your potential
carcinogen and raise you... bone pain." He'd wave a different report.
"Excessive fluoride intake from cheap tea bags. Weakens the bones. We
can spin that into a nice panic about osteoporosis for the over-fifties."

And off we'd go. We became masters of the half-truth, the artfully
decontextualised fact. We never lied. Our legal department, a pair of
joyless ghouls in grey suits who communicated entirely through sighs
and passive-aggressive memos, made sure of it. Everything we wrote
was technically, factually correct. We just never told the whole story.

We'd write a piece about the 'shocking' levels of caffeine in tea,
conveniently omitting the fact that coffee generally had far more per
cup. We'd find a single study about the harsh working conditions on a
specific coffee plantation in a country no one could find on a map, and
we'd spin it into a heart-wrenching exposé on the 'hidden human cost'
of your morning cappuccino. We learned to speak the language of fear,
playing on vague, middle-class guilt and health anxieties. And the mad
thing was, it actually worked. The sales figures proved it. One week,

coffee sales would dip by three percent. The next, tea would take a hit. We were just two young lads in our early twenties—sat in an office, armed with a fax machine and a thesaurus, pulling on the invisible strings of public opinion and nudging the habits of an entire nation.

But even that felt abstract. Our next project was different. The results were so immediate you could almost hear the cash registers ringing in unison across the country. We were commissioned by a massive DIY chain—one of those soulless, aircraft-hangar-sized places on the edge of town that smells of sawdust and domestic despair. Our job was to help produce a TV makeover show.

We called it *Dream Designs*. You know the formula. Take a deserving couple living in a house with all the aesthetic charm of a provincial bus station. Add three experts—an interior designer with a penchant for scatter cushions and the word *fabulous*, a chippy who could knock up a feature wall before you'd finished your tea, and a gardener who spoke about herbaceous borders with the hushed reverence of a priest. Give them 48 hours and a lorry-load of our client's products, and hey presto: a dream home.

Ostensibly, it was a heart-warming piece of light entertainment. But behind the scenes, it was a finely calibrated weapon of mass consumption. The show would air on Sunday night at eight. By nine o'clock Monday morning, there'd be a national shortage of the specific shade of *Lagoon Blue* they'd used in the living room. It was like a switch had been flicked. Tens of thousands of people, simultaneously, would look at their own perfectly adequate living rooms and be filled with a sudden, burning need to change them.

The most absurd example was the railway sleepers. The gardener on the show had a thing for using old railway sleepers to build raised beds and decking. The thing is, our client didn't actually stock them. It was a complete oversight. But it didn't matter. The show created a rabid, nationwide demand for giant, creosote-soaked lumps of wood overnight. A few lucky timber importers thought all their Christmases had come at once. The price for a sleeper doubled, then tripled. People were driving hundreds of miles, putting their names on waiting lists, practically getting into fistfights in salvage yards. And our client didn't even mind. They sold astronomical quantities of decking stain, varnish, and industrial-strength screws to the lucky few who got their hands on them. We could hardly contain ourselves. We were giddy with it. This wasn't a subtle nudge. This was puppetry. We'd put an entertainment programme on the telly, and the next day, a significant portion of the British public would march out in a unified trance to buy the exact same things, convinced it was their own brilliant idea.

That was the moment the penny really dropped for me. If we could do all that, what else could we make people do? It wasn't just PR. It was magic.

The train gave a gentle lurch, shaking me from my reverie of DIY shows and railway sleepers. The green fields of Kent were blurring past the window. I thought about the very campaign that had landed me this cushy seat: the Eurostar *Discoverers* project.

It was a classic example of one of the core tenets of our trade: you don't invent a culture from scratch; you find a new social trend, a little eddy in the cultural current, and you build a hydroelectric dam on it. You watch what people are already doing, what they're starting to talk about, the new things they're trying. You find a fledgling trend, and you give it a name, a story, and a commercial sponsor.

The problem for Eurostar was simple. Their big-budget TV ads were great at selling the *idea* of a high-speed train, but they didn't necessarily make Brenda from accounts think, *Right, I'm booking a long weekend in Bruges.* We needed to create the desire.

The social trend we identified was the idea of the 'Gap Year' which was really starting to bubble up. It was, of course, another manufactured PR campaign, a joint enterprise by the banks—who would be handing out the loans to fund it—and the travel industry who would be raking it in by the students spending it. The whole concept was about to explode with the saturation media coverage of Prince William taking a year away before starting university.

We piggy-backed the Gap Year campaign to encourage a kind of simmering, middle-aged wanderlust. As parents waved their own children off on these new, pre-packaged adventures, watching them set off to find themselves in Thailand or Peru on a once-in-a-lifetime trip financed by a student loan, we were whispering in their ear through the television: *If they can do it, why can't you? You missed out once. Don't miss out again.* We were selling them a cure for a regret we had just reminded them they had.

We invented a target demographic we called the *Discoverers* and hired minor celebrities to take train journeys across Europe. We'd pay them to feature in travel segments, and a key part of the script was to have them sigh wistfully and reminisce. "Oh, this reminds me of when I went Inter-railing in my youth," they'd say, a faraway look in their eye.

This was the masterstroke. It was a direct, surgical strike on the latent jealousy of every mum and dad in the country, the ones who had been too sensible to piss off around Europe for a summer with nothing but a backpack and a questionable haircut.

To complete the strategy, we paid publishers to reissue some classic, musty old travelogues about European train journeys, and we paid a well-known bookshop chain to display them on those little tables marked as "staff picks". We gave people the idea, we stoked their dormant envy, and Eurostar gave them the ticket. It was a stunning success.

And here I was, hurtling towards a conference that promised to take these very techniques—these little games of trend-spotting, emotional manipulation, and manufactured desire—and bolt them onto the engine of the most powerful communication tool ever invented.

The train plunged into the blackness of the Channel Tunnel. A brief, subterranean pause before emerging into a new country, and a new world. It felt fitting.

Chapter Two

Monuments and Code

I COULD HAVE FLOWN direct to Stockholm, of course. The firm would have paid. But I'd chosen the slow route, a meandering two-day train journey across the continent. I told myself it was to decompress, but really, I wanted to see things. To get a feel for the landscape before talking about how to reshape it.

My first stop was Brussels, then a mid-morning train to Cologne. I wasn't there for the beer or the museums—I was there for the Cathedral, the *Kölner Dom*. Even to this day, having spent years of my life promoting the idea that the Great Pyramids were built by aliens with antigravity technology, I still say that nothing man-made on Earth is as mind-bogglingly impressive as a great medieval cathedral.

You step out of the doors of Cologne's main station and there it is, right in front of you, filling the sky. It's not a building; it's a geological event. A Gothic monster of such impossible scale and intricate detail that it seems to defy the laws of physics. It feels less like it was built and more like it was grown—a dark, crystalline forest of stone stretching towards a heaven it seemed determined to personally interrogate. For centuries, men with nothing more than pulleys, brute strength, and an unshakeable belief in God chipped away at this thing, building something that would outlast their own civilisation. It's a testament to what humanity can achieve with faith, patience, and a hell of a lot of stone. It makes you feel small, but in a good way. Grounded. Sane.

From Cologne I ambled on to Hamburg for another overnight stop—I was in no rush—before catching the train to Copenhagen. This was a bizarre journey in those days. The entire train, all several hundred tons of it, would roll directly onto the deck of a ferry. You'd feel the heavy clank as the wheels locked into tracks on the ship's floor, and then you'd either just sit there in your carriage, happily floating across the Baltic Sea, or you could go up on deck to stretch your legs for half an hour, before the whole process was reversed and the train rolled off again onto Danish soil. It was wonderfully, ridiculously analogue, a brute-force solution to the simple problem of a bit of water being in the way.

It also felt like a dying breed. Just a couple of years from then, the magnificent Øresund Bridge would open, linking Copenhagen in Denmark and Malmo in Sweden. I'd seen the plans in a magazine. It wasn't just a bridge; it was a statement of intent from the coming age. A road bridge, a rail bridge, and then, in the middle of the sea, it would just disappear. It would dive down onto a small, man-made island and transform into a tunnel, continuing its journey under the waves. I remember trying to get my head around it. How do you even *build* an island in the middle of the sea? What's it attached to? It was a different kind of marvel to the cathedral. Cologne was about conquering stone and gravity. This was about conquering nature itself, bending the very elements to the will of a computer-aided design. The old world built monuments to God; the new world was building monuments to its own cleverness.

After another short ferry crossing, this time from Denmark to Sweden, I was on the final leg to Stockholm. It was still early evening when I arrived, so I decided to walk to my hotel in the old part of town. It was a lovely little place right next to the Royal Palace, full of old paintings, antique furniture, and crystal chandeliers—very authentic but not at all pretentious. Anne, back at the office, was a genius at finding these places.

I sat for a while in a quiet little courtyard, nursing a beer, the air so peaceful I almost fell asleep. There was a teenage girl, sitting in a corner, silently dancing in her chair. She was listening to music on a device I didn't recognise. It wasn't a Walkman playing a cassette—it was a tiny, solid-looking grey box with no moving parts. I squinted at the brand name. Eiger. The model was an *MP Man*. I'd never seen one before. Another week, another gadget. You could barely keep up. There was always some new bit of kit coming out, some shiny new piece of tech that was quietly changing the way we did everything. The pace of it was relentless. That little box, holding who knew how many songs, felt more alien and more powerful in its own way than the cathedral or the bridge. It was a quiet little omen of the coming strangeness.

Later that evening, lying in the comfortable quiet of my room, I found myself thinking about the hotel and that word 'authentic'. It's a word we use a lot in my trade. And the more you sell it, the less you believe in it. The charming, old-world feel of the hotel triggered a memory of a campaign I'd worked on a couple of years back. It was one of my favourites, a perfect symphony of beautifully crafted nostalgia.

The client was a massive brewery conglomerate, a corporate behemoth we'll call *Albion Breweries*. Albion had spent the last decade buying up hundreds of historic British pubs and gutting them, replacing the sticky carpets and nicotine-stained ceilings with soulless, identikit interiors. They created plastic theme pubs: O'Malley's Irish Fun Pub, The King's Ransom Medieval Tavern, all of them with the same laminated menus and the same three soulless lagers on tap.

The problem was, the public had started to notice. There was a growing backlash, a nostalgic craving for the 'real British pub'. People were getting sick of the plastic shamrocks and fake Tudor beams. So Albion hired us. Their solution? To launch a brand new chain of pubs called *The Cornerstone Taverns Collection*.

The genius of The Cornerstone Taverns was that each pub was designed to look and feel like a unique, independent, slightly scruffy, family-run establishment, with chalkboards advertising a "Quiz Night" or "Sunday Roast". The menu might feel unique, but the core ingredients were all supplied centrally from the same distributor as the other 500 pubs in the chain.

Albion hired theatre set designers to meticulously create the illusion of authenticity. They'd hire specialists to artificially distress the new floorboards and give them the patina of age. They'd spill beer on the new bar and bake it in with heat lamps to create fake, decades-old stains. They'd source mismatched furniture from salvage yards and hang dusty, framed black and white photos of the local area from a hundred years ago. They even invented a folksy backstory for each pub, often featuring a fictional, long-dead landlord named *Henry Wainsford* or something equally credible.

The illusion extended to the beer itself. The craft beer revolution was just starting, a genuine grassroots movement of small, independent brewers. Albion saw the trend. They didn't just buy up the successful microbreweries; they created their own fake ones. They launched a range of "local craft ales" exclusively for The Cornerstone Taverns—beers with names like *Thistledown IPA* and *Old Anvil Porter,* complete with edgy, artistic labels and a backstory about two mates who started brewing in their garage. In reality, they were all brewed in the same colossal, stainless steel factory on an industrial estate outside of Reading.

The campaign was a staggering success. People flocked to *The Fox & Hounds,* or *The Shepherd's Rest*, praising them for their real character and authenticity. They'd sit there, on artificially scuffed chairs, drinking focus-group approved fake craft ale, and congratulate themselves for supporting a proper local and avoiding the soulless chain pubs down the road. They had no idea they were sitting in the most cynically constructed, most perfectly realised theme pub of all, owned and operated by the very same company they thought they were rejecting.

That's the job, I thought, as I drifted off to sleep in my authentic Stockholm hotel room. You don't sell people a product. You find out what they feel they've lost—community, authenticity, a sense of belonging—and you sell them a beautifully crafted, utterly fake version of it. You sell them a story they want to believe. It was an important lesson I'd learned early in my career. And I was about to find out, here in Stockholm, just how far you could take it.

Chapter Three

We Want You To Spread Conspiracy Theories

I WALKED THROUGH THE revolving doors of the conference hotel, and the generic hum of late-nineties corporate ambition hit me. It was a sea of dark suits, sensible haircuts, and the straight-faced, self-important chatter of people using phrases like "low-hanging fruit" and "blue-sky thinking". This was my world, my tribe, and I viewed it all with a deep, almost affectionate, sense of absurdity.

It was impossible to miss Jez. He was holding court with some bloke our age, leaning against a marble pillar, laughing with his whole body. He wasn't wearing a suit, of course. Just an expensive-looking shirt, unbuttoned one notch too far, and that signature mane of unkempt blond hair. He looked less like a delegate and more like the lead singer of a moderately successful indie band who had wandered in looking for the bar. He radiated an easy confidence that the men in suits tried to buy from tailors and never quite achieved.

The moment he saw me, his face split into that big, infectious grin. He cut his conversation short with a quick word and came striding over, weaving through the corporate drones like a golden retriever in a field of sheep. I'm not a hugger, never have been—it's not in my working-class DNA—but Jez doesn't really give you a choice. He threw his arms around me with a boisterous lack of decorum that seemed completely at odds with his upper-crust background, slapping my back with a resounding thud.

"William, my man! What kept you? Christ, it's good to see you. You look like you need a coffee. Or something stronger."

The conference wasn't due to start for another half an hour, giving us a perfect window. We found a small, secluded table in the corner of the lobby café, a little island of reality in a sea of corporate performance. The small talk was dispensed with in record time—work, life, the journey—all the usual filler you use to bridge a gap of a few years. We'd kept in touch since our placement, of course, but only through the odd, stilted email. The technology was still a novelty back then, a tool for work, not for genuine conversation. Most of our old contacts still relied on the telephone and the dying shriek of the fax machine.

After about a minute of pleasantries, Jez leaned forward, placing his elbows on the table. The familiar, mischievous twinkle was back in his eye. "Anyway," he said, waving a dismissive hand at the memory of our last three years. "Never mind all that. I have something far more interesting for you." He paused for effect. He always loved a bit of theatre. "We want you to come and work on something a bit different," he said, his voice dropping slightly, drawing me in. "Something a bit unusual. Something I know you'll love."

"Right..." I replied, a familiar sense of professional caution kicking in, though I couldn't quite suppress a smirk. "Go on."

He grinned, the cat that hadn't just swallowed the canary, but had also re-mortgaged its nest and sold the film rights. "We want you to help spread conspiracy theories."

The words just hung there in the air between us, so composed yet utterly ridiculous. Outside our little bubble of insanity, serious-faced PR executives were busy discussing market penetration and brand synergy. My brain felt like it had been unplugged and plugged back in too quickly. *Conspiracy theories?* That was the domain of bedroom-dwelling teenagers, not a serious business proposal in a four-star Stockholm hotel.

"What?" I finally managed, letting out a laugh that was half-genuine amusement, half-shock. "You've dragged me all the way to Sweden to turn me into a fourteen-year-old boy? You actually want me to sit in my bedroom and tell people that Adolf Hitler lives in a secret base on the moon, or that Arnold Schwarzenegger murdered Lord Lucan while he was working in London in the seventies?"

Jez threw back his head and laughed. "That Arnie one is new to me—you can tell me more about that later. But no, not those ones exactly. And you won't be sitting in your bedroom posting on some geeky message board that only other teenagers know about. This is serious. Professional. You'll be posting on stand-alone websites and web journals that we're setting up as we speak—*VeryTopSecret.com* is one of them, I think it's called. You'll be promoting a very specific, curated group of conspiracy theories. We'll do the hard work of providing the information, you'll be doing what you do best—helping to make people believe it."

He was serious. My laughter died in my throat. This wasn't a joke. He had piqued my interest, which he knew he would. Jez had a great talent for it, he knew which buttons to press.

"It won't just be you," he continued, sensing he had me on the hook. "I'm busy recruiting a few others. Mainly people in PR like us, people who understand the mechanics. That guy I was talking to when you came in? He's a Kiwi, been over here working but he's going back home soon. He's well-skilled in PR, but he's also massively into his music. So we'll be setting up a website where he can push a narrative about the music industry. Everyone gets their own little parish."

"So what will I be pushing?" I asked, the question feeling absurd on my lips. "What's my parish?"

Jez leaned in even closer, his voice a conspiratorial whisper. "You've heard of the Illuminati?"

"Well, I've heard the term, yes," I replied. "It's a punchline, isn't it?"

"Not anymore," he said, his smile unwavering. "You'll be promoting that, the Illuminati—amongst other things."

"But Jez, the Illuminati is a myth, a joke—a secret group of su-per-villains running the world. No one actually believes that kind of thing—not really."

"Oh, they do believe it, of course they do! And it's our job to make more people believe," he said, his smile unwavering. "You know the rules, Will. We'll keep repeating it, over and over again, in enough different ways, through enough different channels, and it will soon become true. *Repeat Till Real*—that's how it goes, you know this. You made people believe their daily cuppa was causing memory loss and mood swings. We could convince people the sky is green and the grass is blue if we used the right expert to tell them, and provide them with the right necessary 'evidence'. They'll believe it. It will become real."

It sounded ludicrous. It also sounded like every campaign I'd ever worked on.

As he spoke, a memory surfaced, sharp and clear. I was twenty, sitting in a dusty lecture hall at university. Our PR professor was a former agency man, a chain-smoking Machiavellian type who thought PR was just psychology with a better wardrobe.

He stood at the front of the room that day and said, "Let me show you how bacon became a belief." He played it out for us like theatre. The client was Beech-Nut, a company in the 1920s with a warehouse full of bacon and not nearly enough demand. Americans back then weren't big on breakfast meat. Most had toast, maybe a coffee. So what did the man they hired, the legendary Edward Bernays, do? He didn't push bacon. He reshaped breakfast.

He didn't launch an ad campaign. He simply asked a doctor if a "hearty breakfast" might be healthier than a light one. The doctor, naturally, said yes. Bernays then sent a survey to 5,000 other doctors asking the same leading question. Most agreed. Of course they did. Now, here was the trick. The doctors had endorsed *hearty breakfasts*. That's all. Not bacon. Not eggs. But Bernays took that survey and splashed it across the newspapers: *Doctors Recommend Big Breakfasts!* And in every article, bacon and eggs were presented as the quintessen-tial example of a hearty meal.

It was genius. He hadn't made bacon healthier. He hadn't changed the product. He just changed the story people told themselves about their morning routine. And it worked so well that, to this day, a *Full English* isn't a meal—it's a cultural institution. And every greasy-spoon café in the country owes the PR industry a big kiss and a thank-you card.

I remembered sitting in that lecture hall, utterly fascinated. Not because it was manipulative—I already knew PR companies weren't run by the local vicar—but because it was so *elegant*. He hadn't sold bacon. He had sold a belief. And that's what people buy more than anything. They buy beliefs.

Jez was right, of course. You could make people believe anything—you just had to tell them in the right way. He leaned forward, a mischievous glint in his eye. "These people here," he gestured vaguely at the conference delegates around us, "they spend millions trying to get someone to switch from one brand of washing powder to another. We're aiming higher, Will. Our new product is far more compelling. We're getting people to switch belief systems."

Chapter Four

The Psychological Comfort Blanket

WE DIDN'T GO TO the conference. We didn't even pretend to. The moment Jez had dropped the word *Illuminati* into the conversation, the idea of sitting through a lecture on *'Leveraging Brand Identity in the Digital Space'* seemed spectacularly pointless. We spent the rest of the day in a series of quiet Stockholm bars, the conversation circling around Jez's proposal like a shark—occasionally darting in for a bite before retreating to the safer waters of reminiscing about our early days in the playground of PR.

He was slowly, patiently, reeling me in. He knew better than to dump the whole insane plan on me all at once. He was doing what we had always done with a difficult client or a sceptical journalist: building a relationship, establishing a baseline of trust, and then carefully, incrementally, introducing the core idea until it seemed not just plausible, but inevitable.

I barely slept that night. My hotel room, which had felt so charming and peaceful the night before, now felt like a holding cell. My mind was a washing machine on full agitation mode, churning with a chaotic mix of excitement, disbelief, and a professional admiration for Jez with his bizarre offer. How could spreading conspiracy theories possibly be a serious, well-funded enterprise? Who was paying for it? And more importantly, the question that burrowed deepest into my brain: w*hy?* What was the end game?

The next morning, I met Jez after breakfast. He seemed fresh, energetic, completely untroubled by the world-altering insanity he was proposing. "Forget the conference hall," he said. "I'm taking you somewhere much nicer." He was talking about the Skogskyrkogården, the Woodland Cemetery, a place that had recently been granted UN-ESCO World Heritage status. An odd choice for a business meeting, but I was past questioning the strangeness of it all.

We spent the morning walking through the pines. It was beautiful, tranquil, a masterpiece of design where nature and modern architecture blended into one. It wasn't a grim, Victorian boneyard full of weeping angels and morbid pronouncements; it was a place of quiet contemplation. We passed simple, elegant chapels and long, silent rows of graves half-hidden by the trees. It felt less like a place of death and more like a park dedicated to the memory of life.

Finally, Jez stopped near a crest overlooking a quiet lawn, a large granite cross standing solitary against the horizon. He turned to me, his expression suddenly serious, the usual mischievous glint gone from his eyes.

"You know all this new technology we're seeing?" he began, his voice low. "The internet, the MP3 player at your hotel...this mobile phone?" He gave me a flash of his new toy. "Well, it's not just about cool new gadgets, Will. It's not about making things faster or a bit easier. That's the surface level. This is fundamental. It goes way, way deeper than that."

He took a breath, gathering his thoughts. "What we're living through right now, this very moment, is the start of the Technological Revolution. It's not just another chapter in human history; it's a completely new book. Everything—and I do mean *everything*—is about to change. How we produce our food, how we treat disease, how we harness power, how we reproduce, how we communicate, how we form communities. It's all up for grabs."

He started pacing slowly, his hands in his pockets, his expensive shoes crunching on the gravel path. "There'll be new institutions, new infrastructures, new social classes. New forms of government, new laws, new monetary systems. All of these things are going to happen, Will, and plenty more besides. Make no mistake, this is the biggest change ever in human behaviour. Way more than when we stopped roaming as hunter-gatherers and settled down to become farmers. Way more than when we first invented cities. Way more than the Industrial Revolution. This is the Industrial Revolution on steroids, with microchips for a brain."

"It's like those first proper settlements, Will, when large groups first came together and they had to start doing things differently. Imagine a village on one of Europe's great rivers..."

...Beneath the timbered roof of the meeting hall, the elders of the Danube settlement gathered in the fading heat of late afternoon. Smoke from the hearths drifted lazily overhead as the settlement's first watchtower cast long shadows over the packed-earth paths.

What had once been a scattering of thatched huts along the riverbank had grown into a bustling community of hundreds. Grain from the outer fields now arrived in woven baskets. Artisans shaped polished stone and baked clay pots in open courtyards. Scribes—or their earliest form, using knotted cords and carved tokens—had begun to track the flow of goods. But with change came disorder. Petty theft in the gathering spaces. Disputes over grazing rights. Fights between households. The oral customs that had guided village life for generations no longer held sway.

"We are too many now," said Tava, the high elder. "The spirits watch, but they no longer settle quarrels." Heads nodded. Others spoke in turn—of youths shirking field work, of surplus barley going missing from the communal store.

The settlement needed more than ritual and harvest. It needed rules, agreed upon and recorded. A council to judge disputes. A record of stores, marked by neutral hands. Perhaps even a watch—young men trained not for the hunt, but to keep peace within the palisade.

In that smoky chamber, the elders of the Danube did not know they were building the foundation of law, governance, and administration. They only knew their community had outgrown memory and needed something firmer to stand on.

Jez kicked at a pinecone, a rare flash of frustration. "You know that maxim, *'Those who do not learn from history are doomed to repeat it.'* It's a cliché, but it's true. And for the first time, we actually *have* the history. We have the studies. We have the reports from historians, sociologists, anthropologists. We've seen what happens when society goes through a massive upheaval like this. The turmoil, the chaos, the social breakdown. The shock of the new. A bloke called Alvin Toffler wrote a book about it—*Future Shock*. He said that when change happens too fast, it overwhelms people. It leads to mass disorientation, anxiety, violence even. It's group psychological trauma on a planetary scale."

He stopped and looked me dead in the eye. His voice was intense, passionate. "But this time, we can get ahead of it. We can manage it. We know what went wrong in the past—they weren't prepared, they didn't see it coming. This time we have an opportunity to do something about it, to try and negate some of the turmoil. We have to prepare society for these changes, Will. We have to get them ready, psychologically, for the world to be turned upside down. We need to soften the blow."

He paused, letting the words hang in the still, respectful air of the cemetery. "We have to offer them a psychological comfort blanket. A brand new way of looking at the world that makes sense of the chaos."

"And that's conspiracy theories?" I said, the words sounding feeble in the quiet woods. "Aliens and the Illuminati? That's the comfort blanket?"

"Yes!" He looked relieved that I was finally getting it. "That's precisely what it is. These stories will provide a new way of looking at the world, and will act as the psychological comfort blanket."

This serious version of Jez was still new to me. He stopped walking, and his expression, already intense, hardened into a still, focused certainty.

"Think of it like this, Will. What do you do when a child is scared of the dark? You don't give them a lecture on optics, and the rods and cones in their eyes. You don't explain that the monster under their bed is a statistical improbability. That won't work. It doesn't address the *feeling*. No, you give them a story. You tell them about guardian angels, or you give them a 'magic' teddy bear that will protect them. You create a comforting narrative that makes the darkness feel manageable."

He gestured to the quiet, peaceful woods around us. "The modern world is full of new, grown-up monsters. They're not under the bed; they're in our bank accounts, our workplaces, our governments. Technological unemployment, systemic complexity, the collapse of old certainties...these are huge, abstract, terrifying things. They make people feel small and powerless. They create a profound, free-floating anxiety."

"Our job," he said, his voice dropping with intensity, "is to give them a new story. A new philosophical worldview that helps them cope with it all. And the way we're going to deliver it is through the biggest, most ambitious astroturf campaign in the history of mankind."

I stared at him. *Astroturfing*. I knew the term, of course. It's a classic piece of PR jargon, a beautifully knowing word for a beautifully deceptive practice. It's the art of creating a fake grassroots movement, and is now so common that you hardly even notice it.

Normally, you'd do it for a corporate client. Imagine a big soft-drink company wants to fight a proposed sugar tax. A direct campaign from them would look self-serving and greedy. So, you create a 'grassroots' organisation from scratch—something with a wholesome name like *Britons for Sensible Choice*. You build a website, you write passionate articles from the perspective of "concerned parents," and "small business owners" who are worried about the tax's impact on their freedom. You encourage people to write to the newspapers or their MPs. You make it look like a genuine, spontaneous outbreak of public opinion. In reality, it's a completely artificial movement, a manufactured outrage, funded and directed by the very corporation that stands to profit. It's called 'astroturfing' because it has fake grass-roots.

And here was Jez, proposing to use that same technique not just to sell a product or fight a policy, but to reshape reality itself—to create a whole new worldview, a whole new belief system.

He saw the look of dawning comprehension on my face and clapped me on the shoulder, the old, familiar grin returning. "That's what this is all about, mate. Getting ready for the big transformation." He started walking back towards the entrance, his step suddenly lighter.

Jez gestured around us, at the graves half-hidden by the trees, at the new leaves growing on the branches. "You know that game people play, *Which period of history would you like to go back to?'* Well, in the future, people are going to choose this time. Right now. This is a monumental moment in human history. The old world is about to die, and a new one is about to be born—all because of advancements in technology. Life and death, existing as one, as it is right here in this cemetery. Our job, Will, is to be the midwives for the new world. To make the birth as painless as possible."

"Come on," he said, his voice full of excitement. "I'll introduce you to some people. You'll love Hendrik. He's a complete madman."

***

"This will all be a thing of the past soon," Jez remarked, holding up his passport with a theatrical sigh as we stood in the check-in queue for the flight to Germany. He'd bought my ticket in advance, of course, correctly assuming I'd find his offer too intriguing to refuse. He'd even had someone call my boss, Jeff, to let him know I'd be taking a few extra days. The man had contacts for everything.

"What—passports?" I asked, playing along.

"Borders," he said, with a sweeping gesture that took in the entire departure lounge. "The whole idea of a nation-state. It's a 19th-century concept and its time will soon be up. Why pay taxes to a government for services and protection when a tech company can provide you with a better, more personalised version online? Think of them as digital city-states. Their headquarters in California, or wherever they might be, will be the new capital cities. It's going to happen."

I must have looked baffled.

"It's part of the package, Will," he explained, lowering his voice. "The *New World Order* stuff we're pushing? *The One World Government?* It's a cover story. A way to get people used to the idea that

24

borders are becoming meaningless. We prime them to fear a shadowy global government so they won't even notice when global tech corporations become the actual real power."

"I thought the Illuminati were running things?" I said, trying to keep the ever-expanding cast of characters straight in my head.

"Oh, we throw everyone in the pot," he grinned. "The Royals, the Vatican, the Freemasons, the Rothschilds...they're all on the list. The more potential villains you have, the more believable the whole thing becomes. It's a tapestry of terror."

"And they don't mind you slagging them off?"

"God, no. They're all in on it. Most of them, anyway. Remember James? From that club night after the awards do? Paid for your taxi home because you'd spaffed all your cash on snakebite and black?"

I vaguely remembered a posh, affable bloke in a tweed jacket who seemed amused by everything and everyone. "Yeah. What about him?"

"He's a Rothschild," Jez said, as casually as if mentioning he was a postman. "A good lad. Heard he's planning on rowing the Atlantic solo."

We made our way through to the departure lounge, and as Jez made a series of calls on his mobile phone, I wandered off to waste a bit of time. A quiet little exhibit caught my eye: *Flight: From Dreams to Departure Gates*. I wasn't expecting much—just the usual airport filler—but something made me stop.

There wasn't too much on the jet-age. Instead, it went back—to the 1800s. Cayley, Lilienthal, Chanute. Men gliding off hillsides and scribbling equations in notebooks. And the Wright brothers, of course—two bicycle mechanics who, by 1903, had built wind tunnels in their workshop and solved the puzzle of controlled flight long before anyone else believed it possible.

But what really pulled me in was a faded newspaper behind glass, dated 1896: *Mysterious Airship Startles Sacramento*.

There it was: a glowing object hovering in the night sky, with descriptions of cigar-shaped hulls, mechanical wings, even voices overheard from above. Similar sightings followed across the country in 1897. Reports of strange flying machines—years before powered flight was public knowledge. Some claimed inventors were testing secret technologies. Others were sure they'd seen visitors from another world.

And I remember smiling—because the pattern was so clear. People had always seen things in the sky they couldn't explain, and when the facts weren't available, imagination filled the gaps. Aliens, omens, government cover-ups—it was never really about the object itself. It was about belief.

I didn't know it then, standing in that airport with my boarding pass in my pocket, but those old stories would stay with me. One day soon, I'd need the public to believe in things that weren't quite real—or weren't real *yet*. And when that time came, I'd think back to those 1890s airship sightings. How easy it had been to stir wonder. How even vague, conflicting accounts had taken hold.

Because the truth was simple: If people believed in alien visitors *before* aeroplanes even existed, I'd have no trouble making them believe again.

I returned to Jez just as our flight was being called. "See this, Will? " he held up his phone as he was putting it in his jacket pocket, "would have been a godsend to us back in the day. One easy call and suddenly *he's* the misunderstood genius, *she's* the loose cannon, and we're back at the bar before the ink's even dry."

Jez fell asleep almost before the plane took off, as effortlessly as he did everything else. He was completely untroubled, a man at ease with the strange realities he inhabited. I, on the other hand, couldn't rest. The flight became a strange, suspended limbo. Trapped in a pressurised tube at 30,000 feet, hurtling towards a future I couldn't comprehend, I watched the patchwork of northern Europe scroll by beneath us. It all looked so neat and orderly from up here, a quiet map of fields and towns. It gave no hint of the chaotic, invisible wars of belief and perception that Jez was suggesting were being waged down on the ground. It was a potent reminder of how easy it is to miss what's really going on if you're not looking for it.

Part 2

The Special World

Chapter Five

The Ministry of Truth

WE ARRIVED LATE AND checked into a nondescript hotel in a small town not far from Frankfurt. The next morning, Jez drove us to a building that formed part of a satellite campus of the main university. It was all concrete and brutalist angles, a grim 1970s architectural statement, the last place on earth you'd expect to find the nerve centre for a global psychological operation. We buzzed our way in and went up to the top floor.

The room was a long, open-plan office. Down one entire side, stretching for what must have been fifty feet, was a sprawling, inter-connected series of those dark blue, felt-covered display boards you see used as room dividers in large offices, or in primary school classrooms. They were covered in a chaotic, overwhelming collage of photos, di-agrams, handwritten notes, and newspaper clippings, all linked by a spider's web of coloured string and arrows. Above it all, scrawled in thick black marker pen, were the words: *THE DOTS*. This was *The Long Blue Wall*.

"Here it is," Jez said, with the quiet pride of a new father showing off his baby. "The blueprint. The instruction manual. The largest astroturf campaign in the world. This is what you'll be helping us build in people's heads." He led me to the beginning of the display boards. "First, let me introduce you to the team," he said. The room wasn't just a collection of data; it was a functioning office. A handful of people were dotted around at various desks, absorbed in their work. Jez gestured towards one of them. "Dave!"

A man in his mid-fifties looked up from a desk cluttered with vinyl records and academic journals. He had a long white beard, a stripey grandad-collar shirt with the sleeves rolled up, and a black pork-pie hat perched on his head. He looked like he should be playing banjo in a folk band, not running a focus group on the controlled reboot of Western civilisation. He touched the brim of his hat in acknowledgement.

"Dave here is our demolition expert," Jez said. Dave ambled over, a warm, easy-going smile on his face.

"Alright, mate?" he said, his voice a gravelly London rasp. He gestured at the first two boards, which were covered in pictures of world leaders, banks, oil rigs, riot police, and the cover of Orwell's *1984*. "This is my parish. The old world. The institutions. Government, finance, medicine, law and order... the lot. It's all knackered. Outdated. Built for a world that's about to disappear. It all has to go."

"So we attack it," he continued, tapping a picture of the Houses of Parliament with a nicotine-stained finger. "We wind people up. We show them the corruption, the lies, the incompetence. We make them angry. We make them demand change. We're creating the public mandate for a complete system upgrade. It'll get messy, of course. Hence this lot." He waved a hand at the second board, covered in images of civil unrest, FEMA camps, and headlines about martial law. "Got to prepare them for the chaos. Cultural Lag, know what I mean? Happens when the rules of society can't keep up with the tech. You've got to give 'em a bloody good scare, so when the changes come, they're relieved instead of terrified." He gave a wry smile. "Hope for the best, prepare for the worst. That's what we're working to. We sow the panic now so they'll welcome the new world like it's a warm bath."

Jez led me further down *The Wall*, towards a section covered in pyramids, UFOs, and New Age symbols. A woman with long, curly dark hair and a pleasant, academic smile was pinning up a picture of a pop star. Standing next to her, carefully adjusting a piece of string connecting a medieval painting to a picture of a crop circle, was a small, middle-aged man with a neat side-parting and an enamel CND badge on the lapel of his tweed jacket.

"Will, this is Beth, our chief architect," Jez said. "And this is Bertil. He's our resident expert in semiotics and cultural history. He's the man who understands the secret language of symbols." Bertil gave a shy but friendly nod. "And over there—that's Charlotte. She handles genealogical research and the bloodline myths. You'll hear more from her later—fascinating stuff."

"Nice to meet you," Beth said warmly. "My job is to build what comes next—but up here." She tapped a finger to the side of her head. "People need something to believe in. A worldview. We're giving them a new updated one—Religion 2.0 but with better special effects. This for example, it's a long-term project..." She pointed to a mock-up of a movie poster called *Zero Day: 2012*. "We're building a foundational myth for the coming age. We're creating a story that future generations will remember as the origin story of their entire epoch. We're writing the first chapter of a new history."

Bertil chipped in. "Yes, and the date—2012. It is perfect," he exclaimed. "2-0-1-2: It has the look of computer code, totally suited as the birth date for our new technological age."

"And the single zero," Beth added softly, "the void in the middle. It represents the divine presence, the mystery from which all things emerge. It's a good choice, it works well."

Just as she was speaking, a man in his late forties with wild, grey-streaked hair and eyes that burned with a manic intensity strode over. He wore a rumpled linen suit and carried a sheaf of papers, already talking before he'd even stopped moving.

"The initial data on the social media platforms is conclusive!" he announced to the room in a rapid-fire German accent, tapping one of the papers. "The memetic contagion vectors are exceeding all projections! It confirms the briefing papers! The disruption is accelerating!"

Social media platforms? I thought. I hadn't heard the term before. It had a strange, clinical ring to it. I pictured vast, digital territories, online nations where people lived and interacted. I had no idea what form it would take, but I knew instantly that a label like that had been designed with a purpose. It was the kind of language that could shape a new reality.

Jez grinned. "Will, this is Hendrik. He's a... consultant." He said the word with a certain weight, a clear signal that it meant more than it seemed. "He advises some very old families on some very new problems." Hendrik's intense gaze fixed on me. He seized my hand and shook it vigorously.

"Ah, the new recruit! The storyteller! Good! You are essential. These academics," he gestured at Dave and Beth, not with disrespect, but with a sense of distinction, "they understand the past. I am here to translate the future. A future that, I assure you, is arriving far faster than the public timetables suggest!"

He leaned in, his voice lowering to a whisper. "Forget the Illuminati. That is a smokescreen! The real threat is not a secret society; it is the technological wave that is about to hit us. It is the decentralised finance making central banks irrelevant. It is the CRISPR technology allowing us to program our own evolution! It is the artificial intelligence making entire professions obsolete in a single afternoon. We are facing a crisis of meaning on a planetary scale. We are giving them bogeymen and aliens so they do not see the real monsters at the door!" He stood back, breathless, looking utterly triumphant.

I was trying to process this torrent of information when something on Beth's board caught my eye. Pinned right next to a diagram of The Great Pyramid was a crudely drawn picture of something that seemed totally out of place.

"And that?" I asked, pointing. "Is that... *a newt?*"

Jez burst out laughing. "Ah, that's new. That one's about to break. We needed a new bad guy for the new worldview. A replacement for the Devil." He turned to face me straight on. "You know Michael Wright?" he asked.

The name clicked instantly. "Michael Wright, the old comedian?" I replied, somewhat taken aback.

"That's him—he's one of ours," Jez said, very matter-of-factly. "He's about to announce that the world is secretly run by a race of giant, shape-shifting lizards from another dimension."

I stared at him, then at the drawing, then back again. I couldn't help it; I started to laugh. Properly laugh. "Jez, come on! That's too far. They might believe in a shadowy group of bad guys who run the world behind the scenes, but they're not going to believe that they're actually giant lizards. No one on earth is going to believe that."

He just smiled. "Of course they will."

We reached the end, where we were met with a miscellaneous collection of faces and ideas—Princess Diana, a modern stone circle, some sci-fi illustrations. "And these?" I asked.

"Our new myths," Beth replied. "Every society is built on them. We're just preparing these for the next generations."

Jez clapped me on the back. "You know what Plato said, don't you Will?"

"I'm sure he said plenty of things, Jez. But nothing about giant lizards, I'd bet."

"Those who tell the stories rule society," he said, his eyes shining. "It's all about controlling the narrative. He was talking about propaganda, of course."

I looked back at the Long Blue Wall—the insane, brilliant, terrifying roadmap for the future. "Or Public Relations as it's called now," I corrected.

Jez roared with laughter. "Yes, Public Relations, darn right!"

***

That evening the team met for dinner at a traditional German bistro. The heavy oak tables, steins of beer, and hearty portions of schnitzel were a nice contrast to the sterile, high-concept environment of the university block from earlier in the day. It was a chance to see the architects of the new world in a more relaxed setting—their guards down, their mischievous, insider humour on full display.

I was the last to arrive, and I found myself sitting between Jez and Beth. Before I'd even had a chance to look at the menu, Dave, with a theatrical flourish, announced that he'd already ordered for me.

"A little game, Will," he said, his eyes twinkling over the top of his beer glass. "Have a look at the menu. Point out to Beth what you *would* have chosen."

Intrigued, and slightly suspicious, I played along. I scanned the list of German delicacies and, turning to Beth, discreetly pointed at the *Jägerschnitzel*—the pork cutlet with the mushroom sauce. A few minutes later, the waitress arrived with our food. In front of me, she placed a plate of Jägerschnitzel. It was exactly what I'd picked. Everyone applauded as Dave stood and took a mock bow.

"Ha! ... that's good!" I laughed. "Come on then, how did you do it?" Dave took a huge gulp of beer before going on to explain. Before he was a full-time sociologist and part-time overseer of societal collapse, he had a modest career on the university circuit and at holiday camps as a stage mentalist. He'd dress up in ponchos and feathers, calling himself *The Great Fabiola, Amazonian Mind-Reader*. He claimed to be descended from a long line of tribal shamans. As he'd later tell me, "People are way more suggestible if they think you're the authentic article. Wear the right uniform, use the right lingo, and they'll swallow anything." The fact that his parents were both from Hemel Hempstead and had never even owned passports, was an irrelevant detail. He still maintained, with a completely straight face, that Derren Brown had stolen his entire act.

"I knew you were in showbiz!" I exclaimed.

The conversation flowed as easily as the beer. Eventually, my attention turned to Bertil, the quiet Swedish academic I'd been introduced to earlier at the university. I'd barely noticed him since I'd sat down. He was one of those unassuming presences, perfectly content to listen rather than speak. It was Jez who brought him into the spotlight.

"Bertil here," Jez said with a mischievous laugh, "he helps people believe in aliens."

Before I'd had a chance to question Bertil about this intriguing revelation, the conversation had already moved on, this time to Charlotte, our quiet, intense genealogist. "So, Charlotte," I said, "tell me about your role here. What's the mystery behind the *Ancient Bloodlines* stuff I saw on the boards earlier?"

Charlotte took a calm sip of wine, a slight, enigmatic smile on her face. "Mystery? There's no real mystery, Will. It's just history. Very well-documented history. The upper echelons of Europe and early America—royalty, presidents, banking dynasties—you could call them the most inbred club on Earth. They're all interlaced, not just socially, but genetically."

Dave glanced at his beer. "Ah yes, the Global Elite: keeping it in the family since Charlemagne."

"Yes," said Charlotte. "Charlemagne is the great-great-grandfather of everyone in this room. You, me, the waiter, that baby with the alarming eyebrows two tables over."

Beth laughed. "Wait, I'm related to royalty?"

"If you have European ancestry, yes." Charlotte nodded. "Go back forty generations, and the number of your theoretical ancestors actually exceeds the number of humans who ever lived. You have too many—the branches have to collapse. Your family tree isn't a tree at all—it's a hedge, trimmed into a circle and gently set on fire."

Charlotte confirmed. "Nearly every living European can trace their lineage to Charlemagne. And from there, it's just a hop, skip, and a regrettable cousin marriage to Queen Victoria."

"And the higher up the social ladder you go," she continued, her voice precise and academic, yet laced with wit, "the smaller the gene pool gets. It wasn't about love. It was about land, titles, alliances. Keep the bloodline, keep the power. The Habsburgs practically folded in on themselves. Charles II of Spain was the result of generations of strategic inbreeding—his parents were uncle and niece. He couldn't chew, couldn't read, couldn't rule."

"And let's not forget the U.S. presidents," she went on. "George W. Bush is related to Franklin Pierce, Abraham Lincoln, and even his political rival Al Gore. In fact, almost every U.S. President has some documented link to King John, signer of the Magna Carta."

"So America didn't actually reject monarchy," I said. "It just changed its job title?"

"That's a good way of putting it," said Charlotte. "Less crown, more waistcoat. And the banking dynasties—the Morgans, Rockefellers, Rothschilds, Du Ponts—did the same. They didn't just marry wealth. They recycled it. Consolidated it. They built dynasties like greenhouses: controlled breeding, high-yield ambition, consistent jawlines."

"The Rothschilds married into European nobility," she went on. "Quietly underwriting empires while their cousins wore crowns. That line between the throne and the vault? Very thin indeed."

"And what about the Vatican?" Beth asked, jumping in. "That's always been the third pillar of the *Big Three* theory, hasn't it? The idea that the world is run by a trinity of city-states: Washington D.C. for military power, the City of London for finance, and the Vatican for spiritual control. The whole narrative is built on the idea that it's three branches of the same family business, with the same ancient bloodlines pulling the strings in all three."

"Indeed," agreed Charlotte. "Half the Popes of the Renaissance came from the same handful of families: the Medici, the Borgias, the Farnese. They made nephews into cardinals and daughters into duchesses. The papacy wasn't above the family game—it was built on it."

"So the Pope, the banker, and the king walk into a bar..." Dave began.

"Yes—for a family reunion!" Charlotte finished the line with a little giggle. "So when people talk about the West as a network of power—it's not a conspiracy. It's genealogy. A very old, very pale family tree, passing around land, titles, and elections like the silverware at a very long and drawn-out family party."

"So," I said, trying to put it all together. "This is where the Ancient Bloodlines stuff comes from? You just present these facts?"

Charlotte smiled, that cool, professional glint returning to her eye. "Oh no, Will. The facts are just the foundation. They're the boring, verifiable bit that gives the story credibility. We don't just present the facts. We build a story on top of them. We provide the *interpretation*."

She leaned forward. "We take these interconnected family trees," she explained, "and we ask a simple, leading question: *Isn't it a bit of a coincidence?* We frame it as a deliberate, centuries-long breeding program. We hint that they are preserving something special in their bloodline. Something... not entirely human."

"This is where we connect with Beth's work," she went on. "We take my genealogical charts and we lay them over the myths of *ancient aliens* and *fallen angels*. We create the narrative that this 'one, big family' isn't just descended from Charlemagne. They are the descendants of an alien race that crash-landed here millennia ago. The 'blue bloods'. The Illuminati. They aren't just protecting their wealth; they are protecting their alien DNA."

"Okay, so you take the fact that they're all cousins," I said, a sense of dizzying, admiration washing over me, "and put it all together and spin it into the Ancient Bloodlines story."

"Precisely," she said. She looked directly at me, her expression turning from academic to professional. "You're in PR, Will. You know how it goes." She smiled. "It *is* the truth. It's just not the *whole* truth. It's only the part we want people to see, dressed up in a much better story."

Chapter Six

The New Gods

THE NEXT MORNING, I went down for breakfast and found Beth and Bertil already in the hotel restaurant, sitting at a corner table with coffee and a selection of newspapers. They looked at home—this was clearly their regular spot when they were in town. I joined them, and a few minutes later, Jez appeared, looking as effortlessly put-together as ever.

"Morning, all," he said cheerfully. "Beth and Bertil are heading into Frankfurt today, Will. A pilgrimage to the Städel Museum. Fancy going along?"

"The Städel?" I said. "What's that?"

"It's one of the great art museums," Beth explained. "Famous for its collection of Old Masters. Lots of Renaissance and mythological paintings. It's practically Bertil's second home."

It sounded like the perfect opportunity. A chance to talk to two of the quietest and perhaps most thoughtful members of the team, away from the chaotic energy of *The Wall*. I was still trying to get my head around the sheer scale of the project, and I was keen to understand their roles more deeply. "Yeah, I'm in," I said.

Jez wouldn't be coming. "I've got other business to attend to," he said vaguely, leaving us to wonder what clandestine meetings or aristocratic favours he was dealing with.

An hour later, the three of us were standing in the magnificent, light-filled atrium of the Städel Museum. The place was a temple to art, and the main atrium felt like its high altar—a vast, vaulted space filled with a hushed, reverent silence. I felt a familiar sense of awe, the same feeling I'd had looking at Cologne Cathedral. This was history, tangible and real.

We wandered through the galleries, past portraits of stern-faced merchants and luminous Madonnas. We stopped in front of a huge, dramatic painting by a Flemish master. It was a chaotic, beautiful scene, full of suffering and heroism.

"This is it, isn't it?" Beth said softly, her eyes fixed on the canvas. "This is what we do."

I looked at her, confused.

"Art," she explained. "It's the same as poetry, the same as mythology. You don't just look at it; you *feel* it. It speaks to a part of you that words can't always reach. A life without myth, Will, is like a life without art or music. It's just...grey. Empty. Meaningless. Like those old concrete towns from the Eastern Bloc. Functional, but soulless."

We moved on, stopping in front of another painting, this one depicting a scene from Greek mythology. "Myths aren't just fairy tales for children," Beth continued, her voice filled with a quiet, academic passion. "They are the operating system for a healthy society. They provide the framework for the type of person we want to be, the kind of society we want to live in. Think of the *Ten Commandments*. Forget the religious aspect for a moment. At its core, what is it? It's a foundational social contract. A set of ten, simple, agreed-upon rules for how we can all live together without killing each other and stealing each other's things. It's a blueprint for a functioning society."

"It's why we have to teach children right from wrong," she said. "A child doesn't instinctively know how to behave. We teach them through stories. And we still use these stories, these moral blueprints, every single day, even if we don't realise it. We ask ourselves, *What's the right thing to do?* What we're really asking is, *What would the person in the story do?*"

She smiled. "What would Luke Skywalker do when faced with tyranny? He'd fight back, even when the odds are impossible. What would the Magnificent Seven do when a village is being terrorised? They'd defend the powerless, even if it costs them their lives. Would Wonder Woman just stand by and ignore the wrongdoings of the politically corrupt? Of course not. Her very existence is a call to fight for truth and justice."

"These aren't just characters," she said, her voice intense. "They are archetypes. The Good Samaritan, who teaches us compassion for strangers. Icarus, who teaches us the dangers of hubris. They provide us with emotional scripts for how to act in a crisis. Without those scripts, that shared moral framework, society would crumble into a collection of self-interested individuals."

She let the thought hang in the air for a moment, the painted eyes of long-dead gods and heroes staring down at us. "And that," she said, her voice dropping to a near-whisper, "is why our work is so important. The old myths—the Ten Commandments, the story of the Good Samaritan—they were wonderfully effective. They gave us a solid framework for a stable, pre-industrial society. But they are becoming insufficient."

She turned from the painting and looked at me directly, her expression serious. "Those stories weren't designed for the world we are about to enter, Will. They don't have anything to say about the ethics of artificial intelligence, or the social considerations of lab-grown meat, or what it means to be human when you can edit your own DNA. The new Technological Era will create new institutions, new social structures, and new moral dilemmas that our ancestors could never have dreamed of."

"We are heading into uncharted territory without a map," she continued. "A society without a coherent story for its current reality is a society on the verge of collapse. We need new myths. We need new stories to explain how these new things came to be, and we need new fables to teach us lessons for situations that are completely new to human experience."

She gestured around the grand gallery. "Our job isn't to replace these old gods. It's to build the new ones. We have to create the myths for the world that is being born right now. It's the most important work in the world."

41

We broke for lunch at the museum's elegant rooftop restaurant. Over plates of *wurstsalat* and glasses of crisp German Riesling, the conversation continued. I was still trying to process Beth's lecture on the necessity of myth, but I'd been itching to question Bertil on what Jez had said the previous evening.

"So, Bertil," I began, "what's this about aliens?" I smiled politely.

"Ah, yes." Bertil laughed. "It's a good conversation starter, is it not? It's my job to find the evidence to support the theory that aliens have visited us throughout history."

"And where do you even start with that?" I pushed him further.

Bertil dabbed his mouth with a napkin, a shy but enthusiastic smile on his face. "Well, my formal job helps. I'm an art historian, a cultural historian, and I'm well versed in semiotics. But we are also very fortunate. The groundwork has already been laid for us by pioneers like Erich von Däniken. His books were wildly popular. He showed that there is a huge public appetite for these ideas."

"Our work is always a work in progress," Beth chimed in. "We are not the originators of these myths. We are simply curators. We borrow stories that have already gained a foothold in popular culture, and we amplify them, shape them. And future generations of people like us will come along and add their own layers. That's how a myth stays alive."

"And the alien story," Bertil continued, "is the big one. It's the most important myth we are building, because it's our new *Story of Creation*, our new origin myth."

He explained that all societies, across all of history, have a foundational myth to account for their own existence. It answers the profound, universal questions that science can't touch: *Who are we? Where did we come from? Why are we here?*

"The human mind has an innate need for causality," Bertil said, his voice quiet but intense. "It cannot tolerate a vacuum. It needs an answer for the cause of everything. And it doesn't much matter what the answer is, so long as it is an answer of some kind. A creation myth gives people an anchor point in time, a reason and a purpose for their existence."

"And our old anchor, the story of Adam and Eve, is dragging," Beth added. "So we are simply building a new one." She held up four fingers. "It's a simple, four-step process."

"Step One: *Make us believe in human-looking aliens.*"
Bertil took over again. "Have you noticed how aliens in popular culture have become very human-like in recent years? Gone are the days of the Little Green Men or the pink blob with a built-in antenna. Now, we have the iconic 'Grey'—humanoid, upright, two arms, two legs, a head, and large soulful eyes. This is deliberate. It's a process called anthropomorphism. We give them human characteristics so we can relate to them, so we understand their supposed reasoning. We can't empathise with a blob, but we can empathise with a creature that looks like a sad, skinny version of ourselves."

"Step Two: *Make us believe they have visited Earth in the past.*"
Beth continued. "This is where we resurrect the work of von Däniken and Sitchin: we take the great, unexplained mysteries of the ancient world—the Pyramids of Giza, the colossal stone platforms of Baalbek, the statues of Easter Island, the Nazca lines in Peru—and we present them not as feats of human ingenuity, but as evidence of extraterrestrial intervention. We ask the simple question: 'How could primitive humans have built these things?' And we provide the simple, exciting answer: 'They didn't. It was aliens.'"

"Step Three: *Make the method of creation believable to our new technological mindset.*"
Bertil's eyes lit up. "This is a most crucial step. Our current level of understanding can no longer accept the biblical account of Man being created from soil. But we can certainly accept its modern equivalent: genetic engineering and DNA manipulation. So that is our new story. A superior alien race visited Earth long ago and created modern humans by splicing their own advanced DNA with that of a prim-

itive hominid. It's a creation myth for the age of biotechnology. It's high-tech, it's plausible, and it speaks to the world we live in now."

"And **Step Four**," Beth said, looking directly at me, a wry smile on her face, "**Repeat. Repeat. Repeat.**"

"And that, Will, is where you come in. We provide the ammunition. You, and the others, just have to keep firing it."

The list of ammunition was long and varied. I was to push the narrative about ancient structures being built by aliens. I was to promote the 'evidence' from paintings and artwork that Bertil had so cleverly re-contextualised. I was to talk about the Anunnaki gods of Sumerian mythology as if they were a literal historical account.

"Actually, we have a new recruit on this," said Beth. "Only an organic asset mind—a signal booster—but they're very useful. I can't remember his name—the scientist who used to be a pop star?"

I knew who she meant. A young, pretty-boy physicist who had a hit single in the charts. He had nice hair and a PhD. The media loved him.

"He's perfect," Beth continued. "He's not one of ours, not consciously. He's just an ambitious young guy who enjoys being on stage. He'll be good for the alien origins narrative. We got him on the BBC to talk about his mix of music and physics. The public loved him—the handsome genius pop star. They've decided they like him, therefore they trust him, and they'll go along with whatever he says."

"So he'll be invited back, and we can move it on a bit. This time he can be asked more about the *big questions*, and he can use his expertise in physics and mathematics to tell the nation that the existence of alien life is a statistical certainty. He'll say that the numbers are simply too vast for us to be alone. And it will sound incredibly logical and intelligent, and people will adopt it as their own viewpoint."

"But he's a physicist..." she continued. "He understands probability, of course—he can talk very convincingly about the Drake Equation, about the billions of stars and the trillions of planets. But his expertise isn't in biology or chemistry. He doesn't understand the astronomical, near-impossible odds of abiogenesis—of life actually starting from non-living matter. He wouldn't be able to explain that part. And the producers at the BBC, guided by our friends, will *never* have a biologist on the same sofa to offer the counter-argument."

"So the public gets a one-sided, comforting, and 'scientific' argument from a man they trust, who just happens to be confirming a key tenet of our new creation myth. He's not lying. He'll just be providing a single, compelling data point. And we'll make sure it's the only data point the audience will hear. It's nice, isn't it?"

After lunch, we continued our walk through the museum. But now, as I looked at the paintings, I saw them in a completely new light. A halo around a saint's head no longer looked like a symbol of divinity; it looked like a helmet on a space-traveller. A stylised cloud in the background of a crucifixion scene now looked suspiciously like a flying saucer. My eyes had been educated. I could no longer un-see the story I was supposed to be telling. Bertil and Beth had given me the gift of their professional vision, and in doing so, they had corrupted my own forever.

As we stepped out of the museum and back into the crisp Frankfurt air, my head was spinning. It was one thing to manipulate public opinion about a brand of coffee or a new train service. That was just business. It was another thing entirely to be told, in the calm, academic halls of a world-class art museum, that my new job was to convince the entire Western world to believe in aliens.

Aliens. It was almost too much to comprehend. This wasn't just a marketing campaign; it was a theological one. They were proposing to rewrite the foundational story of human existence—to replace an old, outdated biblical story with a new one imported from a science fiction novel. And I knew it would work.

Because the groundwork had already been laid. I thought about the cultural landscape back home. It wasn't just *The X-Files* on a Friday night. It was everywhere. It was a massive, ongoing drip-feed, a campaign that had been running so successfully, for so long, that most people didn't even see that it *was* a campaign. It was seen, simply, as reality.

I thought back to that little exhibition I'd seen at the airport, with the old newspaper clippings from the nineteenth century reporting sightings of airships as reconnaissance vehicles from Mars. This wasn't new. This conditioning had been going on for generations.

And the result was a stunning, almost total success. I tried to think of a single person I knew who didn't, on some level, believe. Not just the cranks and the true believers, but normal, everyday people. My own friends, my family. They might not believe in abductions or flying saucers, but they all accepted the fundamental premise: the strong *possibility,* or even the actual *probability,* that alien life exists. The conversation had been so completely normalised that the existence of extraterrestrials was now a perfectly normal everyday topic of discussion in any pub in the country. It was as if they were already here, a quiet, accepted part of our cultural landscape, just waiting for the official announcement.

I wondered, standing there in the crisp Frankfurt air, just how long this programme had been running. Who had started it? When had they decided that we, as a society, needed to start believing in little green men—or more accurately, humanoid-looking greys as Bertil would correctly point out? It was the biggest, most ambitious, and most utterly insane project I had ever heard of. It was priming on a civilisational scale. And I couldn't wait to get started.

***

The Sky Between Us

The fire hissed low, and the old woman leaned forward.

"There are many beginnings," she said, her voice slow and thick as smoke. "Ask ten peoples from where we come, and you'll hear ten truths."

The children watched her, wide-eyed.

"In the north, they say the world hatched from an egg. Sky from shell, land from yolk, beasts from the white.

"Across the sea, some say a tree dreamed. It dreamed of walking, and its fruit grew mouths. When those fruits split, we spilled out—still half-dreaming."

She let the silence settle before continuing.

"In the dry lands, they say something fell—a star, or a voice, or a thought—and where it touched the earth, man stood up, blinking."

She paused, as if choosing whether to go on. Then nodded.

"But it doesn't matter which story you heard first. What matters is why we tell them."

The flames reflected in her eyes, flickering like a secret.

"We tell them because there is a space inside us that needs filling. A hunger that isn't for food, or warmth, or safety. A hunger for belonging. For meaning. For knowing what we are in the middle of all this sky and blood and time."

She looked around the circle, her voice softer now.

"You see, we were the only beasts who woke up afraid. Who saw our own shadows and asked, *What am I? Where did I come from? What am I meant for?* And in the asking, we made stories."

She opened her hands to the fire.

"They don't need to be true in the way a stone is true. They are true in the way music is. In the way grief is. They are how we carry ourselves through the dark."

A log shifted, and the sparks jumped upward.

"The stories remember for us, when we forget. They help us live in a world too big to hold all at once. They give shape to the void—not to close it, but to stand beside it, and not be swallowed."

She leaned back, letting the weight of her words settle.

"Maybe we came from stars. Or trees. Or bones. Maybe all the stories are half-true. Maybe none are. But we keep telling them because something inside us still longs for the first fire—the moment we opened our eyes and saw that we are here, and had to make sense of it."

The children said nothing. They didn't need to. The silence was full.

Chapter Seven

Nothing Up My Sleeve

THE MORNING AFTER MY return from the trip to what Dave had so aptly christened *The Ministry of Truth*, I sat at my desk, the quiet of the office feeling strangely charged, as if the air had changed. The world outside looked exactly the same—the same grey sky, the same delivery lorries rumbling past—but I knew what was humming beneath the surface. I felt like I'd glimpsed the blueprint behind the wallpaper. And now I had a choice to make.

Jez's offer wasn't a job offer in the traditional sense. There was no contract, no salary, no formal job description. It was an invitation. A key to a secret door. And I could, in theory, just say no. I could thank him for the interesting chat, go back to my life of promoting a new line of industrial-grade floor polish, and getting D-list celebs to open garden centres, and I could pretend the whole bizarre trip to Germany had never happened. I could choose to remain a simple storyteller, a professional narrative consultant in the service of commerce. But I knew I wouldn't. I couldn't.

My mind kept replaying the last few days. The mind-blowing, audacious scale of The Long Blue Wall. The manic, world-altering pronouncements of Hendrik, Dave's pint-in-hand philosophical wisdom, and Charlotte's encyclopaedic, almost supernatural, recall of every royal birth, marriage, and secret. But most of all, it was the time spent with Beth and Bertil at the museum that had truly sealed my fate. Listening to them deconstruct history, art, and mythology, and then reassemble them into a new, coherent narrative was art in itself. They weren't just selling a product; they were painting a new map of reality, landmark by careful landmark.

How could I possibly say no to that? How could I go back to writing press releases about low-fat yoghurts after being offered a chance to write a new Book of Genesis?

This was a once-in-a-lifetime opportunity. It was a glimpse behind the ultimate curtain, a front-row seat at the greatest show on Earth. The pull of it was irresistible, a force far stronger than the quiet satisfaction of a successful commercial campaign. It was the intellectual thrill of the puzzle, the creative challenge of the story, and the dark, intoxicating allure of being one of the few people in the world who was in on what was happening.

To say no would be to choose the grey, concrete reality that Beth had talked about. To say yes was to step into the painting. I took a deep breath.

My first assignment was simple: start writing. Jez had given me a list of nascent websites—*VeryTopSecret.com*, *GlobalAwakening.net*, and a few others. My job was to populate them with content. To start connecting the dots for the public. But first, I needed to join the tribes.

That evening I fired up my dial-up modem—that horrible, screeching, electronic handshake with the digital world—and went looking for the existing communities. Websites back then were a different species entirely—digital fossils in the making. Clunky, text-heavy forums built on basic message board software. They felt more like bulletin boards than the sleek sites we know today. Places like *Above Top Secret*, *GodLike Productions*, and the *Biblioteca Pleyades*. They were the Wild West of the internet, ugly and chaotic, but also vibrant with a raw, unfiltered energy. The fonts were too small, the backgrounds were often a headache-inducing black, and they were littered with blinking, low-res animated GIFs of spinning pyramids and alien heads.

I created a stable of anonymous profiles. I was no longer Will Camden. I was *Veritas_2012*, a handle that sounded both portentous and vaguely futuristic. I was *TruthSeeker77*, a no-nonsense handle for the more nuts-and-bolts forums. I was *AgentM*, a deliberately mysterious and provocative persona.

I lurked for a while, learning the language, understanding the dynamics. These people were already a tribe, united by a shared sense of alienation and a belief that they were smarter than the "sheeple". They were primed. They just needed a guide.

My first move had to be perfect. I decided to start with Edward Bernays, using the propagandist's own confession as supposed-proof of the phantom Illuminati. I posted a thread on the *VeryTopSecret* forum titled:

THEY ADMIT IT! The Opening Line From the Secret Elite's Playbook

—and I quoted the first sentence from his book, *Propaganda*.

"The conscious and intelligent manipulation of the organized habits and opinions of the masses is an important element in democratic society. Those who manipulate this unseen mechanism of society constitute an invisible government which is the true ruling power of our country."

The next morning, I logged on with the same nervous excitement a fisherman must feel checking his lobster pots. Had I caught anything?

The thread was buzzing. It was like I'd tossed a grenade into a nest of ants. The replies were a perfect cross-section of the human mind, a beautiful mess of belief, suspicion, and outright hostility. There were the instant converts, the ones who had been waiting their whole lives for someone to articulate what they already felt.

User: StarChild82

OMG, this is it! I always knew it! It's right there in black and white. Thank you for posting this, Veritas. The truth will set us free!

Then came the sceptics, the ones who smelled a rat and delighted in trying to expose it.

User: Logic_Bomb
Hang on, people. This is a quote from a book about PUBLIC RELA-TIONS. He's talking about advertising and marketing, not a shadowy group of elites running the world from a hollowed-out volcano. It's a metaphor. Don't be morons.

And in between, there was the vast, undecided middle. The curious, the cautious, the ones who wanted to believe but needed a little more convincing.

Watching the debate unfold, I was reminded of a stage mentalist Emma and I had seen a while back. Not the one Dave insisted had stolen his act, but one whose costume was at least a little more conventional than an Amazonian shaman costume which had been rented from the local fancy dress shop.

The show Emma and I went to see was a masterclass in the same techniques. The highlight was when the performer would get a dozen people up on stage and, through what he claimed was mass hypnosis, made them forget their own names, or to eat a lemon as if it was an apple.

But the real trick wasn't what he did on stage; it was how he selected his volunteers. He'd get the whole audience to perform a series of suggestibility tests. Clasp your hands together and imagine they're glued tight. Imagine a balloon tied to your wrist, pulling it up. Most of us would just sit there, feeling a bit daft. But he was scanning the crowd, looking for the tells. The people whose hands genuinely seemed stuck. The ones whose arms started to drift upwards, their faces a mask of confused belief. Those were the ones he invited up on stage.

"He's looking for the easy marks," I'd whispered to Emma.

"The suggestibles," she'd replied. Emma's a nurse; she sees it every day. She calls it the 'white coat effect'. Patients who report feeling better simply because a doctor gave them a sugar pill and told them it was a powerful new medicine. It's the placebo effect, and it's one of the most powerful forces in human psychology.

That's the fundamental truth of the human herd, and it's the bedrock of our business. As Dave would say, people respond less to facts than to perceived authority. If something sounds official or comes from the right source, we're far more likely to believe it—and act on it. In any given population, about twenty percent of people are like the first group on my forum thread—the true believers. They are highly suggestible. They *want* to believe. They are the volunteers from the audience, eager to get on stage and play the part of the Amazonian Mind-Reader's willing subject.

Then you have the twenty percent at the other end of the scale. The hard sceptics. The *Logic_Bombs* of the world. Their default setting is 'no'. You can't convince them, so you don't try. You use them. Their angry denials add legitimacy and drama to the debate.

And then there's the big prize: the sixty percent in the middle. The persuadable majority. They could go either way. They are the audience watching the show, and my job was to convince them that the magic is real.

I cracked my knuckles. The curtain was up. First, I logged in as *Veritas_2012* to nurture the believers.

Reply to: StarChild82
You are welcome, brother. It's time for those with eyes to see to stand together. More truths will be revealed soon. Stay strong.

Next, I logged in as a different persona, *Skeptic_Sam*, to engage the 'Maybe Men'. This persona was designed to seem reasonable, just asking questions.

Reply to: MaybeMan
I had the same thought. I did some digging into this Bernays fella...he was involved in helping to overthrow the government of Guatemala for a banana company. The guy was more than just an ad-man. Logic_Bomb is right that it's from a PR book, but maybe that's the whole point? Maybe they've been hiding in plain sight all along?

Finally, I used a third account, *AgentM*, to counter the main sceptic, not by arguing with his facts, but by questioning his motives—a classic logical fallacy, but brutally effective.

Reply to: Logic_Bomb
Funny how quickly you jump to dismiss this. It's classic damage control. Who do you work for? Why are you so desperate to shut this conversation down? What are you so afraid we might find?

I hit 'Post' on all three. I was no longer just the author. I was the believer, the doubter, and the accuser. I was a digital puppeteer, creating the illusion of a growing movement. All I had to do was keep the show entertaining enough for the audience to stay in their seats.

Three personas. One thread. A full-blown ideological argument, crafted entirely by me.

I pushed back from the desk and went downstairs. The house was quiet. Emma was in the living room, sitting on a yoga mat in the soft light of the early evening sun. Her head was tilted up slightly, her eyes closed, her palms turned towards the sky, open to the world. She was meditating. Connecting with the 'Universal Force', as she called it. On the mantelpiece, next to a photo of our wedding, sat a collection of crystals—rose quartz for love, amethyst for calm. Her spirituality wasn't found in a dusty book or a cold stone church; it was personal, internal, something built from breathing, feeling, and 'energy'.

It was so different from her mum's way. She was old-school. A good Catholic woman who found her faith in the shared ritual of the Mass, in the grand, ancient stories of the Bible, in the solid, comforting presence of the church itself. She would kneel on a pew, her head bowed, her hands clasped tightly together, a part of something much bigger and older than herself.

And then there was our daughter, Ellie. She was just a toddler, playing on the floor. Her favourite toy was my old Nokia phone. The thing had a user manual as thick as a brick, yet Ellie, with her tiny, uncoordinated fingers, could somehow navigate the menus with an instinct that was utterly alien to me. She would press the chunky plastic buttons with a strange, innate logic, her face lit by the green-tinged glow of the monochrome screen, making the pixelated snake dance to her will.

Three generations, all in one room. My mother-in-law, a citizen of the old world of fixed institutions. My wife, a transitional figure, building her own bespoke spirituality from the ruins of the old one. And my daughter, a true digital native, for whom technology was not a tool to be learned, but a toy to be mastered.

It was all happening, just as Hendrik had preached. The great institutional shift wasn't some abstract theory. It was right here, in my house. I was being paid to pour petrol on that fire, but here was the gentle, real-world version of it. I stood there for a moment, watching them. The loving husband, the proud father, the secret architect of the new reality. It was a strange triple-life to be living. And I was only just getting started.

***

The Subliminal Sleep Merchant

In the summer of 1977, in a dusty corner of a rented flat above a butcher's shop in Leeds, Arthur Winlow ran a peculiar business.

Every Sunday, Arthur placed small ads in the classifieds section of regional newspapers across the UK. The ads were always the same:

> *"SLEEP BETTER TONIGHT—Subliminal Cassette Therapy. No effort. No drugs. Just results. £3.95 inc. postage. Money-back guarantee."*

Arthur's product was simple. He mailed out blank cassette tapes. Not silent tracks—*blank*. No subliminal messages, no gentle waves, no carefully engineered frequencies. Just magnetic tape, wound neatly in a plastic shell, doing absolutely nothing.

He didn't consider himself a fraud. He wasn't selling truth. He was selling the idea of truth. And in the end, for most people, that was more than enough. His money-back guarantee was genuine, and he honoured every request. But here's what fascinated him: only about 20% ever asked for a refund. Another 20% wrote letters full of praise: *"I haven't slept this well in years!" "Your tape is a miracle!"* Some even claimed to hear whispers guiding them to sleep.

Arthur understood something most didn't: people are suggestible. He'd learned it by watching the world. He saw how advertisers on TV and in newspapers shaped people's wants—not by logic, but by repetition and confidence. He watched politicians stir crowds into agreement with nothing but slogans and certainty. He read headlines that told people *how to feel* before they even got to the facts. He saw how easily minds could be led—not forced, just nudged—into belief.

The truth, he reckoned, was that if you wrapped a blank tape in the right words, the right setting, and just enough hope, people would do the rest themselves. Not out of foolishness, but because the human brain wants stories to be true—especially stories that promise change.

Some believed the tape worked, and for them, it did. Others didn't believe, and it didn't. But most never questioned it too closely.

Arthur didn't see himself as selling tapes. He was selling expectation. Wrapped in newspaper print and a polite guarantee, it was enough to change how people felt. Or at least, enough to make them think it had.

And so, from his little flat in Leeds, Arthur kept mailing out his blank tapes, sipping his tea, and marvelling—quietly, with a smile—at the strange and powerful magic of belief.

Chapter Eight

How to Build a Hero

It's one thing to build a fire online—to orchestrate a debate between your own sock puppet personas from the anonymous safety of your desk. It's another thing entirely to go out into the field and watch one of your star performers work his magic on a live audience. A few weeks after my first online foray, I got a call from Beth. She was in London.

"Will," she said, her voice as crisp and academic as a freshly printed journal article. "You need to see this. Michael Wright is doing a talk in a community hall in Croydon. It's early days for him, still a small crowd, mostly his own mailing list. It's the perfect time to observe a high-potential asset in its natural habitat before the signal gets too noisy."

Michael Wright. The name itself was a signal. I thought back to my visit to The Ministry of Truth, to Jez laughing at the crude drawing of a lizard and telling me with a grin about the ex-comedian who was preparing to deliver their most outlandish narrative. I'd been aware of his work for some time now, but this was my first chance to see him live.

I met her outside the hall that evening. It was a drab, brick building from the sixties, the kind of place that smelled faintly of damp coats, stale tea, and the quiet desperation of town council meetings. The crowd milling inside wasn't a mob; they were quiet, intense, a collection of seekers. There were sensible-looking men in sensible walking shoes, women in floaty scarves clutching well-thumbed paperbacks, a few younger lads with the wide-eyed look of recent converts. They were the people who felt something was wrong with the world but couldn't quite put their finger on what it was. They were looking for an answer, someone to give them a story.

And then I saw him. Michael Wright. He wasn't backstage psyching himself up. He was out front, working the room with the easy confidence of a man who had spent two decades on stage. He was moving from group to group, shaking hands, a warm, reassuring smile fixed on his face, looking people directly in the eye with a practised sincerity. He had a natural charisma that filled the slightly shabby room. This was no nervous novice fumbling with his notes. This was a professional.

And he was wearing the jacket.

The deep indigo jacket. It had become infamous after his disastrous first book launch, and was now as much a part of his persona as the theories themselves. The press had mocked it mercilessly, calling it a cult leader's robe, a dressing gown, a wizard's cloak. But what the media meant as ridicule, his followers had embraced as a badge of honour. To them, the jacket, with its intricate gold-thread patterns and shimmering crystal disc, wasn't a costume; it was a symbol of his unique connection to the cosmos, a "resonance map" as he'd once called it. It was the uniform of their guru.

When he took the small, hastily erected stage, the transformation was complete. He was not Mickey Wright, the comic. This was Michael Wright, the visionary. The friendly charm was still there, but now it was underpinned by a powerful, righteous fire. He spoke for two hours, his delivery flawless—the modulated tones, the confident gestures, the expertly timed pauses that drew the audience in. He had the timing of a stand-up, with the fire of conviction. And behind the professional polish was something else, something I hadn't expected: absolute, unwavering, white-hot belief. I was a professional, I knew how to spin a yarn, I knew how to spot a lie. This man wasn't lying. He believed every word he was saying. The audience was utterly captivated.

He told his story, his conversion narrative, weaving a tale of personal discovery and persecution. He talked about a pivotal, life-changing trip to Lake Titicaca in Bolivia, to the Isla del Sol—the 'Island of the Sun'. There, he had climbed a hill the locals called Palla Khasa. I was somewhat familiar with the story as I'd read some of his early books. My wife Emma has them, the New Age stuff.

Excerpt from *'Revelation on The Sacred Hill'* – by Michael Wright

I didn't hear it with my ears.

It wasn't a voice in the way you hear someone shout across a room. It was...everywhere. It was *through* me. Like it had been waiting there—patient—until I finally shut up long enough to feel it.

The light didn't blind me. It *revealed* me. That's what it felt like. And then the words came. Not one by one, not like sentences, but whole—complete.

"You made them laugh as Mickey.
Now you will make them listen as Michael."

It stopped me cold. Michael. That was my name, of course. My real name. But I hadn't heard it like that in years. Not like a name. More like...a command. Or a remembering.

"You were chosen for this before you were born.
And now—the veil lifts."

At that point, I couldn't stand. I didn't fall to the ground—the ground came up to meet me. My body couldn't hold the energy. My hands were shaking. My face was hot. I felt like I was about to explode, and then be rebuilt at the same time.

Then came the core of it. The reason:

"You will go out on a world stage.
You will reveal the truth behind the illusions of the world.
You will show them what lies beneath the surface—
the hidden hands, the silent structures,
the vibrational field that holds their minds in sleep."

Now...I didn't *understand* it. Not in that moment. But I felt it. Every word landed in me like it had always been there, just waiting to be unlocked.

"You were not sent to persuade—you were sent to speak—and many will fear you for it. But speak anyway. The ones who are ready will hear you."

And then:

"In the time still to come, they will speak of this hill,
and of the man who stood upon it, when the world was still asleep."

Then it was gone. Just wind. Just stone. Just me—sweating, blinking, breathing in a new reality I couldn't explain to a soul. Not yet. But I knew, as clearly as I know my name now: I'd gone up that hill as Mickey. I came down as Michael. And nothing—*nothing*—would ever be the same again.

—

The story was told with such passion, such raw emotion that, even though I was there only to observe, I still felt a flicker of something. The audience was rapt.

Then, just as he was wrapping up, he leaned into the microphone, his voice dropping to a conspiratorial whisper.

"But my friends," he said, "there is a deeper truth. A truth so shocking that the human mind struggles to comprehend it. I'm talking about the true nature of our leaders, the ones who pull the strings. They are not like you and me. They are...something else. Something cold-blooded."

The word "cold-blooded" hung in the air, a sudden, jarring note in his performance. The room, which had been buzzing with fervent energy, went instantly, eerily silent. You could feel a collective intake of breath. People shifted uncomfortably in their seats, glancing at each other with wide, confused eyes. A woman in front of me literally shook her head, as if trying to clear water from her ear. He had taken them to the edge of what they were willing to believe, and for a moment, it seemed like he might have gone too far.

It sent a jolt through me. *That's new*, Jez had said. *That one's about to break.* This was it. It was breaking, right here, in a damp community hall in Croydon.

But then, something remarkable happened. The initial shock didn't curdle into ridicule. It softened into a kind of fearful curiosity. I could see people leaning forward, desperate to understand. The silence was broken by a low murmur that rippled through the crowd—not of rejection, but of hesitant acceptance. A few people nodded slowly, their minds working to assimilate this new, impossible piece of information into the worldview they had already bought into.

He was their leader. And if he said it was true, then no matter how ridiculously far-fetched it sounded, it *must* be true. He had built up so much trust, so much charismatic authority, that he could now introduce a concept of pure, barking madness, and his followers would dutifully try to make it fit.

I whispered to Beth, my voice barely audible, "The lizard thing? I thought Jez had been joking about that."

She just gave a small, almost imperceptible nod, her expression a mask of cool, clinical observation. "The *monstrous enemy* archetype," she murmured back, her eyes still scanning the crowd's reaction. "A classic fear trigger. It's fascinating to see it deployed in real time."

***

After the talk, as a queue of people formed to thank him, we slipped out and found a nearby pub that looked like it hadn't been decorated since 1972.

"He's good," I said to Beth over a bottled beer. "Very good in fact. He's got great stagecraft, and he actually believes what he's saying too. That's a potent combination." I paused, swirling my bottle. "And that story about Bolivia...it's powerful stuff."

Beth took a slow sip of her wine and smiled, a knowing detached smile that didn't quite reach her eyes. "Yes, I'm happy with how that's turned out," she said. "It didn't quite happen the way it's told of course, but that's mythology for you. It's not entirely fabricated, but let's just say it's been...creatively enhanced."

I stared at her. "So that was your doing? But enhanced—why? He's already got them eating out of his hand."

"Because his original story was good, but it wasn't *mythologically sound*," she said. "What happened in Bolivia completes his narrative. It transforms his personal journey into a perfect, resonant myth. It turns Mickey Wright into *The Hero*."

She saw the puzzlement on my face. "It's my job, Will. I advise Hollywood studios on their scripts, and authors on their fantasy novels. I analyse story structures. And the most powerful, most enduring story structure we have, the one that's hard-wired into our collective consciousness, is *The Hero's Journey*. It's a template as old as time, and Michael Wright's life story—with a few of our own edits—is now a textbook example."

Her expression shifted from casual analysis to that of a professor about to explain a core concept. "You're seeing a perfect, real-world application of the Hero's Journey," she explained...

"The journey is always split into three acts," she began, now in full lecture mode. *"The Departure, The Special World, and The Return."*

"Act One: The Departure always starts with The Ordinary World."

"We meet the hero, but he's just an ordinary person. He feels like something is missing from his life. Think of Luke Skywalker on his moisture farm, bored out of his mind. Rocky Balboa, a washed-up boxer who knows he wasted his talent. Harry Potter, sleeping in a cupboard under the stairs."

She gestured with her glass. "For Michael Wright, he frames his own ordinary world perfectly in his book, *The Harmony Within*. He presents his life as a successful stage performer, yes, but he describes a growing spiritual unease. He talks about odd physical sensations, a feeling of being watched by some unseen force. He is establishing the classic 'hero in waiting,' the man who knows there must be something more to life."

"Next," she continued, "comes the **Call to Adventure.** Something unexpected happens. Destiny shows its hand. A holographic message from a princess, an offer for a title shot. For Wright? It was when the woman gave him a book at the Mind & Light Fair. '*I was told in a meditation this morning that a man with a troubled spirit would come to my stall today, and that I should give him this.*' She handed him a copy of a small paperback book, *Whispers from the Void*. That's his call."

"Then you always have the **Refusal of the Call**. The hero hesitates. Rocky turns down the fight. Luke says he has to get back to work on the farm. Wright reads the book: '*If there's anyone there...give me a sign! A proper one! Don't just send me books via nice ladies at mind-body-spirit fairs! Show me something real!*' This is his moment of doubt, his refusal to fully commit without more proof."

"And he gets his proof by **Meeting the Mentor**, that's the next stage," she said. "Every hero needs a guide—Obi-Wan Kenobi, Mickey Goldmill, Morpheus. The mentor sees the hero's potential. He is *The One*. For Wright, it's Madame Helena the spiritualist whose shop he happens to stumble on while walking round Covent Garden. She reads the tarot cards, the spirit speaks directly to Michael, referencing the specific doubts he shouted in his living room days before. '*You asked for a sign. You asked for something real. Here I am*'. The spirit then tells him he has been chosen, that he has a great purpose, and that he must write down what he learns to *awaken the others*. This is the undeniable proof and the direct guidance he was looking for. It's structurally perfect."

I listened, fascinated, as she laid it all out with the dispassionate air of an engineer describing a blueprint, and it followed exactly what I had already read in Emma's book about his spiritual awakening.

"Act Two: The Special World."

"The hero finally commits. He **Crosses the First Threshold**. There's no turning back. Harry gets on the Hogwarts Express; Neo takes the red pill. For Michael, this is when his spirit mentor tells him he will '*go on to the world stage and reveal great secrets.*' He has accepted his destiny."

"And in this special world, he faces **Tests, Allies, and Enemies**. This is the bulk of the story. It's where the hero trains and grows. Luke meets Han and Chewie. Dorothy meets the Tin Man, the Lion, and the Scarecrow. For Michael, his 'allies' were the other psychics and spiritualists he met. And his 'enemies'? The media. That book signing appearance where he was ambushed by those reporters and their cameramen?" she said with a glint in her eye. "We arranged that. He needed a powerful ordeal to create the 'test' element. Public humiliation was perfect for his future mythology."

"Then," she said, her voice dropping, "the stakes get higher. **The Approach to the Innermost Cave**. The hero nears his ultimate goal, but it's the most dangerous part of his journey. This is his journey to a strange and distant land, his trip to Bolivia and our enhanced storyline where he has his conversion on the hill."

"It's Saint Paul on the road to Damascus—the blinding light, the voice from Heaven, his new purpose. It's classic mythological symbolism. The hill is a place of transformation, a point of contact with the gods. The disembodied voice is a direct reference to the mythic nature of the story we're creating for him. Then comes ***The Reward***. He survives and seizes the sword. He now has a superpower: the ability to access secret knowledge."

"Act Three: The Return Home."

Beth concluded. "He's not the same man. He has the magic elixir, the gift. He takes ***The Road Back***, returning to the ordinary world to face his biggest challenge yet."

"He just needs his final ***Resurrection***. We're arranging something suitable right now. This time, he'll be treated seriously. It will complete his transformation. After that, he will be unstoppable."

"He has 'died' a figure of fun and is 'reborn' as a serious prophet. He has ***Returned with the Elixir***. He is triumphant. He has the gift that will save the world—the secret knowledge that will free humanity from the evil Illuminati."

She sat back and took a final sip of her wine. I was stunned into silence. It wasn't just a story. It was a formula, ancient and powerful, and they had applied it to a living man like a fresh coat of paint.

We talked more about the Hero's Journey. Beth explained how common the template was.

"It's not just the obvious epics like *Star Wars* or *The Lord of the Rings*," she said. "It's everywhere. Children's stories: *The Lion King, Aladdin, The NeverEnding Story*. Then there's *Groundhog Day*...I could go on and on and on. Comedies, too. Even *Monty Python and the Holy Grail*. King Arthur gets his Call to Adventure from God, he meets a Mentor in the form of Tim the Enchanter, he faces a series of absurd Tests—the Knights who say 'Ni!', a killer rabbit, the Bridge of Death—before finally reaching his goal. The structure is universal because it's the story of personal transformation."

"We're creating the new mythologies for our new society," Beth said, simply. "And Michael Wright is one of our first living myths. The stories he tells now will become some of our future mythologies—and his own story of transformation will also become one."

"My God," I said when she'd finished. "You've reverse-engineered his life to fit a story."

As we were getting ready to leave, she gave me a thoughtful look. "You know, Will," she said, her tone shifting from academic to friendly, "you're very good at this. You have a natural instinct for it. But you're wasting your time in that agency."

"It pays the bills," I shrugged.

"Jez was saying you should set up your own shop," she continued, a light, conspiratorial sparkle in her eye. "Go independent. It would give you more time and freedom to focus on...the more interesting work. And of course, there are perks. You've seen the kind of doors Jez can open. If you're going to be part of the project, you might as well get something out of it."

It was a gentle nudge. A friendly suggestion from a colleague. But I knew what it was. It was an invitation. The next step on my own journey.

Chapter Nine

The Signalroom

"Just quit," Jez had said over the phone, his voice breezy with the casual confidence of someone who has never had to fill out a job application in his life. "Don't faff about. Hand in your notice. We need you focused. It's time to set up your own shop."

And so I did. I walked into my old office—cluttered but familiar—and gave my boss, Jeff, four weeks' notice. He looked at me with a mixture of pity and confusion, probably assuming I was having an early midlife crisis and was about to go and buy a motorbike. If only he knew. He was surprisingly decent about it though, even offering me some old office furniture as a goodwill gesture—a couple of filing cabinets, a desk with a coffee ring etched into its surface, and a swivel chair with a persistent squeak.

I found the perfect place on the edge of a forgotten industrial estate, a part of town that time had forgotten and town planners had decided to ignore. It was an old, two-storey railway signal box, a red-brick relic from the age of steam, stranded at the end of a disused freight line now choked with weeds and cigarette ends. It had been converted into a cramped office space years ago and then promptly abandoned. It was all draughty sash windows, dusty venetian blinds that rattled when a lorry went past, and a kettle on top of a filing cabinet. The broadband connection was patchy at best, a hesitant, stuttering link to the new world from a building firmly rooted in the old one. I called the new business *Signalroom*. It felt right.

Emma helped kit it out. We crammed in Jeff's old desk, a knackered sofa we bought for a tenner from a charity shop, and a magnificent wall-mounted Bakelite telephone—purely aesthetic, but it completed the look. I set up my old, heavy typewriter on a side table for drafting statement quotes—there's something about the percussive, definitive clack of the keys that makes the words feel more authoritative. For decoration, we stuck up posters from past campaigns, a kind of personal greatest hits: The Millennium Dome and a faded *News of the World* front page that we'd helped seed brought back happy memories.

There was also my very first client who was assigned to me when I started out on my career proper all those years ago with Jeff—a well-known football manager. Like me, this manager was just starting out on his professional career, and he instinctively knew the power of a good positive image. He always wore sharp suits, he had his teeth whitened, and he hired a communication coach to help him perfect his speech, body language and presence.

My job wasn't to help him become a good football manager; it was to ensure that people's perception of him was one of a highly skilled, forward-thinking tactical visionary. It was a simple process. My client would keep me informed of any dressing room gossip he heard on the football grapevine regarding transfers of players, and I would then pass this on to our pet journalists on the sports desks. In return, they would ensure regular write-ups praising his credentials as a top coach, and one that any chairman would be lucky to have at their club. After a bad loss, the narrative was never "he got his tactics wrong." It was always "he was desperately unlucky with that refereeing decision," or "he hasn't been given the funds for the players he needs." I would also arrange for him to be invited onto radio phone-ins and TV punditry shows, where he could talk a good game, and come across as intelligent and passionate. It was a continuous, drip-feed of positive spin.

To most people, the £1,000 per week he paid our agency sounds like a fortune. But that investment kept his reputation intact, ensuring he was always seen as an 'unlucky tactical genius' rather than a bang-average manager. That perception could easily add a million pounds a year to any new contract he was negotiating, meaning the £50,000 each year he was paying us was money well spent. We weren't just managing his press; we were managing his market value. And business was good.

A week after we settled in, Jez called again. "Favour to ask, Will," he said. "Friend of my father's has a son. Bit of a handful. Needs a real job, a bit of grounding. Name's Crispin. He's smart as a whip, but a first-class git. Think you can take him on?"

It wasn't a question. It was the first tug on the golden leash. In his father's world, you didn't get an invoice; you got a phone call about a friend's son who needed a job. It was just the price of admission. "Send him over," I said.

Crispin arrived the next day, stepping out of a taxi that he clearly felt was beneath him. He was tall, slim, and dressed in clothes that cost more than my first car. He looked around my signal box with an expression of faint, aristocratic disgust, as if he'd just found a slug in his salad.

"Quaint," he said, the word dripping with a kind of pained conde-scension. "Frightfully... rustic. Does the little man still come out with a flag to wave the trains past?"

He was everything Jez promised: obnoxious, rude, and with an undisguised contempt for anyone who hadn't been to a school with its own crest and a complicated uniform. But he was also fiercely intelligent, with a cutting wit and a natural, born-to-rule grasp of how power worked. He was a perfect, horrible fit for the world of PR. Emma and I took to calling him 'Crispy', purely to reclaim some sense of satisfaction.

We were talking about the project, and I mentioned my trip with Beth to see Michael Wright.

"Oh, him," Crispin sniffed, examining his fingernails as if looking for imperfections. "The shouty man in the purple trench coat. A bit much, isn't he? One imagines he rather enjoys the sound of his own voice. Frightfully sincere. Never trust a man that sincere. It's terribly performative."

It was the first time anyone in the circle had passed a negative comment on Wright. At the time, I dismissed it as typical Crispin snobbery. But the comment lodged in my mind like a piece of grit in an oyster, and years later, I had to accept that he'd been the first to see the pearl of a very ugly truth.

***

The first contract for Signalroom came a few days later, and quite out of the blue. It was a big one: promote the Glastonbury Music Festival. But the client wasn't the festival organisers, or even a record label, nor the ticket agency. It was a new, high-end mobile catering collective called *Field & Flame – Artisan Festival Kitchens*. In my work, it's not always the obvious candidates who foot the bill—there's often less visible stakeholders behind the scenes whose whole business depends on the success of the main event.

"Right, Crispy," I said, laying the brief on the desk. "The client wants to sell posh burgers and wood-fired pizzas for fifteen quid a pop, so they need people with money. The problem is, Glastonbury is seen as a mud-bath for teenagers who live on warm cider and regret. How do we get middle-aged people with low mortgages and disposable income to sleep in a field and pay a premium for their dinner?"

Crispin didn't even blink. "Simple," he said. "We don't sell them a festival. We sell them their own youth back. We weaponise nostalgia. We make it emotionally indefensible for them to not go."

And just like that, we were off. It was a masterclass in the dark arts, our dusty signal box transformed into a campaign headquarters. Our target was anyone who grew up on Bowie, The Jam, and Blondie; anyone who now owned a slow cooker and thought their festival days were over. Our strategy was to reframe Glastonbury not as a youth event, but as a cultural pilgrimage. Not going wasn't just missing a gig; it was missing a piece of your own history.

"First, the radio," I said. "Radio 2, Capital Gold, Virgin. We hit them with the classics. Thirty-second spots." I started scribbling. "Bowie's '*Let's Dance*' as an intro...a warm, familiar voice-over, maybe someone like Trevor Nelson...'*You danced to it. You kissed to it. You lost yourself in it. Now it's time to hear it live again.*'"

"Good, but we need to inject the fear," Crispin added, pacing the small room. "The Fear of Missing Out. FOMO. The tag-line should be something like, *Come, or spend the next year lying about it.*"

"More subtle," I countered. "We'll do a post-festival FOMO campaign ready for next year—posters everywhere saying: *You Had to Be There.* But for now, we build the social pressure for this year. We need to make it seem like everyone is going."

"We need to create social proof," I said, sitting at my desk swirling a pen. "Everyone is going. Not just the kids, but people their own age, people just like them."

"The National Treasures," Crispin said with a smirk. "The ones who feel like a comfortable old jumper. Joanna Lumley," he said after a moment to think.

"Yes! She's perfect. It's *Absolutely Fabulous* goes to Glastonbury. What's her line?"

Crispin thought for a moment. "Something self-deprecating but inspiring. '*I thought I was too old for festivals. I was wrong. Turns out I was just out of practice.*' It's warm, it's relatable, it gives other middle-aged women permission."

"Brilliant," I said, writing it down. "Okay, someone else. A male this time."

"Billy Connolly?" suggested Crispin. "'*It's not about tents or toilets—it's about stories.*' It's poetic," Crispin offered. "Everyone loves Billy Connolly's stories, and they won't want to miss this one—they can be a part of it."

"What about a musician?" Crispin was going for the clean sweep of getting all three. "What about...now, what's his name...Socks?"

I had to think. "Suggs? From Madness?" I offered.

"Ah, yes. That's the chap," agreed Crispin.

"No, not a musician, they already belong at these festivals. We need someone who doesn't belong, someone more normal, someone who's a bit out of place. I've got it, Michael Caine! I'm sure he was actually there last year on stage with Socks, joining them for that song they wrote about him. See if we can find a photo of him in his wellies."

71

We spent the next hour putting together a list of six or seven celebs who fitted the bill.

We also developed the *Adult-Comfort* framing. We'd create a 'Glastonbury for Grown-Ups' insert for the *Observer Magazine*, with tips on dry camping and coffee hacks. We emphasised the morning yoga and the late-night jazz lounges rather than the mosh pits. We partnered with M&S and Barbour to create the illusion that this was a civilised, middle-class pursuit.

The final piece was explaining to Crispin *how* we'd seed the celebrity quotes. "Right," I said. "Time to use the bibles." I pulled out a couple of hefty, paper-based industry directories. "In this business, you never call the celebrity. You call their keeper—the agent, the manager, the publicist."

Crispin nodded, already way ahead of me. "A soft pitch. No payment, just an opportunity. Mutual alignment." He sat down at the computer, his fingers flying across the keyboard, drafting the perfect, non-committal, ego-stroking email. It was beautiful to watch. The boy was a natural.

It was a two-pronged attack. For the bigger names, it was about 'publicist coaching'—we'd send them a list of *messaging cues* and *themes,* and they would feed them to their client before a radio interview.

To: caroline.preston@publicity-prime.co.uk
From: crispin.devere@signalroom.co.uk

Subject: Light Touch Media Mention – Glastonbury 2001

Hi Caroline. Hope you're well.

Just reaching out with a very light touch opportunity that might be a nice fit for Anneka ahead of her upcoming radio appearances.

I'm currently heading up a quiet little nostalgia-led campaign around this year's Glastonbury Festival. The angle is very much about celebrating the festival's heritage and encouraging the post-youth demo of festival-goers to reconnect with live music. It's less about the mud and more about the memories.

We're not asking for formal endorsements or anything so crass. We were simply thinking that if Anneka happens to be discussing summer plans or nostalgia, a soft, off-hand mention of Glasto could be a wonderful, authentic-feeling moment for her audience. Something natural and conversational, along the lines of:

"I nearly said no this year, thought I was past it. Then I thought—when was the last time I did something truly unforgettable?"

It's just a thought-starter, of course. The key themes we're seeing resonate are "reconnection," "making new stories," and the idea of it being a "cultural pilgrimage" rather than just a music gig. As a small thank you from our end, we'd be delighted to arrange full VIP hospitality for Anneka and a guest should she decide to attend. We're working with premium food partners, so think less burger van, more artisanal sourdough and a decent Sauvignon Blanc.

No obligations of course. Just a thought in case it aligns with her media schedule. Let me know if this sounds workable.

Warmest regards,
Crispin de Vere
Senior Partner, Signalroom PR

For the smaller fish, the daytime TV presenters or *Loose Women* panellists, it was *informal prompting*. Crispin would call a publicist he knew.

"Darling," he'd purr down the phone, "if your lovely client happens to be talking about his summer plans on next week's show, do feel free to mention he's considering Glasto. We've got VIP passes with his name on them—full access to the nice food stalls, none of that dreadful mud. It would be a marvellous nostalgia angle for his audience."

It always worked. A week later, you'd be watching the telly and a presenter would say, completely 'spontaneously',

"I caught myself saying no to Glastonbury. That's when I realised—I was dangerously close to becoming sensible."

And I'd be sitting at home, grinning. The quote was ours, but the audience heard it from someone they liked and trusted. It was the third-party technique in its purest form.

That evening, feeling smug after a productive day, I got a call from Jez. "Heard you're getting the middle-aged to embrace mud and wet wipes," he said. "Field and Flame. Good work. Solid contract."

Ah... Jez. The penny dropped. It had come from him. "Yeah, it's a good start," I said proudly. "Classic campaign. Should be a piece of cake."

There was a pause. Then Jez said, his voice laced with that familiar, knowing amusement, "It's a great contract, Will. But it's not just about selling burgers."

"What do you mean?"

"Glastonbury," he said. "Beth and Bertil will explain more when you next see them at The Wall. Just make sure people turn up."

He hung up. I stood there, looking out the window of my signal box at the dark, derelict freight yard. Of course. It was never just about the burgers. It was never just about the music. It was also a job for the Ministry. Every signal I sent out served two purposes. There was the job you got paid for, and then there was the real work.

Chapter Ten

A Portfolio of Paranoia

AND SO, LIFE AT *Signalroom* settled into a strange, dual-natured routine. Our days were a patchwork of the mundane and the magnificent, the legitimate and the utterly insane.

On the one hand, we had our official work. We drafted monthly press releases for a dial-up internet service provider, trying to find new and exciting ways to say "our internet is slightly less slow than it was last month". We handled the media relations for a local political candidate—a lovely, little old man with such a small budget that our main strategy involved trying to get his cat featured in the local paper. We even had a brief, disastrous contract for a MySpace clone targeting older adults, which was called *GreySpace*. It never took off. Turns out most of the people it was aimed at didn't want to be online and thought MySpace was still a bit too wild. The client ditched the whole thing and started a mail-order pen pal club instead. Clever.

This was the stuff that paid the bills, our legitimate day job. But it wasn't what made us excited to come into the office in the morning. The real fun, the real purpose, began when we put the commercial projects to one side and logged into the forums. This was our assignment from the Ministry. Our primary role was to act as the ground crew for the grand narratives being spun from The Long Blue Wall. We were tasked with building the foundations for Beth's new mythologies, and hammering away at the old-world institutions for Dave's demolition project.

I concentrated on promoting the myth of the Illuminati. It was a beautiful, multifaceted project that allowed me to attack from three distinct angles, all designed to muddy the waters and create an unsolvable, compelling mystery.

First, I started with the easy one: the *real, historical Bavarian Illuminati.* They actually existed. It was a matter of public record. This gave me a kernel of truth to build my story upon. The original group were Enlightenment-era thinkers who wanted to promote reason over superstition and push back against the power of the church. My job was to misrepresent their goals, to twist their rational ideals into a sinister plot for world domination, and to frame their historical demise not as a failure, but as a strategic decision to "go underground" and continue their work in secret.

Second, I weaponised satire. There was a cult classic sci-fi book from the seventies called *The Illuminatus! Trilogy.* It was written as a joke, a brilliant, chaotic send-up of the very nature of conspiracy culture by connecting dozens of unrelated dots—Atlantis, the Kennedy assassination, UFOs, rock music—into one giant, absurd pattern. The supreme irony, of course, was that the authors themselves were horrified and amused that people were taking their fiction literally. They'd written the book to mock the very nature of blind belief, to show how easily the paranoid mind can connect unrelated dots. And what was the result? An entirely new generation of believers who used the book not as a warning, but as an actual roadmap. We helped them along the route.

And third, I connected our work directly to Michael Wright's. He was already pushing the idea that the Anunnaki gods of Sumerian mythology were alien visitors who had created humanity as a slave race. This was the perfect place to continue the alien creation story.

I would get regular emails from Beth with *talking points*, explaining how Wright's work was based on a deliberate misreading of Zecharia Sitchin's already-fringe theories, and how he had added his own reptilian layer on top. My job was to go online and defend Wright's 'research', to provide a second wave of 'evidence' to support his claims.

And woven through it all was the constant, background drumbeat of general anti-establishment rhetoric. Anything to support Dave's demolition job. We'd fire off posts about the Vatican being a front for the world's largest money-laundering scheme—with the Jesuits as the Pope's secret hit squad. We'd resurrect the old classics about the moon landings being faked by NASA. And we'd always, always, blame every war on the Rothschild and Rockefeller banking dynasties.

It was a full-time job, managing this portfolio of paranoia. We were the weavers, pulling threads from history, fiction, and pseudoscience, creating a story so vast, so contradictory, and so compelling that it was impossible to unpick. And in the quiet of our little signal box, surrounded by the ghosts of the steam age, we were building the foundations of the new one.

Crispin, meanwhile, with his natural flair for the outlandish, took charge of the broader Alien agenda. His main task was to convince people that humanity was the result of a cosmic experiment.

"Right, Crispy," I said one afternoon, pushing a packet of Hobnobs across the desk. "Today, we're giving humanity a new set of parents."

"Oh, good," he said, inspecting a biscuit for imperfections before deigning to eat it. "Are they from a decent family, at least? One does hope we're not descended from riff-raff."

I explained Beth's theory to him again: the old creation myth of Adam and Eve was losing its power. Our job was to replace it with a high-tech equivalent. The Garden of Eden story, at its core, is about a superior intelligence creating life through biological manipulation. We were just swapping a bearded God for a grey-skinned alien, and a divine miracle for a bit of advanced genetic engineering.

Crispin immediately logged in as one of his personas, *The_Antiquarian*, and started a new thread:

Title: *Genesis Revisited - Was the 'Garden of Eden' an Alien Laboratory?*

Post by The_Antiquarian:
A thought has been troubling me. We, as a culture, have dismissed foundational texts like Genesis as simple superstition. I find this to be a rather unimaginative and intellectually lazy position. What if we are not reading it correctly? What if the text is not a theological document, but a primitive anthropological account of a technological event?

Consider the key elements: a "God" (a superior, non-human intelligence) creates humanity from the "dust of the ground" (the planet's existing genetic material). He places them in a "garden" (a perfectly controlled biosphere or habitat) where all their needs are met. He forbids them from eating from the "Tree of Knowledge" (accessing a data terminal or supercomputer that would reveal their true situation?). Viewed through this lens, the story is no longer a fairy tale. It is a startlingly coherent, if primitive, description of a genetic engineering project. I submit that it's time we stopped dismissing these old stories and started re-examining them for the truths they are trying to tell us.

The replies came quickly. The believers loved it. The sceptics piled in with scorn. It was time for the show.

A user called *AstroNutter* posted a detailed, scientific takedown of the theory, citing the fossil record and the principles of evolution. This was our cue. "He's taken the bait," I said to Crispin. "He's trying to have a reasonable debate. I'll go first." I logged in as my *Skeptic_Sam* persona. My job was to look reasonable, to win over the undecided middle:

Skeptic_Sam replies to: AstroNutter
Some good points, mate. But evolution doesn't explain everything. What about the massive, unexplainable leap in human brain capacity 200,000 years ago? Science calls it a 'mystery'. This theory at least offers an explanation. Just saying...

I turned to Crispin. "Righto, your turn." Crispin's fingers flew across the keyboard. He logged in as *Patrician_Gaze,* his insufferably smug, aristocratic alter-ego:

Patrician_Gaze replies to: AstroNutter

Oh, do be quiet. Another tedious little man from the 'Science' cult, desperately trying to protect his crumbling worldview with his dusty old textbooks. It's so tiresome. Your 'facts' are terribly boring. Have you ever considered having an original thought, or do you just regurgitate whatever your grant-awarding committee tells you to? Please, go back to cataloguing pottery fragments and leave the big ideas to those of us no longer in short trousers.

It was a masterpiece of ad hominem. He hadn't addressed a single one of the man's facts. He had attacked his intelligence, his profession, his motives, his very worth as a human being. "A bit harsh, isn't it?" I said, taking a biscuit.

"Nonsense," Crispin replied without looking up from the screen. "It's like watching a hamster trying to reason with a python. He's completely bewildered. Now, while he's composing a tearful, point-by-point rebuttal, you need to create a distraction."

He was right. The sceptic's thread was spiralling into chaos, exactly as planned. While Crispin kept him pinned down with ad hominem attacks, it was time for me to perform the classic misdirection. I logged in as *Veritas_2012* and started a brand new thread on a different part of the forum, designed to look like a much more serious, intellectual discussion:

Title: *The Playbook: The Real Weapon is Your Mind*

Post by Veritas_2012:

Forget the ray-guns and the secret bunkers for a minute. The real weapon they use against us every single day is called 'Public Relations'. Look up a man named Edward Bernays. He wrote the manual on how to control the masses, how to 'engineer consent'. All the tricks the media and politicians use—the fake grassroots movements, the 'trusted experts', the emotional manipulation—it's all his work. They're not just selling you products; they're selling you what to think. And they're doing it right out in the open because they think we're too stupid to see it.

I hit 'Post' and leaned back in my chair. It was a beautiful piece of work, and the kind of move that made me love my job—it was a perfect piece of professional hypocrisy. Here I was, warning people about the hidden dangers of propaganda and astroturfing, while using a fake online persona on a forum that was part of a larger, even more sophisticated astroturf campaign. I was exposing the very techniques that I, and the websites these people trusted, were using on them at that very moment. We were the disease masquerading as the cure.

Crispin leaned back in his chair, a look of immense satisfaction on his face. "A job well done," he said.

We hadn't proved a single point. We had simply shut down a rational, intelligent discussion with pure, orchestrated chaos. I poured us both a celebratory cup of lukewarm tea from the kettle on the filing cabinet. It was just another afternoon for the Ministry of Truth.

Chapter Eleven

Year Zero

IT WAS A TUESDAY. September 11th, 2001. A beautiful, clear, early autumn day. The sky was a crisp, impossibly cloudless blue. In the Signalroom, Crispin and I were mired in the deeply important business of arguing about the font for a magazine insert. Life felt absurdly, comfortably normal.

Then the phone rang. It was Emma. "Will? Are you watching the telly?" Her voice was strange, thin.

"No, I'm working. Why, what's up?"

"Turn it on," she said. "Just... turn it on. Any news channel."

I switched on our small portable TV. The screen flickered to life, showing a picture that didn't make sense: one of the twin towers of the World Trade Center, a ghastly plume of black smoke pouring from a gaping hole near the top.

"...appears a small, private aircraft has accidentally crashed into the North Tower..." an anchor was saying.

And then we saw it. The second plane. It glided into the frame from the right, not wobbling or struggling, but moving with a smooth, sickening purpose. It banked slightly, like a bird of prey adjusting its trajectory, and slammed into the second tower. The fireball that erupted was silent on the television, a ghastly ballet of fire and falling debris that defied all reason. In that instant, everything changed. The word 'accident' evaporated from the universe.

The days that followed were strange and muted. The world seemed to hold its breath. All the noise of normal life—the petty arguments, the deadlines, the celebrity gossip—just stopped. At the Signalroom, the phones were silent. Our campaigns felt trivial, obscene. We just sat there, like everyone else, watching the endless, looping footage of smoke and dust and falling paper. At home, Emma and I would watch the news for hours, barely speaking. There was a real sense of a line being drawn. A feeling that we were now living in the *after*. Nothing would ever be the same again. And I knew this would be true for both of my lives.

Then, on the Friday, the old Bakelite phone on my office wall rang. I'd had a new business line installed for it just a few weeks prior. I picked it up. It was a woman's voice—clipped, calm, and sounding utterly unaffected by the week's events. She spoke with a cool, precise clarity that left no room for questions or argument. "Is that Mr. Camden?"

"Speaking," I said.

"This is Lord Harrington's office calling," she said. "His Lordship has requested your presence. A car will be with you in one hour. Please pack an overnight bag. The core team is being summoned to Frankfurt."

She'd said it all so calmly, with such an air of absolute authority, that I just mumbled a quick "Okay, thank you," before she hung up. I stood there for a moment, puzzled. *Lord Harrington?* The name sounded vaguely familiar, but I couldn't quite place it. And then a memory sparked. Harrington. That was Jez's surname.

What was going on? I had assumed Jez was the man in charge, the leader of this strange little club. But the call hadn't come from him. It had come from his father, Lord Harrington—a man with a secretary who sounded like she could have someone killed with a single, polite phone call. For the first time, I had the distinct, unsettling feeling that I didn't know whose game I was actually playing in.

My mobile rang, snapping me out of my daze. It was Dave. "You get the call, Will?" he asked, his voice low.

"Just now. From Lord Harrington's office."

"Yep. The high command has spoken," he said with a sigh. "Time to go and see what the grown-ups have decided our new reality looks like. See you there, mate." The summons had come from the very top. The game had just got a whole lot bigger.

The journey was a blur of silent cars and a near-empty private jet. We were all there, assembled in our familiar room on the satellite campus of the Frankfurt university. But this time the atmosphere was different—tense, sombre.

At the head of the room, standing before The Long Blue Wall, was a man I had only seen from a distance. The memory was brief, a ghost from our placement days. He had walked through the open-plan office once, on his way to a meeting with the CEO. I remembered him nodding briefly to Jez as he passed, but otherwise making no fuss—just a man with a purpose moving quietly through someone else's space.

This was Lord Alistair Harrington. The 9th Marquess of Halebury. He was in his sixties, tall and impeccably dressed, but it wasn't his title or clothes that commanded the room. It was his presence. The moment he turned his gaze on you, the air seemed to steady. He had a quality of absolute, unshakable calm, a stillness that made everyone else in the room feel slightly frantic by comparison. It was the quiet, earned authority of a man who had seen conflict, borne responsibility, and had nothing left to prove.

I looked at Jez, standing respectfully a few feet behind him. I could see the family resemblance now. Jez had his father's height and sharp intelligence, but his confidence was expressive and radiant—a bright, charismatic energy that projected outwards and drew people in. Lord Harrington's was different. It was an inward certainty, a quiet, compelling pull that made the room bend towards him. One was a spotlight; the other was a centre of gravity.

"A terrible week," Lord Harrington began, his voice measured and clear, holding us all in its solemn integrity. "A tragedy for the people of America and for the world. We will take a moment to acknowledge that." He paused, letting the silence hang in the room, a genuine mark of respect.

"But," he continued, his tone shifting from pastoral to strategic, "we must now see it for what it is: a catalyst. A paradigm shift. An event that has created a wound in the collective psyche. And into that wound, fear will pour. It is our duty to channel that fear, to give it a narrative that serves our ultimate purpose."

He gestured to a man I hadn't noticed, standing quietly to one side by the board. He was in his late thirties, with a head of thick, dark hair and a formidable moustache that gave him the air of a Cold War chess master.

"To that end, I'd like to introduce our newest colleague, Maks," Lord Harrington said. "He is a physicist of considerable talent, and his expertise will be of great benefit. He will provide the scientific ammunition for our campaign." He then gave a slight nod towards Beth. "Maks will also," he continued, "be lending his equally extensive knowledge of astrophysics to Beth's ongoing work on the *2012* narrative. A project of equal, if more long-term, importance."

Maks, a Latvian with a sharp Russian accent that I could detect even in his silence, gave a short, formal nod to the room. He was clearly a specialist, a man brought in for a very specific purpose.

Lord Harrington's gaze swept across us one last time. "You will hear from my son when we have narratives to push. For now, listen. Watch. Learn. The story is just beginning."

***

That evening, we gathered in the dark, wood-panelled bar of a grand old hotel in the town centre. It was a classic 'lobbyist' bar, a neutral territory of quiet corners, comfortable leather armchairs, and expertly made cocktails—the perfect place to discuss our work in hushed tones. Lord Harrington, with the quiet wisdom of a true leader, did not join us. He knew his troops needed time to relax, to speak freely without the weight of his presence in the room.

The mood was a strange mix of sombre and electric. We were all processing the week's horrific events, but also the cold, strategic purpose of our being there. It was a chance for me to be properly introduced to the team's new recruit.

"Will, this is Maks," Jez said nodding between us. "Maks, meet Will."

Maks shook my hand firmly. He looked slightly older in the dimmed light of the restaurant, with sharp, intelligent eyes and an air of intense focus. "A pleasure," he said, his English perfect but wrapped in a heavy, rolling Russian accent.

He explained that he was a physicist, originally from Latvia, who had come over to the West after the collapse of the Soviet Union. He was now based in Wales, of all places, where his main passion, aside from astrophysics, was amateur dramatics. He was the perfect recruit: a scientific mind with a flair for performance.

At one point, as we waited for drinks, he pulled out a heavy, brass-coloured pen and began absent-mindedly clicking it. "Soviet," he said, catching my glance. "My father's. He got it when he made colonel." He signed the bar receipt with deliberate, precise script. "Still works better than anything you buy today." The pen made a crisp snap as he capped it—an oddly final sound. Then it disappeared back into his inside pocket, like a prop returning to its box.

"Lord Harrington has assigned me the post-mortem of the New York event," Maks said. "My purpose is to analyse the physics of the structural collapses. Early data is always chaotic, but within the chaos, there are always... inconsistencies. Thermal anomalies. Material stress points that do not align with a simple fire. Facts that do not fit a simple narrative. I will find these facts. I will provide the technical and scientific anomalies. Your job..." he said, looking from Jez to me, "will be to build the story around them."

"And for Beth," he gave a slight, almost imperceptible smile, "I provide the hard data for her 2012 campaign. The orbital mechanics, the solar flare projections. I give her the numbers, and she will find the poetry in them."

Charlotte, our resident historian and keeper of the Family Trees, was still buzzing from the meeting with Lord Harrington. "Your father is just incredible, Jez," she gushed, her eyes shining. "The way he holds a room. So much charisma."

"He's just my dad, Lottie," Jez shrugged, clearly uncomfortable with the praise.

"But you're 'The Honourable Jeremy' then, aren't you?" she pressed. "As the son of a peer?"

Jez winced slightly. "Technically, yes."

"What's your full name?" Charlotte asked, her inner fangirl taking over.

Jez sighed, as if preparing for a familiar humiliation. "The Honourable Jeremy Peregrine Uther Harrington."

There was a moment of stunned silence before Dave let out a roar of laughter. "Peregrine Uther! Bloody hell, Jezza! You sound like a wizard from a children's book!" The table erupted, the tension of the day finally broken.

The conversation eventually turned to my Glastonbury work. I mentioned how Jez had hinted that it was about more than just selling tickets.

"Ah yes," Beth said, a knowing smile on her face. "It's the symbols. It's about normalisation through mass exposure. Glastonbury has always been the perfect incubator for the alternative crowd, a spiritual home for the seekers. But that's too small a demographic for our purposes."

She leaned forward, her voice taking on a more strategic tone. "The goal now is to move the entire festival into the mainstream. It needs to become a national institution, a cultural rite of passage that everyone feels a part of—not just the counterculture crowd. That's why your 'Glastonbury for Grown-Ups' campaign is so vital. It will broaden the audience."

"The more mainstream the festival becomes," she continued, "the more the BBC will ramp up its coverage. Soon, it will be a national television event, watched by millions from their sofas. And when that happens, our symbols won't just be seen by a few thousand people in a field. They will be broadcast, subtly and repeatedly, into every living room in the country. You plant the symbols there, and they will seep into the mainstream. You're not just showing them to people; you're making them a normal, unavoidable part of the cultural wallpaper."

"We're talking about the *Eye and the Pyramid?*" I asked.

"Yes, the Eye and the Pyramid," she confirmed. She leaned forward, her tone shifting from casual conversation to a relaxed, informal lecture. "You see, Will, humans are symbolic creatures. We don't just live in a physical world; we live in a world of meaning. And symbols are the shortcuts to that meaning. Think about it. A red light means 'stop'. A tick means 'correct'. A crucifix means—if you put its religious status to one side—it means two thousand years of Western history, morality, and culture, all distilled into one simple shape."

"These types of symbols," Bertil continued as he joined the conversation, "act as unifying anchors for a society. They appear on our buildings, in our art, around our necks. They work on a subconscious level, constantly reinforcing a shared set of values, a group identity. They're a quiet, constant reminder of the rules of the tribe. The crucifix, the star and crescent, the Star of David...Yes, they are religious symbols, but they are more than that, they are cultural symbols. They all perform the same function."

"And the Crucifix—our old primary symbol here in the West—is losing its power," Beth went on. "Its meaning is becoming diluted in a secular age. So we need new ones—new unifying cultural symbols for the coming new era. We chose the Eye and the Pyramid because they're ancient, powerful, and ambiguous. They suggest knowledge, watchfulness, structure, mystery—all perfect themes for our upcoming new age."

"And our colleague in New Zealand—his website is up and running," Jez chimed in. "*The Veiled Signal,* it's called. It's the perfect delivery system. He's a brilliant PR man. He's just like you, Will. He does the promotional work for us. He deconstructs music videos, Hollywood movies, corporate logos, and then presents them all as 'proof' of a supposed Illuminati conspiracy."

"It's a nice piece of misdirection," Beth said. "He makes the symbols seem dangerous, subversive, edgy. He brings massive attention to them. And people, especially young people, react by adopting them. They wear them on T-shirts, they get them as tattoos. They do it to look cool, to act rebellious maybe, but they're actually walking billboards for a huge, subtle branding campaign. They are unwittingly adopting the new corporate logo for the entire Western world."

I thought back to the Glastonbury planning materials we'd been sent—the festival maps, signage mock-ups, merchandise designs. The Eye and the Pyramid were there already, lurking in plain sight. The official branding was full of geometric motifs: rays of light fanning out from a triangle, a pupil nestled inside a stylised sunburst. At the time, I'd assumed it was just a nod to counterculture aesthetics—a sort of psychedelic pastiche.

But now I saw it for what it was: a soft launch. This wasn't just about the festival. This was bigger. This was the slow introduction of a new iconography. They were using mainstream popular culture—and at the same time the entire anti-establishment wing of the Conspiracy Movement—to embed their chosen symbols into the public psyche. A cultural logo for a future that hadn't quite arrived—yet.

I looked around the table at this strange collection of academics, showmen, and aristocrats. Within just a few days of the world changing forever, we were sitting in a German restaurant, quietly finalising the emblems for the new one.

Chapter Twelve

The Cool Dad Mandate

AFTER THE INTENSITY OF the 9/11 summons, it was a sobering jolt to return to the reality of the Signalroom. While we had been making plans to introduce our own narrative for the global tragedy, a new leak had appeared in the ceiling above my desk. The grand sweep of history, I was reminded, doesn't stop the rain from coming in. The roof still needed fixing, the broadband was still rubbish, and there were bills to be paid.

The Glastonbury campaign had been a resounding success, earning us a tidy fee and a reputation for being able to sell water to a fish—or in this case, mud and chemical toilets to the respectable middle-aged. But that contract was winding down. I was starting to feel the familiar churn of anxiety that comes with running your own business—the constant, gnawing fear of the pipeline running dry.

I needn't have worried. Early, one damp Wednesday morning, an email landed. It was from a very senior civil servant at the Department for Social Cohesion and Development, a government body I'd barely heard of. They were inviting Signalroom to tender for a major public awareness campaign.

"I wonder how they found us?" I said to Crispin, who was busy trying to remove a speck of dust from his laptop screen with a silk handkerchief.

He glanced at the email. "They didn't find us, William," he said, without looking up. "We were placed in front of them. One from Jez's father I would wager. Consider it your performance bonus."

He was right, of course. This was the other side of the deal. This was how they paid us. Not with a cheque from a slush fund, but with a gilt-edged, legitimate contract dropped in our laps. A network dividend.

The brief was fascinating. The government had a problem: teenage pregnancy rates were stubbornly high in certain areas. They wanted to bring them down.

"I see," Crispin said, finally giving the brief his full attention. "So, they want us to run a campaign telling teenagers to wear johnnies and stop shagging in parks."

"No," I said, pointing to a key paragraph. "They've tried that. Direct education, safe-sex campaigns in schools...it doesn't move the needle enough. They want something different. Something subtle."

"Subtle?" Crispin raised a perfectly sculpted eyebrow. "The government wants subtlety? That's a first."

"They don't want to talk about sex at all," I explained. "They want to change behaviour. They want to give teenagers something else to do in the evenings besides hanging around with their mates, drinking cheap cider, and fumbling their way to parenthood."

Crispin was silent for a moment, a slow smile spreading across his face. "Oh, this is good," he said, the glee evident in his voice. "This is our kind of work. They don't want a public service announcement. They want a full-blown social engineering project."

"The goal," I said, "is to make it cool to spend time with your parents, to make teenagers actually want to go out and do things with their mum and dad."

Crispin let out a short, sharp laugh. "Good heavens. In my day, being seen socially with one's parents was a fate worse than a public flogging. It was considered a catastrophic failure of one's social independence."

"Yep, me too," I said. "So, how do we do it?"

And so began one of the strangest and most satisfying campaigns of my career. The objective wasn't to sell a product, but to sell an idea: the idea of the family as a social unit. We weren't just a PR agency; we were becoming amateur sociologists.

"You don't lecture them," Crispin declared, pacing the small room. "You colonise their free time. You make their parents' world more appealing than the park bench."

Our first work stream was 'The Cool Dad'. We needed to create an archetype. We worked with scriptwriters on a new family sitcom, subtly influencing the father character. He wasn't a bumbling oaf like Homer Simpson. He was a bit like your mate's dad who not only had the original vinyl of The Stone Roses, but could also tell you which B-side was better. He wasn't trying to be down with the kids; he was just authentically cool in his own right. The kind of dad you wouldn't mind going to a gig with. The idea that your dad could be cool was now out there.

Next, we tackled fashion. The generation gap, visually, was a chasm. We worked with high-street clothing brands, seeding the idea of 'cross-generational' styles. Skinny jeans, classic trainers, retro band T-shirts. They would produce similar styles in both adult and youth sizes. The message, delivered through fashion magazines like *The Face* and *i-D*, was that style had no boundaries. We were subtly eroding the uniform of teenage rebellion, making it harder to tell the parent from the kid.

Then came the activities. We seeded stories in the media of families doing interesting, exciting things together. We had travel writers pitch articles on 'secret' European city breaks, perfect for a weekend away. The subtext was clear: cool parents don't take their family to a boring beach resort; they take them to a brewery escape in Belgium, or a street art festival in a corner of Paris. We influenced TV shows to feature storylines about parents and children going to football matches together, or bowling, or the cinema. And we worked with local authorities to make it easier to receive funding to run evening and weekend workshops like football coaching, martial arts tasters, or local drama clubs—anything that would give the youngsters something new to do, with their parents either chaperoning them or acting as their taxi service. The goal was to fill up the evenings, to replace aimless hanging about with structured, engaging activity.

It was all about the slow, steady drip of suggestion. A story here, a TV character there, a fashion spread, a radio phone-in topic. None of it looked like a government campaign. It just looked like life ticking along naturally.

And it gave me something else to think about too. I had always thought of 'conspiracy' as something dark and sinister—shadowy figures plotting in secret to achieve some malevolent goal.

But this was different. This was a benign conspiracy. A conspiracy of good intentions. A secret, undeclared collaboration between government departments, media producers, and PR agencies, all working together to nudge society in a healthier, more stable direction. There was no evil cabal, just a series of committees. There were no secret handshakes, just budget meetings and strategy documents.

And it was happening everywhere, all the time. It was the reason we all started recycling our plastics, the reason the once-glamorous act of smoking was now seen as a grubby habit. These weren't accidents or organic social shifts. They were the results of patient, well-funded, and entirely covert campaigns. They were the product of thousands of hours of work by sociologists, psychologists, and public relations people like me, all working behind the scenes to gently, invisibly, engineer our consent for the wider good of the whole.

It was, in its own way, far more unsettling than a simple story about the Illuminati or aliens. The idea that a few well-meaning experts could sit in a room and decide to move our collective furniture without any of us ever knowing they'd been there, was a strangely compelling concept. It implied that even the good in our society was as carefully manufactured as the lies—a fact which, professionally speaking, I couldn't help but admire.

I looked at the whiteboard in our office. It was covered in our campaign notes for the *Cool Dad Mandate*. Flow charts, target demographics, key messages. It was a smaller, more focused, and infinitely more straightforward version of The Long Blue Wall—but it was run on identical tactics. The methodology was the same, the only difference was the objective. While we were looking to create a whole new set of beliefs and a new worldview for the upcoming Technological Era—the Department for Social Cohesion just wanted teenagers to stop getting knocked up.

We were all in the business of social engineering. And I was now a key player in both games: the respectable, public-facing one, and the real, world-altering one happening in the shadows.

***

Setting:
Sixth Form Common Room, 2004. A cracked whiteboard, forgotten custard creams, and a knackered projector that takes two minutes to warm up.

Teacher (clapping hands):
"Alright, listen up. This is Leo. He's here as part of your careers advice week. He's going to talk to you about sociology. Try not to fall asleep."

A few chuckles. Someone sips flat Lucozade. Leo steps forward, adjusts his jacket. "Cheers. Right. I'll get straight to it. I studied sociology. And no, before you ask, I don't work at a bank, and I'm not a manager at McDonald's. Not that there's anything wrong with that—someone has to be in charge of gherkin distribution... but it's not me."

A few smirks. One eyebrow lift.

"I work with behaviour. Real behaviour. Not what people *say* they do—but what they *actually* do when no one's looking. Sociologists work with supermarkets, phone companies, bits of government. Some of it's public, most of it isn't. All of it's interesting. It's like having administrator privileges for society's operating system, while everyone else is just a standard user."

Slide 1: *A supermarket trolley.*

"This is Supermarket Trolley Model 9-B. The handle is off-centre. Why? Because it subtly shifts your balance. Makes your *right* hand reach higher shelves—where they put the wholegrains, the organic pasta, the stuff the government wants you to eat more of. We tested it. Healthy purchases up 18%. No signs. No slogans. Just nudging."

A kid up front blinked.

"Why not just tell people what to buy?"

"Because people hate being told, so we have to find a different way. They like finding things out for themselves. Sociology helps them do that."

Slide 2: *Big Brother on screen. Crowd cheering.*

"Anyone watching this? Thought so. A couple of years ago, when these shows were starting out, a bunch of sociologists worked with the TV producers. Not to make it nicer, but to make it feel more human. Less shouting, more moments where people opened up, talked about their lives, cried a bit."

He scanned the room.

"You know what that did? Made it okay for you lot to talk about your feelings online. On Myspace. In texts. In school. That shift didn't just happen. It was nudged along by people like me."

Slide 3: *A Nokia phone—the chunky kind.*

"This one's being worked on right now. You won't notice yet but the next phone you buy, the keypad will be louder when you're texting. Loud clicks make texting less sneaky. If everyone can hear you, it's harder to send nasty messages under the desk. Might cut down on bullying, or dodgy texts. We'll see. That's the idea though."

A boy near the back said, "That's actually smart."

Slide 4: *A CCTV image from a night bus.*

"This one's happening right where I live. They've hired actors to ride late-night buses in high-conflict zones. They perform small acts of kindness: helping with bags, picking up dropped coins, giving up seats. Always quiet, always believable."

"In six weeks, violence has dropped by nearly half. No arrests. No speeches. Just presence. We changed the emotional temperature of a moving vehicle."

Someone at the back muttered "That's mental."

Leo smiled and let it hang in the air. The room was quiet now.

"Sociology isn't about telling people what to do. It's more subtle. It's about shifting the vibe till the new way feels right. From the shadows, from the trolleys, from the bus seats, from the confessional booth of reality TV."

The bell rang, harsh and shrill. No one moved.

Leo put the slides away and zipped up his bag. As he reached the door, he turned.

"If you want to change the world, don't become a politician. Become a sociologist. We're the ones who move the furniture when no one's looking."

Chapter Thirteen

Scientific Smackdown

THE CALL FROM JEZ came on a rainy autumn morning, a couple of years after the attack. The initial raw grief of 9/11 had subsided, replaced by a simmering stew of patriotism, fear, and a thousand unanswered questions. The soil was fertile. It was time to plant our seeds.

"Right." Jez's voice crackled down the business line. "It's time. The official report will be released soon, and it's a mess of contradictions. The American conspiracy scene is bubbling up nicely with their own theories, and will soon go into overdrive. I want us to ride their coat-tails. Our objective isn't to find the truth—that's not our concern. Our objective is to use this event to accelerate public distrust in all official institutions. This is a demolition job, pure and simple. Maks is now on point for all technical queries. He's your new best friend."

I put the phone down and looked over to Crispin. "The Ministry has spoken," I said. "We're going to war."

Crispin's eyes, which had been glazed over with the boredom of writing a press release for a regional accounting firm, suddenly lit up with a predatory gleam. "Splendid," he said. "A proper war. Not just a skirmish. What's the strategy?"

I grabbed a marker pen and went over to the whiteboard we'd installed on one of the signal box's old brick walls. "Jez wants us to hit this from all angles," I said. "We can't just push one theory. That's amateur hour. This is a multi-theory offensive. A narrative for every type of sceptic." I drew a large circle in the middle of the board. "The core message is simple: *You Are Being Lied To.* But the delivery has to be tailored."

I drew four lines branching out from the circle. "We'll have four main pillars to the campaign, each designed to appeal to a different psychological profile."

"Pillar One: The Rationalists → They need science," I wrote.

"This is for the people who are too smart for conspiracies—well, that's what they tell themselves. The ones who need numbers, data, a sense of intellectual confidence. We don't give them myths; we give them science."

"So we data-dominate them?" Crispin said, a smirk on his face. "A scientific smackdown."

"Exactly," I replied. "This is where Maks comes in. We'll lead with his stuff. The controlled demolition argument. The physics-defying collapse of the towers at near free-fall speed. The pools of molten metal in the rubble that jet fuel can't explain. The whispers of military-grade thermite. It's all technical, jargon-heavy, and almost impossible for a layperson to properly debunk. They'll be satisfied to go along with this one."

"Pillar Two: The Cynics → They need motive," Crispin offered, pacing the room.

"The *'Cui bono?'* crowd. 'Who benefits?' This is for the world-weary, the readers of *The Economist*, the people who believe all politics is a grubby backroom deal. We push the *Project for a New American Century* angle. We find that quote about needing a *'new Pearl Harbor'* and we hammer it home. We talk about the oil contracts in the Middle East, the swift passing of the Patriot Act. We frame the whole thing as a simple, grubby, neo-conservative power grab."

"Good," I nodded. "It feels less tinfoil hat and more like a gritty political thriller. It appeals to their sense of worldly cynicism."

"Pillar Three: The Everyman → They need absurdity," I continued, writing it on the board.

"This is the bread and butter stuff. The appeal to pure incredulity. The details that just don't make sense. This is for the man in the pub. We lead with the story of the indestructible magic passport, supposedly belonging to one of the hijackers, found pristine on a New York street. We'll make it so absurd it will make people question the entire official story."

"And the phone calls from the planes," Crispin added. "We can seed doubts about the technology. *Could you really get a clear mobile signal at 30,000 feet in 2001? Just asking questions.* It's wonderfully insidious."

"Finally," I said, writing the last heading.
"Pillar Four: The Mystics → They need meaning,"

"Ah," Crispin said, with a connoisseur's appreciation. "For Beth's lot. Some real life ceremonial magic for the New Agers, the Third-Eye Truthers."

"Precisely. For them, we frame it not as a political event, but as a mass occult ritual. We talk about the destruction of the twin pillars, like Boaz and Jachin from Masonic lore. We find those tarot cards printed years before that seemed to depict the towers burning. We don't claim it's proof; we just post the image with the caption, '*Make of this what you will...*' We give them a sense of cosmic, fated significance. They'll love it."

I stood back from the whiteboard. It was a complete campaign strategy. Four distinct narratives, each targeting a different part of the human psyche: the need for logic, the comfort of cynicism, the shock of absurdity, and the allure of myth.

"Right," I said. "Let's get our new best friend on the phone. We need some ammunition for Pillar One."

I dialled Maks's number. He was now our in-house 9/11 expert, our scientific authority. He wasn't looking for what was true; he was looking for what was anomalous. He had been sifting through the data for anything that didn't quite fit the official narrative, anything we could pry open with a crowbar of doubt.

He picked up on the first ring, his voice a torrent of excited, Russian-accented jargon. "Ah, William! Now listen... The official narrative is an insult to the laws of thermodynamics. It is an engineering absurdity. We have near free-fall acceleration, a near-perfect vertical collapse into the building's own footprint—but, from office fires? No, this is not a random structural failure. This is a demolition. A very clean one, actually. But the story they built on top of it is... clumsy. Very clumsy."

I put him on speakerphone. Crispin and I sat there, pens poised, ready to translate his scientific consternation into a series of simple, elegant, and devastatingly effective lies. He was our scientific weapon; Crispin and I were the artillerymen, tasked with firing his science shells into the digital battlefield. The war had begun.

We dived into the forums. The Americans were already running with a brilliant, simple slogan: *9/11 Was an Inside Job.* As one of the old PR masters said, propaganda must be simple and repetitive. You reduce a complex problem to its simplest terms and then you hammer it home, again and again. It's the same reason *A Mars a day helps you work, rest and play* sold millions of chocolate bars. The masses don't remember nuanced arguments—they remember a catchy phrase.

Our job was to provide the 'evidence' to back up the slogan. We co-opted everything we could find. It wasn't long before we found a perfect little ember flickering in a dusty corner of the internet called *iFilm*, a quirky video site before YouTube made that sort of thing a global phenomenon. Buried in its new 'Underground' section was a 45-minute DIY documentary called *The Shift: Shadows of September*.

It wasn't slick or professional, and that was its superpower. In a world of polished news reports, its grainy footage, slow fades to black, and ominous synth soundtrack felt more real, more authentic. It had the texture of forbidden truth. It was the perfect piece of third-party content. We didn't have to endorse it; we just had to share it. We didn't care if its claims were true; we only cared that they were plausible-sounding and emotionally resonant.

"*Have you guys seen this?*" My *Skeptic_Sam* persona would post on forums like *Something Awful* and early *LiveJournal* blogs. "*A bit rough around the edges, but it asks some important questions.*"

We'd watch as the link spread. iFilm eventually bundled it into a mini-playlist called *Alt Realities,* alongside other low-budget videos about faked moon landings and suppressed technology. It was beautiful. We weren't just promoting one video; we were promoting an entire world-view, a curated library of doubt.

Our campaign had a single, unifying message: *You Are Being Lied To.* By everyone. The government, the media, the scientists.

Dave was thrilled. "This is my department firing on all cylinders!" he chortled down the phone. "We're not just questioning one event; we're questioning the very competence and trustworthiness of every Western institution. It's brilliant!"

***

Excerpt from *"Guidance for the Public Consultant: Influence, Sympathy & Strategic Sentiment" (1928 Confidential Circulation)*

Chapter V: Cultivating Authentic Public Zeal in the Service of Emerging Enterprise.

When introducing a new company, institution, or idea into a market long held by an entrenched power, logic and product alone are insufficient tools. The public's allegiance is not to innovation, but to familiarity. Thus, before adoption can occur, disaffection must be stirred—gently, plausibly, and through trusted channels.

The most effective method is the orchestration of a *citizens' initiative*—not overtly aligned with the client, but composed of concerned individuals who appear to arrive at conclusions independently. Begin by identifying small grievances already murmured among the populace: high prices, worker mistreatment, stifled progress, or distant ownership. Through community figures—teachers, civic leaders, veterans, women's leagues—seed questions, suspicions, and polite outrage. Encourage modest assemblies, editorials, pamphlets. Provide these groups with carefully framed evidence and talking points, but maintain distance. The appearance of spontaneity is paramount.

In time, the old institution will come to seem tired, arrogant, or exploitative. Against this, your client—clean, modern, fair—will be welcomed not merely as a business, but as a public remedy. Remember: the citizen who feels they have discovered the truth themselves will fight harder for it than any paid voice could ever persuade.

***

Crispin was in his element. He'd find a thread where someone was earnestly defending the official report and deploy some of his favourite weapons of attack.

Patrician_Gaze:
One does grow so tired of explaining the basics, but let's try. We'll play a little game. Let's pretend we're simpletons for a moment.

One must, I suppose, admire the sheer narrative tidiness of the official report. It's so wonderfully simple. One only has to ignore the dreary, tedious complexities of physics—things like free-fall speed, the melting point of steel, and the inconvenient existence of Building 7. If one can hold one's nose and disregard all that, then the story they've provided is perfectly adequate. For a certain kind of mind. Now, shall we all have a nice cup of tea?

The post was delivered with Crispin's signature cruelty—a devastating ad hominem attack disguised as intellectual boredom.

If anyone mounted a coherent, factual counter-argument, Maks was our ace in the hole. We'd get him on the phone, and he'd give us a five-minute lecture on eutectic reactions and the melting point of structural steel, which we would then paraphrase into a devastatingly technical-sounding takedown. We were using the authority of science to destroy faith in the scientific establishment. The irony was exquisite.

My job was to play the everyman, just asking questions.

TruthSeeker77:
I'm no expert, but how does a passport of one of the hijackers survive the inferno and land on a street corner, completely intact, when the plane's black boxes were supposedly destroyed? It just doesn't add up.

One of our most effective tactics was brutally simple: repetition. There's a fundamental principle in our trade: *familiarity breeds belief.* The human mind is like an empty room; it abhors a vacuum. If you repeat a single, simple phrase often enough, it will eventually furnish that room, regardless of whether it's true. The official story of 9/11 was complex and full of messy details. Our story was simple. We just kept saying "controlled demolition," over and over, from a hundred different angles, until, through sheer force of familiarity, it started to feel just as true, and just as real, as any other words on any other page.

That evening, I stopped for a quiet beer on my way home. The pub was my sanctuary, a place to decompress. A group of workmen in hi-vis jackets and muddy boots were at the next table, having a loud, boisterous post-work debrief. I couldn't help but overhear their conversation.

"Nah, mate, it wasn't terrorists," one of them, a big bloke with a shaved head, was saying with absolute authority. "It was the Illuminati. They used one of them secret ray-guns from a satellite to bring the towers down. Same way they got rid of Diana." His mates nodded in solemn agreement.

I was fascinated. I was watching my work echo back at me from the real world. After a few minutes, I caught the bloke's eye at the bar.

"Excuse me, mate," I said. "All that stuff you were saying about the ray-guns and the Illuminati. Do you really believe all that?"

He looked at me, took a long swig of his lager, and then a wide grin spread across his face. "Nah, not really," he said. "But it's exciting, isn't it?"

And in that instant, this workman, this normal everyday bloke, had summed up the foundation of our entire project at The Long Blue Wall more perfectly than a thousand academic papers ever could. People don't necessarily want the truth. They want a good story. They want to feel like they're a character in a book, a hero who knows a secret. It wasn't about facts. It was about excitement. And our job was to make our version of reality the most exciting story on offer.

A good story is often more appealing than a boring fact.

Chapter Fourteen

The Veiled Signal

OUR DAYS AT THE Signalroom often felt like running two entirely different businesses under one leaky roof. There was the legitimate work—the Teenage Pregnancy project, Glastonbury, the little old man who was running for Parliament—and then there was the work of the Ministry. Our primary task in those early years was to continue laying the foundations for the grand myths, and one tool that was invaluable in that effort was the website of our colleague in New Zealand.

He had called it *The Veiled Signal: Decoding the Hidden Language of the Elite.* It was a brilliant piece of work, a professional-looking news site dedicated to a single, paranoid purpose: to expose the 'hidden hand' behind modern pop culture by decoding the symbols used to manipulate the masses. It was a key weapon for promoting the Eye and the Pyramid, and for building the mythology of the Illuminati as our new version of the Devil—our new cultural and mythological bogeyman.

Our job was simple: drive traffic to The Veiled Signal. We were the street team, the hype men, handing out digital flyers in the dark corners of the internet.

I would log in as my truth-seeking *Veritas_2012* persona and drop a link into a discussion about a new music video.

Reply to StarChild82:
If you want to see the real proof, you need to look at the symbols. The All-Seeing Eye, the Pyramid...they're everywhere. The pop stars, the movies, the logos. It's their calling card. There's a brilliant site that exposes it all: TheVeiledSignal.com. Prepare to have your mind blown.

Crispin, sitting right next to me and munching on an expensive continental biscuit, would then log in as his "curious newcomer" persona, *Just_A_Bloke*. The character was a masterpiece of subtle recruitment: a normal everyday man who was just starting to question things, dipping his toes into the world of conspiracy and finding it all quite interesting, but still a bit overwhelming.

Reply to Veritas_2012:
Wow, mate, just checked out that Veiled Signal site. Mind. Blown. It's all there in plain sight... How did I not notice this before? I've got a lot to learn. Everyone needs to see this.

It was a perfect, self-validating feedback loop. And it worked. The site itself was a masterpiece of agenda-driven framing. The articles were well-written, deeply researched (in a very specific, biased way), and utterly convincing if you were already inclined to believe. I'd often find myself reading them, half-admiring the craft.

There were the music video dissections, with titles like: '*From Mouseketeer to Serpent Priestess: Deconstructing Britney's VMA Performance.*' Or '*Eminem's My Name Is: The Creation of a MK-Ultra Alter Ego.*' And '*Justified: How Justin Timberlake's Solo Career Was an Illuminati Rebranding.*' They'd break down every hand gesture, every piece of jewellery, every background detail, and link it all back to Luciferian philosophy or rituals rooted in satanic worship.

Then there were the movie analyses: '*The Matrix Reloaded and the Blueprint for Human Control.*' Or '*Finding Nemo's Hidden Message: A Guide to Trauma-Based Mind Control.*'

And there were the 'Signs in Plain Sight' pieces, which were my personal favourite. They'd analyse the 'occult magic' of corporate logos like Apple and Starbucks, or break down the 'occult symbolism' of the Olympic Opening Ceremony.

I understood the *why* of the campaign, but I was still fuzzy on the logistics. "How do they actually get all this stuff into the videos?" I asked Crispin one afternoon. "You can't just ring up Beyoncé's stylist and ask her to stick a pyramid on her leotard."

Crispin looked at me with a touch of pity, as if I'd asked him how the sun comes up. "You don't ring the stylist, William. You ring the person who pays the stylist's invoice. It's the same method as when we're seeding our celebrities, just on a much grander scale."

He explained. It was Lord Harrington's world. The big banks and the financial institutions that underwrite the budgets for Hollywood blockbusters and A-list pop albums. They're all part of the same 'old-world' network. The instructions come down from the top. A quiet word from a banker to a studio head during a round of golf. A clause written into a multi-million dollar loan agreement. It then filters down the chain of command—from the studio head to the producer; from the producer to the director; from the director to the set designer and the costume department.

"The artist themselves?" Crispin scoffed. "They have no say at all. They're just the talent. They wear what they're told to wear and dance where they're told to dance. The people at the bottom of the chain don't ask why—and they wouldn't get an answer if they did. They probably just find it all rather amusing."

I didn't know much about the specific occult motifs, but I knew enough to recognise the bigger picture. The constant refrain on the website was about the "Puppets of the Illuminati"—pop stars, movie actors, celebrities who were supposedly under the direct control and influence of the bad guys. It was a direct, modern equivalent of the Devil and his army of demons, sent out to do his dirty work. I made a mental note to ask Beth or Bertil for a more detailed breakdown of the updated Devil mythology.

I had to admit, I found it all quite interesting. Crispin, of course, was already well-versed in much of it.

"Oh, this is just basic semiotics," he'd say, peering at an article about Masonic symbolism in a film. "We covered most of this in classics.

And Father used to take me to his Lodge meetings for their Christmas party. It's all just theatre and funny handshakes. Terribly dull, for the most part." His father's involvement with the local Freemasons was, he explained with a bored sigh, all very innocent. Less global conspiracy, more arguing about the budget for the summer fête and complaining about the quality of the house claret.

But he understood the power of the imagery. He knew the history, the mythology, the weight of the symbols we were so casually throwing around. I was just a PR man following a brief. He was a product of the very system we were pretending to expose, and he was having the time of his life helping to burn a caricature of it to the ground.

Chapter Fifteen

The Resurrection of Michael Wright

SOMETIMES, IN THE THICK of the digital battles, you could forget what it was all for. You'd get lost in the arguments, the sock-puppets, the scheming. But then a moment would come along that reminded you of the bigger picture, of the real-world myth we were building. This weekend was going to be one of those moments.

It was Friday. I was keen to get home. A text had come through from Beth earlier in the week—just a single, cryptic line:

> *The Resurrection. EvolveFest. This weekend.*

She needn't have bothered—Emma and I were already on it. "We have to go," Emma had said, when she saw the ad in a magazine. It wasn't a work trip for me, not officially. It was a day out. Emma was genuinely excited to go, to immerse herself in a world of alternative healing, organic food stalls, and group meditations. Ellie wanted to come along too and asked if she could bring one of her friends, so we bought a family ticket for the Sunday when Michael Wright had the afternoon slot on the main stage.

We thought back to his infamous appearance at the book signing session all those years ago when he was attacked and ridiculed by the media. The memory was vivid. It was a Sunday morning in the early nineties. We'd only just met then, Emma and I, both of us living in a chaotic shared house in London for young professionals and students. I was at the beginning of my journey in PR, still in university, learning the ropes, and full of boisterous ambition. Emma was a student nurse, full of a genuine desire to help people.

One of our housemates, a trainee journalist, had come into the kitchen waving the Sunday tabloids, a gleeful, scandal-hungry look on his face. "You've got to see this," he'd said. "They've absolutely crucified Mickey Wright."

We gathered around the kitchen table, the pages spread out between the toast crumbs and the coffee mugs. The headlines were brutal. ***"WACKO WRIGHT'S BONKERS BOOK LAUNCH!"*** screamed one. ***"MICKEY'S MADNESS!"*** shrieked another.

The story was accompanied by a series of deeply unflattering photographs. There was Mickey Wright, the famous comedian, standing alone at a signing table in a respectable London bookshop, looking bewildered. He was wearing what the papers described as a "bizarre wizard's cloak"—his now-famous deep indigo jacket. A pack of reporters, their cameras flashing like machine-gun fire, had ambushed him, surrounding him, shouting questions not about his new spiritual book, *The Harmony Within*, but about his claims of talking to spirits and his predictions of a coming global transformation.

It was an uncomfortable read, even for someone like me who knew these tactics would be a required tool of my trade. It was a public crucifixion, a carefully orchestrated media hit job designed to make him look like a lunatic who had lost his mind. The articles were dripping with scorn, mocking his "cult leader" jacket and framing his spiritual awakening as a tragic public breakdown.

We'd all felt a bit sorry for him—a pang of sympathy for this strange man being so publicly dismantled. But he was made of stern stuff. I doubted he'd have wanted our pity. Emma, who had actually read and enjoyed one of his earlier spiritual books, just shook her head sadly. "He'll be okay," she'd said. "He believes in something. That makes him stronger than they are."

I recalled Beth's *Hero's Journey* masterclass in the pub. That first media ambush, she'd explained, had been deliberately arranged. It was part of his *Tests and Enemies* stage, a public ordeal designed to cement his status as a persecuted truth-teller.

But this weekend, now fifteen years on from that disastrous day at the book signing, was to be different. He had been through the subsequent stages of the journey. He had approached the *Innermost Cave* when he climbed that hill in Bolivia. He had overcome *The Ordeal* of the cosmic energy bolt and had *Returned with the Elixir*: the supernatural gift of having access to secret knowledge. He had completed *The Road Back*, and we were now about to be present at the next stage of his story.

We drove the hour and a half to the sprawling country estate where EvolveFest was being held: Eldergrove Hall, tucked away in the Chiltern hills, wrapped in meadows, woods, and something less tangible—a sense of pause, as though the land itself was listening. The atmosphere was peaceful, carnivalesque. The air smelled of incense, freshly cut grass, and vegan curry. Thousands of people drifted between colourful tents, browsing stalls selling crystals, tarot decks, and handmade jewellery. It was a gathering of the tribes, the seekers, the people who felt there was more to life than the nine-to-five.

Ellie and her friend had darted off as soon as we passed through the main gate, their lanyards swinging. Emma waved them away with a smile and a cheerful warning: "No facial piercings or spontaneous soul marriages, please!"

Michael Wright was on the main stage, a huge, open-sided marquee, in the prime Sunday afternoon slot. The tent was packed, the crowd spilling out onto the lawn. When he walked out, dressed in his indigo jacket, the applause was thunderous. It wasn't just appreciation; it was adoration. He stood there, beaming, soaking it in. He looked older, more weathered than the man I'd seen in the Croydon hall, but his confidence was absolute. He was a king addressing his court.

He wasn't giving a lecture; he was being interviewed, sitting on a simple stool opposite the festival's MC, a warm, charismatic woman in her fifties.

"Michael," she began, her voice echoing across the huge crowd, "it's incredible to see so many people here. When you started on this journey, did you ever imagine that so many people would...wake up?"

Michael Wright smiled, a calm, contented smile. "It was never about me," he said, his voice smooth and authoritative. "I was just one of the first to speak the truth. This isn't something I created; it's a natural awakening. People are tired of the lies. They're ready for something real."

His performance was masterful. He didn't raise his voice; he didn't rant. He spoke with a calm, powerful authority, weaving together his familiar narratives about secret histories and cosmic truths. He talked about his journey, framing his public humiliation as a necessary trial by fire. At one point, he gestured towards the small press pit at the side of the stage, where a few journalists were scribbling in notepads.

"And we have some friends from the media with us today," he said, his voice devoid of any malice. "The very same media that once called me a madman, a charlatan, a joke." He smiled. "And I want to thank them. I truly do. Because their ridicule didn't destroy me. It forged me. It was the fire I had to walk through to stand here today. It made me strong, and it showed the world that the truth cannot be silenced."

The MC led the crowd in a roar of approval. It was a brilliant move. He wasn't the victim any more; he was the gracious victor who had transcended his enemies. I watched, a sense of professional, almost detached admiration washing over me. This was the final act of the play that Beth had outlined for me those few years ago in the pub. This was *The Resurrection*. Every part of it was perfectly executed. The carefully chosen venue, the adoring crowd, the softball interview, the magnanimous tone towards his old enemies...it was a textbook piece of reputation management, a masterclass in narrative control. Michael was playing his part to perfection.

I looked around at the thousands of faces, all turned towards the stage, hanging on his every word. The scale of it was staggering. This wasn't a fringe meeting in a dusty hall any more. This was a culture. A belief system. A movement. And we had helped build it.

Michael sat forward slightly, resting his hands on his knees. "The thing people misunderstand," he said, his voice calm but charged, "is that awakening isn't about information. It's about frequency. You don't wake people up by giving them facts. You do it by shifting the signal they're tuned to."

The interviewer nodded. "And how does someone do that?"

Michael smiled. "Start by questioning the most ordinary things. Why do I feel the need to obey? Why do I trust certain voices more than others? Why do I feel afraid when I speak something true?" He paused.

"The systems that govern our world—political, financial, educational—they're all part of a structure designed to hold people in a limited state of awareness. A tiny slice of what we are. It's not just about control. It's about disconnect—from who we really are, and from what we're really capable of."

The audience was silent, locked in. The interviewer let the silence breathe. Then: "Michael, what would you say to those who still laugh at you? Who call this all fantasy?"

He didn't flinch. He smiled, slowly. "They laughed at me when I was Mickey, too. And I laughed with them. That was part of the dance. But there comes a moment when the laugh doesn't feel real any more. When the world looks too strange to joke about. That's when the real journey begins."

Then—a shift in tone. Subtle. His gaze sharpened just slightly.

"There are those who've worked very hard to keep us numb. To keep us small. They hide behind symbols, money, power—but their greatest weapon is our silence." He paused, letting the air carry that weight.

"So speak. Sing. Rebel. And remember—their spell only works if we believe it."

The crowd burst into applause—not wild, but charged. Like something old and waiting had just been named.

I watched, fascinated, as the final stage of the myth clicked into place. This was Rocky Balboa, battered and bruised, going the distance against Apollo Creed. He hadn't won the fight, but he had won the respect of the world and the love of Adrian. This was Luke Skywalker, having faced Darth Vader and returning as a true Jedi Knight, calm and powerful, ready to face his destiny. This was King Arthur—having survived the Knights who say "Ni!" and the Killer Rabbit—being granted his final vision of the Holy Grail. Michael Wright had been knocked down, but he had refused to be beaten. He had returned from the brink, not just intact, but reborn. Stronger. Wiser. A hero. The myth had been completed. The story was now whole. The comedian had died, and the prophet had been well and truly resurrected—right on schedule.

It was time to go home. We found Ellie and her friend—flushed, giggly, and holding paper cups of herbal chai. Ellie's friend was clutching a small velvet pouch with a crystal inside. "Look," she said, turning to show us the back of her T-shirt—a glowing screenprint of the Eye and the Pyramid, ringed by soft flames. "They were selling them at the tent with all the prints and oracle decks. It's cool."

Ellie, her face half-serious, half-lit with wonder, leaned in and said, "We went to see a seer."

I raised an eyebrow. "A what?"

"She had a tent called *The Listening Space*. Candles, feathers, you know," Ellie said with a shrug. "She held my hands, closed her eyes, and just started talking. Like she knew things. Stuff I hadn't told anyone."

Emma was instantly intrigued. "What did she say?"

"She didn't ask me anything. She just held my hands for a bit, then she said this weird line—like she was remembering it, not inventing it."

> *"You'll build something that feels light, but carries weight. People will be drawn to it without knowing why. It will help them think in new ways—quietly, gently, without fear."*

She glanced down, frowning a little. "And then she said:"

"It won't look like truth. But it will act like it."

Emma, who'd been walking just ahead, turned and smiled. "Sounds like it made an impression."

Ellie gave a slow nod. "Yeah. It did."

We walked back towards the car park. I reflected on the day and what it had meant. This wasn't just a comeback. It was a coronation. The myth had been completed. The story was now whole.

The late sun was casting long shadows over the grass. The crowds had thinned, the music was fading into the trees through the last of the happy, smiling people. As we rounded the back of one of the big canvas tents, Emma squeezed my hand and motioned to our right. We caught a glimpse of Michael Wright, half in shadow. He was leaning against a tree, jacket off, cigarette in hand. Next to him stood a young woman—far younger—laughing at something he said, a little too easily.

We kept walking. Emma gave a small, sideways smile. "Even prophets need a smoke break," she shrugged.

Chapter Sixteen

The Prophet of Brixton

It was five years since 9/11, and the official story had begun to crack. The hairline fractures of doubt we had scored into its surface had, with time and pressure, widened into gaping fissures. The whispers we'd started on the forums had become a low, persistent roar in the background of the culture.

This was the world that Michael Wright had triumphantly re-entered a few months earlier at EvolveFest. His *Resurrection* had been a staggering success, and he was now riding a new wave of popularity and influence. He had spent the quiet years writing his new monolithic book *Blueprints of Control*—a grand, unifying theory of everything—and now he was taking it on the road. The Brixton show was the next stop on a tour that felt less like a series of lectures and more like a victory lap. I got a call from Beth. She was, as always, direct and to the point.

"It's time for a temperature reading, Will," she said. "Michael's moved up a weight class, he's playing the Brixton Academy. We need to see how he's capitalising on his new status post-Resurrection. And more importantly, he's starting to roll out his 9/11 material. We need to be in the room to gauge the audience's reaction first-hand."

The Brixton Academy. From a damp community hall in Croydon to a legendary London music venue in just a few short years. He had done well.

The atmosphere this time was completely different. The crowd wasn't a few dozen quiet seekers any more; it was thousands of them. The air was electric, buzzing with the fervent energy of a revivalist meeting. These weren't just curious onlookers; they were followers. Believers. They had the look of people who had found their home, their tribe, their truth.

When he walked on stage, the roar was deafening. He was a different creature to the man I'd seen before. The indigo jacket was gone, replaced by a simple, almost priestly white cotton shirt. He stood there for a full minute, soaking in the adoration, his arms outstretched, a benevolent smile on his face. This was no longer a man sharing his story; this was a prophet addressing his flock.

The performance—and it was a performance—was a masterclass in charismatic authority. He wasn't a speaker; he was a conductor, and the audience was his orchestra. He'd learned the rhythms of the preacher, building the tension with a low, conspiratorial whisper before erupting into a righteous, roaring crescendo. He paced the stage, using powerful, repetitive hand gestures, painting terrifying pictures of a world enslaved, of children being stolen, of a global prison being built around us. He was selling fear, and the crowd was buying it in bulk.

He wove the events of 9/11 into his grand narrative seamlessly. He didn't offer a single, coherent theory. Instead, he just asked questions, his voice laced with sorrowful incredulity. "Jet fuel and office fires, my friends? They tell us that's what brought down three steel-framed skyscrapers. Three buildings. Does that feel right to you?" A low murmur rumbled through the crowd. "And Building 7? The third tower that fell in its own footprint, a perfect, controlled demolition, without ever being hit by a plane? They tell us to ignore that. But we will not ignore it, will we?"

The rumble grew to a roar: "NO!"

He had them. Then, he leaned into the microphone, his voice dropping again. "And they don't want you to look up, my friends. They don't want you to ask about the Moon." He paused, letting the silence hang in the air. "Have you ever wondered why the Moon is always facing the same way? Why it seems to watch us? Why it stirs the tides, the blood, the mind...?"

"The Moon is not what they tell us it is. It's a hollow, artificial satellite. A giant spaceship, parked in our orbit, beaming down a frequency that keeps us trapped in low-vibrational, fear-based emotions. It is the great suppressor. The true source of the madness."

The crowd stared, utterly transfixed. A spaceship? It sounded crazy. But as I looked at the captivated faces in the audience, I understood the logic at play. This was a man who, in their world, had a perfect record. He had predicted a spiritual awakening. He had survived the crucifixion by the media. Everything he had told them had, in their experience, come to pass. So when he presented them with this new, impossible idea, their instinct wasn't to laugh. Their instinct was to wonder, *'What if he's right again?'*

"We've seen enough," Beth whispered in my ear. We slipped out a side door before the applause had even died down, leaving the faithful to their leader. We found a quiet pub nearby.

"Well," I said, still trying to process what I'd just seen. "The Moon is a spaceship. That's a new one. Where did he get that from?"

Beth smiled, that cool, analytical smile I was coming to know well. "He got it from us, of course. Indirectly."

"How do you mean, *indirectly*?" I asked.

"We have an asset—Brian," she explained. "He's been one of Michael's most trusted confidants for years. Brian is the one who brings him the 'inside information', the 'leaked documents', the 'messages from high-level sources'. He's what we call a *feeder*."

She let that sink in for a moment.

"The Moon theory was our latest delivery," she continued. "But he's been the primary source for much of Michael's new book. The scientific anomalies in the 9/11 report? That's Maks's research, distilled down and passed to Brian. The historical parallels and mythological connections? That's Bertil and me. The predictions about the coming societal collapse? Hendrik, of course. Brian takes our complex, strategic narratives and delivers them to Michael in a way that makes him feel like a prophet receiving divine revelation. He is the quiet, final link in our information supply chain."

"So why the thing about the Moon? I mean, it's not actually a spaceship, is it—so *why*?"

Beth took a sip of her drink. "Because the Moon has always been our greatest monster. The one we can't escape." She leaned forward, her voice dropping slightly, taking on the tone of a storyteller. "Think of the old tales, the folklore. What does the full moon do? It stirs the madness. It brings out the beast." She leant in and whispered a short verse—

"Not all monsters howl or bleed—some just change beneath the light.
Becoming what they always were, but only under night."

"It's another updated myth. Folklore has always linked the Moon to madness—lunacy, werewolves, erratic behaviour. It's an ancient archetype. All I did was give it a modern, technological gloss. Instead of the Moon bringing out the beast, we now have a giant frequency generator. It still alters our personality as before—only now it keeps us subdued. It's the same story, just with better props for a scientific age."

She looked at me, her expression serious. "You must realise, Will, that full acceptance isn't necessary right now—what's important is that people begin to engage with the idea, even if it still seems unlikely to some. Michael is a vital tool, but he is just laying the groundwork. He's the John the Baptist of this movement. In future generations, people will look back on him as the first great prophet of our new worldview. He is normalising the concepts, tilling the soil. He's making it possible for others to follow." She paused. "The next one, the next great prophet who will build on his foundations, has already been identified, I'm hearing." The casual, chilling foresight of it all left me speechless.

We finished our drinks and left. Beth's hotel was on the way, so we shared a taxi. As we drove through the West End, we passed a large bookshop. There was a long queue snaking out of the door and down the street.

"You see there," gestured Beth. "That's where Michael had his first book launch all those years ago."

I tapped on the dividing window, "What's that all about?" I asked the driver.

"Oh, it's that professor bloke," he said. "The one who's always on the telly, going on about evolution. One of those *New Atheists* I think they call them. Doing a book signing."

I looked at the queue of people, clutching their hardback copies, waiting patiently for a moment with their hero, for his signature in their book.

Beth followed my gaze, and nodded slowly. "Look at them," she said softly. "They're here to see a famous professor of evolutionary biology, a man who built his career on mocking religion and the irrationality of belief. And yet, they are queuing up for his autograph, for a personal relic, a tangible connection to someone they consider special. They want his mark in their sacred text."

She smiled. "They think they've replaced the old superstitions with science and reason, but all they've done is swap a lock of a saint's hair for a scribble of a scientist's ink. They want to retain something of the essence of their idol, their god, a permanent reminder of their faith."

***

Excerpt from 'Enigma' magazine, Arts & Culture section.

Title: The Prophet of Brixton?
By Tom Fletcher

When my editor told me to go and see Michael Wright speak, I expected a joke. Like most of the country, I remembered Mickey Wright the comedian; the infamous book signing session from the nineties; and a man in an Indigo jacket, a national laughing-stock. But after his recent, remarkably dignified 'rehabilitation' on this summer's festival circuit, my curiosity was piqued. The man who was once a punchline was now selling out the Brixton Academy. Something strange was happening.

And strange it was. The atmosphere inside the iconic music venue was less like a gig and more like a rally, or perhaps even a sermon. The crowd was a diverse mix—students, middle-aged couples, tradesmen, spiritual seekers—all united by a fervent, almost religious devotion to the man on stage. And Wright, it must be said, is a master performer.

Gone is the bewildered man from the tabloid photographs. In his place stands a charismatic, confident figure who commands the stage with the polish of a seasoned performer and the fire of a street-corner preacher. For four whole hours, he held the audience captive, weaving a grand, overarching narrative of secret control and hidden truths.

His material on the 9/11 attacks was a masterclass in Socratic manipulation. He offered no definitive theories, but simply asked a series of unsettling questions about the collapse of Building 7 and the physics of falling towers, leaving the audience to connect the dots themselves. It was slick, effective, and unsettling.

He seamlessly moved on to the true seat of global power, and was alive with historical misrepresentations and distortions. He didn't talk about governments or banks; he went deeper, further back. He spoke of the Vatican, not as a religious institution, but as a corporate entity, the surviving remnant of the Roman Empire hiding behind robes and incense.

"They tell you to look at Washington, at London, at Brussels," he boomed, his voice resonating through the hall. "A distraction! The real power doesn't sit in parliaments. It sits on a throne in a tiny city-state, surrounded by priceless art and the darkest secrets in human history."

And then, he took a left turn into sheer, glorious madness.

He told the packed-out venue, with a completely straight face, that the Moon is not a natural satellite, but a hollow, artificial construct—a 'death star' parked in our orbit to control us with low-vibrational frequencies. The room was silent for a moment. Did I believe him? Of course not. It's patently absurd. But then again, I was one of the people who laughed at him all those years ago. He was ridiculed by the entire country, and yet here he is, fifteen years later, vindicated in his own way, his following larger and more passionate than ever. It gives one pause. When a man has been so spectacularly right about his own resilience, you hesitate to be so spectacularly certain that he's wrong about everything else.

The show is a powerful, anti-establishment cocktail. It's a two-fingered salute to every official institution: government, science, the media, the monarchy, the major religions. It's a compelling narrative for a generation that has grown to distrust all of them.

Leaving the venue, I couldn't shake a strange, nagging feeling. The whole thing was so polished, so professional. The narrative was so perfectly constructed, the emotional beats so expertly timed—it felt less like one man's rambling obsession and more like a carefully designed product. I can't put my finger on it. It just feels like there's something else going on here, a hand guiding the story that remains just out of sight. Maybe that's just the paranoia rubbing off on me. Or maybe, just maybe, that's the whole point.

Chapter Seventeen

The Keepers of The Stories

THE INVITATION ARRIVED ON thick, cream-coloured card, the ink a deep, regal blue. It wasn't an email or a phone call. It was a summons from another era. Lord Harrington was requesting the pleasure of our company for a weekend gathering at Ashcombe Hall, his family estate. It was, the card noted, a small token of his gratitude for our "vital work".

A fleet of sleek but understated cars picked us up, whisking us out of London and into the rolling, impossibly green heart of the English countryside. The gates of Ashcombe Hall appeared suddenly, two ancient stone pillars topped with weary-looking lions, opening onto a long, sweeping drive. And then we saw the house. It wasn't just a house; it was a statement. A sprawling Jacobean masterpiece of warm stone, mullioned windows and towering chimneys, sitting in its landscape with the comfortable, settled weight of centuries.

Lord Harrington greeted us on the steps, not with pomp and ceremony, but with the warm, easy grace of a man welcoming friends into his home. Beside him stood a small group of his peers—fellow aristocrats, men and women of a certain age, all exuding the same quiet, unshakeable self-assurance. These were the backers. The old-world power.

Also present, looking slightly uncomfortable in their expensive but conspicuously casual clothing, were a couple of people from the world of tech. One I recognised as the founder and owner of a major US software giant. The other was a younger, intense-looking man from a data analytics firm I'd never heard of. They were here, Jez whispered to me, to "pay their respects" and thank us for our help in "managing the transition."

The afternoon was a surreal blend of formal garden tour and informal strategy meeting. As we walked through the magnificent grounds, a man with a ruddy, good-humoured face introduced himself as Crispin's father.

"Thank you for taking the boy on, William," he said, clapping me on the shoulder. "Seen no bloody change in his behaviour, of course, but one appreciates the effort!" He roared with laughter. I found myself smiling. I'd grown quite fond of Crispin, with his caustic wit and his horrible, brilliant competence. It was strange how we show different versions of ourselves depending on the company we're in.

Lord Harrington led the tour, his voice a calm, narrative thread weaving through the history of the place. This was more than a garden; it was a piece of England's soul. He pointed out an ancient oak tree under which, he said, plans for the D-Day landings had been refined. He gestured towards a crumbling folly where one of his ancestors, a signatory on some long-forgotten charter of liberties, had hidden from the king's men. Every stone, every vista, had a story. The gardens were a beautiful, managed wilderness, where wild roses tumbled over ancient walls and deer grazed peacefully by a shimmering lake. It was poetic, evocative—a living museum of the nation's history. I glanced at the tech executives. They were shuffling their feet, looking at their shoes, utterly out of their element. This was a world of history and bloodlines; theirs was a world of algorithms and data points.

Inside, the story continued. The air was cool and smelled of beeswax and old paper. We were shown the library, a magnificent, double-height room lined with leather-bound books from floor to ceiling. Lord Harrington ran a hand along a row of spines with a faint, wistful sadness.

"Selling them off, one by one," he said quietly. "To keep the roof on. A necessary sacrifice."

That evening, we gathered for dinner in the grand dining room, a portrait of a stern-looking Harrington ancestor glowering down at us from above the fireplace. To my surprise, Dave was in his element. He might have been a boy from Hemel Hempstead who used to pretend to be an Amazonian shaman, but he held his own with the landed gentry, trading witty barbs and hilarious anecdotes with a duchess as if he'd been doing it all his life.

Charlotte, who was normally so calm and analytical, was in heaven. She was practically vibrating with excitement, peppering one of the lords with questions about his family tree. "The *Almanach de Gotha* is my absolute favourite bedtime reading," she confessed, with a quiet, nerdy enthusiasm that was oddly endearing.

The conversation eventually turned to Michael Wright.

"He's becoming quite the sensation," one of the ladies commented. "A thrilling performer."

"He was here, you know," Lord Harrington said casually. "Sat right where you're sitting, Will. A very fervent man. We explained his role in the new architecture. We didn't give him a doctrine, of course. We just gave him a simple instruction: *make them believe*. A new worldview if you like. Not an organised religion—but certainly with similar elements—not one of bricks and mortar, but one of ideas."

The Duchess who Dave was getting on so well with—a sharp, funny woman who insisted on being called Eleanor—giggled into her wine glass. "He asked my permission, ever so politely, if he could include my family name in his new theory about the ruling classes being descended from... well, you know."

"Lizards?" Jez grinned.

"The very same! I told him, 'Of course, my dear boy, I wouldn't dream of stopping you!'"

The table erupted in laughter. It was a laugh of shared, surreal amusement. They were the wizards behind the curtain who found the sheer absurdity of their own grand project deeply, privately entertaining.

I took the chance to find out more about this shapeshifting Lizard thing that seemed so ridiculous to me. "I still don't get that one," I said to Beth. "It seems so... absurd. What's it about?"

Beth smiled, leaning back as the port came her way. "Well, it's not a new thing," she said, "it's the oldest story in the book, just with a different dust jacket."

Lord Harrington nodded in agreement. "A necessary fiction. Just as the *2012* narrative is a necessary piece of historical stage-setting."

It was Beth's turn to nod in agreement. She continued, "The Illuminati is our new version of the Devil, Will. And every Devil needs a set of characteristics. We've simply updated these as well."

"It's the fear of reptiles," Bertil said, his academic passion ignited. "It's evolutionarily hard-wired. The Gorgons of Greek myth with their snake hair, the dragon Fafnir in Norse sagas, the feathered serpent god Kukulkan of the Maya. We've always cast our greatest enemies in a reptilian form. We're just swapping the serpent in the Garden of Eden for a lizard in a bespoke suit."

"But why do they need to shapeshift?"

"Well they can't actually be seen in lizard form, can they mate?" scoffed Dave, "seeing as they're not actually lizards, and all that. So we claim that they change to their natural self when they go home for their tea, or if they're in a bad mood."

"Ah yes, shapeshifting," one of the lords joined in, swirling his brandy. "A classic literary device. From Ovid's *Metamorphoses* to werewolves and vampires. A creature that can change its form is inherently untrustworthy, supernatural. It triggers a primal fear."

"So, the Devil from the Bible—he was a serpent in Eden, an angel of light, a dragon in *Revelation*, a tempter in the wilderness, and you'll find him in many films and literature portrayed as a charming stranger or trickster."

"Then there's Stephen King's Pennywise..." added Beth, "the Skinwalkers from Native American lore, and of course, most of the Greek gods."

"Loki, the god of mischief, he's in a comic," said Bertil, "and Mystique, she's another one. They're all shapeshifters."

"The T-1000 Terminator?" suggested Dave.

"Oh, I love that film!" said Charlotte who was by now a bit tipsy and giddy. "I'll be back!" she laughed.

"And how about the magic and sorcery?" Dave added, thoroughly enjoying the game. "The supernatural powers? The Devil had his box of tricks for deception, temptation, for controlling nature; but our Reptilians have secret advanced technology, weather control systems, energy weapons. They can destroy your crops or conjure up a plague of locusts anytime they want."

"Of course, that was actually God himself," corrected Lord Harrington, "but the idea is the same."

"Okay, I'm getting it now," I said. "Just like these *Puppets of the Illuminati* on The *Veiled Signal* website. They're a modern retelling of Satan's army of demons, being called upon to do dastardly deeds on his behalf?"

"Yes!" the table said in unison.

"You've got it, Will, that's absolutely what it is!" Beth said with a smile. "And the stories of mind control? The claims of individuals being programmed, even *remote controlled*, to commit acts of evil?" she encouraged, looking at me expectantly.

I thought for a moment. I hadn't considered this. Then it came to me. "Demonic Possession?" I offered.

"YES!" they all shouted, then erupted into laughter and applause.

***

Setting: A Lecture at Saint Albans College for Young Gentlemen
Class: Foundations of Statecraft
Instructor: Mr. Wexley
Pupils: Sons of dukes, MPs, and one rather quiet foreign prince

Mr. Wexley stood at the front of the class, hands clasped behind his back. The late afternoon sun threw long bars of gold across the oak-panelled room. Behind him, chalk dust clung to the blackboard like the last smoke of a battle.

"You, gentlemen," he said, "will one day inherit constituencies, cabinets, perhaps even crowns. Some of you will command armies. Others, newspapers. And a few of you, God help us, may even run banks."

A few of the boys smirked. One yawned. Wexley ignored them. "But tell me this," he said, turning sharply. "Who rules the world?"

"Kings," offered Ashbridge, the tall one with the polished accent.

"Capital," said Patel, who read *The Economist* under the desk most days.

"America," muttered someone near the back.

Mr. Wexley smiled, the kind of smile that meant someone had missed the point entirely.

"No," he said. "None of them. The world is ruled by those who tell the stories."

He let the words settle like dust on leather shoes.

"Think. Before you ever knew what 'honour' meant, you were told tales of Arthur and his knights. Before you understood the law, you heard of Robin Hood stealing for justice. Before you could spell 'democracy,' you were made to cheer for underdogs and despise tyrants. Why? Because someone, somewhere, wrote it that way."

He began pacing now, voice steady and deliberate.

"The story defines the hero. The story names the villain. The story decides whether a rebellion is a revolution or a riot. And the men who broadcast the stories—the writers, the editors, the speechmakers, the playwrights—they do not need to sit on thrones. They only need to speak first, and often."

One boy, the quiet prince from the Balkans, raised his hand.

"But sir...isn't that dangerous? If lies can rule as easily as truth?"

Wexley turned to him, not unkindly.

"Very. Which is why you, all of you, must learn not only how to govern countries, but how to shape the story told about them. Or someone else will."

He paused. The room was still.

"Power," he said, "is the story told not to explain the world, but to command it—a tool for gaining control, and a shield to keep it."

He let the silence return, the kind that made boys sit straighter without knowing why.

***

Later, after dinner, I found Lord Harrington alone in the library, standing before a portrait of a beautiful woman, speaking to her in quiet, conversational tones. He turned as I entered, not with embarrassment, but with a calm, knowing smile.

"My late wife, Catherine," he said simply. "I still speak to her from time to time. There's no harm. It's a normal human instinct, after all—the desire to reach for something just beyond the veil. To imagine we're not entirely alone in the silence." He gestured slightly. "When Jeremy was a child, he had imaginary companions for years. It's the same impulse, the same instinct. And *God*, of course, is the greatest example of them all. Humans have always needed to feel they can make contact with the great spirits on the other side."

He poured two glasses of whisky from a heavy crystal decanter and motioned for me to sit in one of the deep leather armchairs.

"The concept of God is not a static thing, Will," he said, handing me a glass. "It evolves with a society's own level of understanding. We have gone from a world where God was in the trees, in the rivers, in the beasts of the field, then on to the more structured pantheon of the Greeks and Romans, a kind of celestial aristocracy on a mountaintop. And then, finally, on to the single, all-powerful, omnipresent God of the West. A king on a heavenly throne, an external authority perfectly suited for an age of empires and monarchies."

He took a slow, thoughtful sip of his whisky. "That model has served the West for two thousand years, but it's time to move on. Western man now sees himself as secular, rational and free from superstition—but of course, he is not. The instinct remains. It simply requires a new form."

"That was precisely the purpose of our work with places like the Esalen Institute," he continued. "All those bright young things discovering themselves, learning yoga, exploring Eastern mysticism...what they were really doing, what they have been *taught* to do, is simply to move the idea of God to its next logical stage."

He looked at me, his gaze clear and steady, delivering the final, crucial point.

"It's the difference between a generation that was taught to kneel in prayer to make contact with a divine, *external* power, and a new generation that is being taught to sit in meditation to make contact with a divine, *internal* power. It is the same human impulse, just expressed through a new and more sustainable mythology. Our job was simply to ensure the transition was a smooth and managed one."

A lightbulb went on in my head. Emma. Her yoga, her crystals, her talk of 'energy' and 'vibrations'. All of it had been seeded, cultivated, and spread from places like the Esalen Institute in California, a project quietly steered by people like my host. The new, bespoke spirituality that was replacing her mother's Christianity wasn't an organic evolution. It was a product, designed and rolled out like any other campaign.

"This is a long game, Will," Lord Harrington continued, his voice low. "We had to be ahead of this."

"How do you stay ahead?" I asked, the question feeling both impertinent and necessary.

"By listening to the right people," he said simply. "Men like our friend Hendrik. He's not just a consultant, you understand—he's part of a very old, very discreet advisory body. A private think tank, of sorts. It has advised families like mine for generations, long before any of us were born. They don't concern themselves with quarterly reports or election cycles. They look at the long arc of history. The deep currents of technological and social change."

He swirled the whisky in his glass, the amber liquid catching the light from the desk lamp.

"There's a dinner at *White's*, once a year," he said, his voice dropping to a near-whisper. "No notes are taken, nothing is written down. It's the only place you'll hear the real timeline for what's coming. The briefings they provide are... comprehensive. They were accurately modelling the impact of decentralised, non-governmental digital currencies back in the 1960s, when the rest of the world thought a credit card was a space-age novelty."

He took a slow sip of his whisky, his gaze distant. "But foresight, Will, is useless without the character to act upon it. To receive such warnings, to understand the sheer scale of the coming disruption, it requires a certain temperament. A steadiness."

He leaned back in the chair. His tone was not boastful, but firm with a conviction that felt as old as the house itself.

"The hereditary peers—the true Lords—carry something that cannot be taught. It's more than education. It's bred. A memory of the nation, if you like. A sense—an instinct—for when to yield and when to hold firm. In times of peace, we may seem like relics, decorative and faintly absurd. But when the foundations shake—when war comes, or in times of unrest—it is the old families who know how to steady the centre."

There was no arrogance in his voice, only certainty. A man stating a fact he had lived, not simply believed.

"We've been cultivating relationships and partnerships with the technology sector for years. The young men from today," he gestured vaguely, "they think they are building the new world. They think the power is all theirs. They don't yet realise that the oldest networks are still the strongest." He looked at me, and for a second, I saw the same sharp, calculating intelligence I saw in Jez. He tapped the side of his nose. "It's not over for our kind yet. Not by a long shot."

Chapter Eighteen

The Illusion of Choice

After a weekend spent discussing the clandestine reshaping of global society at a magnificent country estate, returning to the mundane reality of Signalroom felt like stepping into a different dimension. One week I was drinking vintage whisky in a library older than most countries; the next I was back in our dusty railway office, arguing with Crispin over the tagline for biodegradable bin liners.

It was a jarring shift—but a necessary one. The grand, overarching mission of The Long Blue Wall was going to be a long, slow burn—not a fireworks display. But the reality of day-to-day life meant I had more immediate things to deal with. The engine of the Ministry ran on favours and influence, but my own little engine ran on client satisfaction and hard cash.

I needn't have worried. The network was still providing. A couple of weeks after our trip to the country, an email popped up on my screen that made me sit up a bit straighter. It was from a newly formed consortium representing the "Big Three" UK supermarkets. They were inviting Signalroom, my tiny two-man operation, to pitch for a major national campaign. It was another gift from Lord Harrington's circle of influence, a lucrative contract dropped in our laps to keep us sweet.

The brief was a masterpiece of corporate doublespeak. The big, global food brands—the Nestlés, Unilevers, and Krafts of the world—had a "brand perception stranglehold" on the public imagination. People, they argued, reached for Heinz ketchup and Nescafé coffee out of pure, unthinking habit, assuming the higher price meant higher quality. Their mission, they claimed, was to *empower the consumer* and promote *informed choice*.

Crispin glanced at the email over my shoulder, a thin, knowing smile on his face. "How utterly transparent," he said. "Translated from the original corporate waffle, it means: *the margins on our own cheap stuff are enormous, and we'd like to sell more of it.* It's hardly a philanthropic endeavour."

"You've got it," I said. "They want higher profits, so they want us to convince the great British public to stop buying the expensive, branded stuff and start buying the supermarket's own, cheaper version. But we can't just say, 'Our stuff is cheaper!' because that just reinforces the idea that it's cheap and nasty."

Crispin's eyes lit up with a familiar, intellectual glee. "Oh, this is delicious," he said. "A textbook case for our peculiar talents. We need to expose the cynical marketing tricks of the big brands—and we'll do it as part of an even more cynical marketing trick of our own. It's hypocrisy squared."

I agreed. "We need to make the consumer feel like a savvy insider who is 'beating the system' by seeing through the con," I said. "We need to give them the illusion of choice, while we guide them to the actual choice our client wants them to make."

The perfect vehicle was obvious. "We'll pitch a one-off TV documentary," I declared. "A classic 'consumer champion' special. We'll call it something like *Shopping for Secrets: The Supermarket Insider*."

A low chuckle escaped Crispin's lips. "Oh, that's good," he said, shaking his head slowly in admiration. "That's not just devious, William. That's art. The public trusts those programmes implicitly.

They see the host as a modern-day Robin Hood, fighting for them against the big, bad corporations. It's the perfect Trojan horse."

"It's the first rule of the game, isn't it?" I agreed. "The public always thinks the consumer champion is on their side, but you have to ask that old Latin question again: *Cui bono?* Who really benefits? And the answer is... not the person watching it on the telly."

I leaned back in my chair, warming to our theme. "The person who benefits is always the person who commissioned the campaign—that's why they do it, after all. The trick is that it's often not the obvious one. Remember the Glastonbury contract? You would think it's the bands who would benefit, or maybe the festival organisers themselves. But the real winner, the one quietly reaping the rewards of the new clientele, was the catering company selling the posh burgers."

"It's a beautiful piece of misdirection," I continued, "and the Americans are absolute masters of it. They have a thing called a Video News Release, a VNR. It's a work of art."

I explained it to Crispin. "A big corporation—let's say a pharmaceutical giant—wants to promote a new drug. They don't just send out a press release. They produce their own, pre-packaged news segment. They hire an actor to play the role of the reporter, they film interviews with 'experts' who are on their payroll, and they edit it all together so it looks exactly like a real news report from a local TV station. They then send this VNR out to hundreds of small TV stations across the country—free of charge. And the stations, desperate for content to fill their airtime, will often run the whole thing, uncut, without ever telling their audience that it was produced by the company whose drug is being praised. The message is laundered through the credibility of the local news."

"We're a bit more subtle over here," I said, "but the principle is the same. It's all about branded content masquerading as helpful advice. Imagine—you're watching morning telly, and there's a five-minute segment on *back-to-school health tips*. The friendly TV doctor tells you all about the importance of vitamins and having a well-stocked medicine cabinet. It all seems like useful public service information. But if you look closely, you'll see the whole segment is *in association with* a major high-street pharmacy chain. Or you see a feature on *The*

Hottest Holiday Tech Gifts, and every single product just happens to be available to buy from the same online retailer. It doesn't feel like an advert. It feels like a recommendation from a trusted friend. And that's why it's so effective."

I pointed to the whiteboard where I'd written the title of our proposed TV show. "And that," I said, "is what we are doing here. *Shopping for Secrets* is just a more sophisticated, feature-length version of the same thing. We're wrapping our client's commercial agenda in the comforting, trustworthy disguise of a consumer-rights programme. It's perfect."

"It reminds me of the old days with Jez," I told Crispin. "We used to work on these lifestyle magazines. They looked innocent enough—full of horoscopes and human-interest stories. But they were just elaborate fronts, owned by PR companies, designed to sell our clients' products and services."

"I remember," Crispin said with a faint, dismissive shudder. "Ghastly publications. Endless pages of human misery, repackaged as light entertainment. Terribly depressing, really."

"Not for us—they were fantastic for our purposes," I corrected him. "We'd run a two-page feature on some bloke called Dave from Doncaster who'd had a hair transplant. The story would be all about how it had changed his life, how he'd found new confidence, a new girlfriend, a new job. It was framed as an inspirational, heart-warming tale. There wasn't a single 'buy now' message. But every middle-aged man reading that story who was feeling a bit thin on top would suddenly think, *Maybe... maybe a hair transplant is what I need.* We weren't selling them a product; we were selling an insecurity, then gently offering the solution. This TV show is the same idea, just with a bigger budget."

The plan for our TV show, Shopping for Secrets, was to expose all the classic marketing tricks used by the big brands to get you to buy their products.

"We'll start with 'Eye-Level is Buy-Level'," I said, scribbling on the whiteboard. "We'll show how the expensive brands pay a fortune to be placed right in the shopper's eye-line, while the own-brands are hidden away on the top or bottom shelf."

"The Packaging Myth," Crispin added. "We get a fancy box of branded biscuits and a plain supermarket box, and reveal that the biscuits inside are identical, made in the same factory, coming off the same production line. Nothing shatters brand loyalty like seeing your £2.50 luxury chocolate digestive is the same as the 99p one."

"And the blind taste test," I said. "It's a classic for a reason. We'll get members of the public to compare a famous brand of coffee with the supermarket's own brand. The results, of course, will be miraculously in our client's favour."

We'd back it all up with a print campaign: *The Savvy Shopper's Guide: 10 Tricks the Big Brands Don't Want You to Know.* And Crispin, with his natural talent for the subversive, would craft a "leaked" viral email chain—the late-2000s equivalent of a viral tweet—supposedly from an industry insider exposing all the dirty secrets.

The tagline for the whole campaign was simple, empowering, and deeply manipulative: "*Don't Buy the Hype. Buy the Biscuit.*"

Crispin was in his element, gleefully deconstructing the very psychological tricks he admired. "It's all so simple, isn't it?" he said, shaking his head. "The *Health Halo* effect. Slap a picture of a farm and the word 'Natural' on a box of processed sugar, and people will believe it's good for them. Honestly, William, the human mind is a profoundly disappointing instrument. You could wrap a dog turd in sufficiently elegant packaging and people would queue up to buy it."

As Crispin and I sketched out the campaign, a grim smile spread across my face. The hypocrisy was beautiful, but it was also deeply, deeply familiar. We weren't just running a campaign for a supermarket; we were running a perfect microcosm of the entire Conspiracy Movement.

I thought of Michael Wright on stage, his voice laced with a deep frustration—the sound of a man who has seen behind the curtain and is filled with a genuine pity for those still content to watch the shadows on the wall. A crucial part of his act was dedicated to exposing the propaganda tactics used by the mainstream. He'd talk about Edward

Bernays and Ivy Lee. He'd explain to his audience how governments, the media, and a hundred other institutions use these same techniques to mislead us, to put their own spin on world events, and to keep us all dumbed down and distracted while the *real* agenda is pushed through behind the scenes. He wasn't just pulling back a curtain; he was dragging them out of the cave and into the blinding light of the real world.

And they loved him for it. They saw him as a truth-teller, a man brave enough to expose the lies. And yet they never seemed to notice that he was using the exact same playbook to sell them his own equally one-sided view of the world. It was a masterclass.

He'd use the *bandwagon* effect constantly: "Millions of people are waking up all over the world! Are you going to be left behind?" He'd employ classic logical fallacies, like the *straw man*, creating a ridiculous caricature of the 'official story' and then heroically tearing it down. His reports were a beautiful example of *card stacking*, presenting only the evidence that supported his narrative while ignoring anything that contradicted it. And he was a master of the a*d hominem* attack, dismissing anyone who disagreed with him—not with facts, but by labelling them a 'shill,' a 'gatekeeper,' or a 'sheeple.'

He was exposing the con, while running a parallel one of his own. He was just selling a different brand of truth. And I had to remind myself of one of the first and most important lessons I ever learned in this business: the opposite of a lie is not always the truth. Usually, it's just another lie.

Looking at our campaign plan laid out on the whiteboard, I had to smile. The tactics were the same ones we used for the Ministry. The methodology was identical. We were creating a *secret knowledge*, empowering a group of insiders to see through the official story, and guiding them towards a pre-determined conclusion. The only difference was that this time, the secret cabal we were exposing wasn't the Illuminati. It was Mr Kipling.

Chapter Nineteen

The Message and the Mouthpiece

OUR MORNING ROUTINE AT the Signalroom had become a kind of unspoken ritual, a perfect summary of our odd-couple partnership. I'd arrive first, usually with a greasy paper bag from the little café down the road containing a bacon and baked bean sandwich. I'd put the kettle on, flick on the radio, and start sifting through the morning's emails.

Crispin would arrive about half an hour later, impeccably dressed, looking as though he'd just stepped out of a gentlemen's club rather than off a commuter train. He would survey my breakfast with a look of theatrical disgust before producing his own from a pristine paper bag from an expensive French patisserie: a single, perfect almond croissant.

"Honestly, William," he'd say, dusting a stray flake of pastry from his trousers. "The smell of fried pig fat. It's so agricultural. How you can function after consuming that is a mystery of modern science."

"It's called *fuel*, Crispy," I'd reply, taking a large bite. "Something your lot will have to learn about when the revolution comes."

This was our normal. By day, we were just two blokes in a dusty old signal box, running a surprisingly successful PR agency, fuelled by bacon and fancy pastry. But by night, when I went home, the other

141

side of my life would bleed through in unexpected ways. The real work, the work of the Ministry, had a way of echoing back at me when I least expected it.

"Have you seen this, Will?" Emma said one evening, flicking through the obscure end of the satellite TV guide. "It's called *Open Minds TV*—it's brilliant."

I glanced over. The on-screen graphic was a crudely rendered pyramid with an eye in the middle, set against a swirling purple galaxy. The channel itself was a bizarre smorgasbord of esoteric content: grainy documentaries about UFO sightings in the seventies, dull-looking men in tweed jackets talking about ley lines, new-age gurus explaining crystal healing, and increasingly—conspiracy theories.

Emma was fascinated by it. It tapped into her open-minded spirituality, her belief that there was more to the world than just the dreary, official version of reality. And to be honest, a lot of it interested me too. Not just because I was watching my own secret work being broadcast, but because, like Emma, I've never been one to believe that what we see is all there is. While I knew for a fact that much of our alien narrative was fabricated, I wasn't entirely shut off to the idea that something might be out there. But I was also a pragmatist. I knew there was absolutely zero hard proof. The modern belief in aliens, much like the old belief in angels, was based entirely on pure faith.

One week, we had tuned in to watch a programme featuring Michael Wright. He was being interviewed in a studio that looked suspiciously like a converted garage, by a man named Theo.

Theo was a cuddly-looking bloke in his sixties with rosy cheeks, a warm smile, and the gentle, non-threatening air of a favourite uncle. He was the perfect interviewer for this kind of material, his gentle questions allowing his guests to spin their yarns uninterrupted.

"Now," Theo began, his voice warm and inviting, "my next guest is a man who has been on a remarkable journey. A man who, for many years, has been speaking truths that many were not ready to hear. He has, at times, been like a modern-day Cassandra—the prophetess from Greek mythology who was cursed to see the future but never to be believed. But it seems the world is finally starting to listen. Please welcome the one and only, Michael Wright."

Out walked Michael, to the warm applause of the small studio audience. Theo got straight into it—he asked Wright about people who dismissed his theories. A flicker of contempt crossed his face. "The sheeple," he said, the word dripping with scorn. "They're not ready to wake up. They're too comfortable in their little pens, chewing on the cud of lies the mainstream media feeds them. You can lead a sheep to the truth, Theo, but you can't make it think."

I looked at Emma. She frowned slightly. "He's getting a bit *narky*, isn't he?" she said.

"He cares," I replied, the words feeling sour in my mouth. But I could see she was right. Was it the adoration going to his head? Was he starting to believe his own myth, maybe?

The channel was also attracting wannabes. A few nights later, we saw a new face: a slick oil executive from Milton Keynes of all places, his face a mask of ruddy, overplayed sincerity, peddling a theory about free-energy devices. He was a grifter, and I could spot him a mile off.

But the most surreal moment came a week later. A show called *Secrets of the Kremlin* featured a supposed ex-Russian military intelligence agent named 'Mikhail Volkov.' The opening titles finished, and out walked someone I recognised. It was Maks. *Our* Maks. Dressed in an ill-fitting grey suit, he delivered a mind-bendingly technical, utterly fabricated explanation of how a "secret Soviet electromagnetic weapon" was used to bring down the Twin Towers on 9/11. His natural Russian accent, combined with his scientific know-how and his secret love of amateur dramatics, made him utterly, brilliantly convincing. He even had that old Soviet pen in his hand, twiddling it as he spoke, like a prop from an old Cold War theatre.

"He's very compelling, isn't he?" Emma said, completely drawn in. "Yeah," I said. "He's a natural."

I sat there on the sofa, watching my colleague pretend to be a KGB spook on a fringe satellite channel that my wife was enjoying as a genuine source of alternative information. The layers of deception were starting to make my head spin.

A few nights after that, we were watching a show about the crop circle phenomenon. An artist, a jovial bloke with a West Country accent, was claiming responsibility for creating many of the most famous formations, demonstrating his techniques with planks of wood and bits of rope.

Michael Wright was on again. This time, the topic was money. Theo, the cuddly host, lobbed him a softball question about the economy.

"The economy isn't just in trouble, Theo," Wright began, his voice dropping to a low, ominous tone. "It's being deliberately dismantled. The Illuminati, through their global banking network, are preparing their final move. They are going to crash the system. They want to steal your savings, your pensions, your children's future."

He leaned into the camera, his eyes burning with conviction. "They want to get rid of cash, the money in your hand, the last thing that gives you any freedom. And what will they replace it with? A one-world digital currency. A currency they control completely. A currency where every single transaction you make is tracked, traced, and logged. A currency whose value they can move up and down with the flick of a switch in a data centre in Switzerland."

He shook his head, a look of sorrow on his face. "They want to take the power away from our governments and give it to faceless, unaccountable machines. And the people? We get left behind. Again. You think inflation is bad now? Wait until the value of your savings can be wiped out overnight by a system glitch or a market correction that they engineered. This isn't just about money. This is about control. This is the final phase of the enslavement plan."

Emma looked over at me, her face creased with concern. "That's terrifying," she said.

"Yeah," I replied, my mind racing. "Terrifying."

Because I had heard this story before. The core concepts, the key warnings about the collapse of traditional banking and the dangers of digital currency—it was pure Hendrik. A few years ago, I would have just marvelled at the echo, at how Michael Wright's mythological sermon was a perfect, dumbed-down reflection of Hendrik's complex predictions. But now, I knew more. I knew it wasn't an echo. It was a delivery. And I knew the delivery boy's name. It was Brian.

Beth's casual revelation in the pub after the Brixton show had been the final, missing piece of the puzzle. And now, sitting on my sofa, I could see the entire, breathtaking information supply chain laid out in my mind for the first time.

It started in the 1960s, in a private dining room at *White's*, with Lord Harrington's predecessors listening to a briefing from Hendrik's predecessors. A quiet, theoretical discussion about the potential future impact of decentralised digital currencies, happening decades before the technology even existed.

That initial intelligence was then passed down through generations, refined and updated by the advisory body, until it landed on the desk of Hendrik himself. He then translated that complex, long-range forecast into his own manic but brilliant presentations for The Long Blue Wall.

From there, our team—Beth, Dave, Bertil—would take Hendrik's terrifyingly rational data and strip-mine it for emotional triggers. They'd craft it into a simple, compelling narrative, complete with a villain and a coming apocalypse.

And then, the final step. The script would be passed to a trusted asset, a man like Brian, who would then feed it, piece by piece, to Michael Wright, who would receive it not as a strategy document, but as a divine, prophetic revelation.

And finally, it would end up here. On a fringe satellite channel, broadcast into my own living room, where the final product—a fifty-year-old piece of strategic forecasting, laundered through half a dozen filters—was being consumed by the viewers as a piece of revelatory, insider knowledge.

I looked at the television, at Wright's passionate, sincere-looking face. He was acting as a prophet, revealing a shocking, hidden truth. I remembered his early books, the ones Emma still had on our shelf. They were littered with references to Nostradamus, Edgar Cayce, Mother Shipton—all the great prophets of the past. It was clear now what he was doing, what he had always been doing. He was priming his audience, subtly placing himself in that same hallowed lineage.

But he wasn't channelling divine insight. He was just an ex-comedian with a gift for performance, laundering the contents of a fifty-year-old classified briefing paper from Hendrik's consultants and presenting it as his own, mystical prophecy. He was a vessel, not for cosmic truth, but for the most patient and well-funded PR campaign in human history.

***

[EXT. SPRINGWELL – DAY – Reporter stands outside a modest semi-detached home. Cloudy skies, a light breeze. The street is quiet.]

Reporter (to camera):
"Behind this quiet front door in Springwell, Mark and Rachel Adams have lived a steady, ordinary life for over 30 years. But when the UK banking sector completed its shift to a fully digital platform earlier this year, the couple found themselves unexpectedly caught out."

[Cut to pre-recorded clip]
(Mark sitting at kitchen table, hands folded, mild Midlands accent)
Mark:
"We're not anti-technology or anything. We use cards, online banking...we're not daft. But our savings—just vanished from view. No warning. Just a message saying: 'Balance unavailable'. What do you do with that?"

[Cut back to reporter outside]
Reporter (voiceover):
"Mark and Rachel had recently moved their retirement savings into a government-backed digital account tied to Astra, the national crypto platform. They were told it was safe, stable—ideal for long-term savers."

[Cut to Rachel in living room, soft-spoken, a little weary]
Rachel:
"They kept saying it wasn't lost, just 'inaccessible'. But when you can't buy food or pay your bills, it feels lost. And it's frightening. We didn't invest—we just saved."

[Cut back to reporter – walking slowly down the pavement]
Reporter (to camera):
"They've since regained partial access, but confidence, they say, hasn't fully returned. Mark now keeps a small float of cash tucked away at home. Rachel has gone back to using a basic bank account, with no ties to digital assets."

[Cut to Rachel, smiling faintly]
Rachel:
"It's not about going backwards. It's just...we trusted the system. Now we're a bit more careful about where that trust goes."

[Reporter back on location, closing line – camera widens to show quiet street]
Reporter:
"Their story is becoming increasingly common, as Britain navigates life after cash. And while the technology may be moving quickly, for many people, the feelings around money—and trust—are changing at a slower pace."

Gemma Rayson, BBC News, Springwell.

Chapter Twenty

The Princess and the Tunnel

I NEEDED A BREAK. The relentless cycle of running Signal-room—juggling legitimate clients by day and fighting digital proxy wars by night—was starting to wear me down. I hadn't been over to the Ministry of Truth for a while, and I used that as a pretext to get out of the office for a couple of days. A change of scenery, a chance to get a view from headquarters.

"I'll come with you," Crispin announced, not so much asking as informing. He was standing by the window, inspecting the sleeve of his jacket for imaginary lint.

"You will, will you?" I said.

"Naturally," he replied. "It's time I saw the fabled nerve centre for myself. Besides, I need to pick up some proper mustard. You can't get it here."

I ran it past Jez, who gave it the green light without a moment's thought. "Of course mate, take Crispin with you. The boy's made of the right stuff. Time he saw The Wall."

Crispin insisted on flying first-class, but as there were no flights available at short notice, I said we should fly economy. He looked at me as if I'd suggested we travel by sewer.

"Absolutely not," he sniffed. "I'm not sharing recycled air with screaming infants and the great unwashed. It's uncivilised."

So, we decided on the Eurostar. It was a good excuse, anyway. The London terminal had moved from Waterloo to the newly refurbished St Pancras, and I was keen to see how they had managed to fit a modern, high-speed train terminal into the grand, historic shell of the old Victorian station.

The journey was smooth. A quick change at Brussels, and then on to our final destination in Germany. Our trip was only momentarily disturbed by a brief disagreement with an elderly German couple who insisted we were in their reserved seats. Before I could even begin to untangle the situation, Crispin switched gears. He addressed them in fluent, flawless, and utterly imperious German. I didn't understand a word, but the tone was unmistakable. It was a verbal dressing-down of such clinical precision that the poor couple visibly shrank, muttered apologies, and scurried off down the carriage looking thoroughly defeated.

I stared at him. "I didn't know you spoke German."

"One picks things up," he said with a dismissive wave of his hand, before returning to his newspaper.

We arrived at the university campus and were soon in the lift heading to the top floor. The place was exactly as I remembered. I introduced Crispin to a few of the team members who were milling about. He was polite but distant, examining everything and everyone with the cool, detached air of an anthropologist at a slightly disappointing museum.

Then he saw it. *The Long Blue Wall.* He walked its entire length slowly, taking in the chaotic web of strings, newspaper clippings, and scrawled notes. He wasn't fazed in the slightest—as if it was a normal everyday occurrence for him. He nodded occasionally, a flicker of professional recognition in his eyes, as if appraising the brushstrokes of a moderately interesting painting.

I watched him, thinking of Lord Harrington, of his belief in the aristocracy's duty to guide the nation. I thought of the great public schools where their children are trained to become princes and world leaders, where they spend their days learning political philosophy, statecraft, and Machiavelli. While Crispin was likely theorising about political manipulation, I would have been pinching someone's sports bag from the changing rooms and blaming it on someone else.

We heard Hendrik before we saw him. "*Meine englischen Freunde!*" he boomed, bounding over to us, his eyes alight with a familiar, manic energy. "Welcome, welcome!"

After a quick handshake and an introduction, Hendrik and Crispin were off, rabbiting away in German. Hendrik, as ever, was a torrent of barely contained excitement, brandishing a new set of briefing papers.

"*Die nächste welle ist schon da!*" he proclaimed, tapping the documents. "The next wave is already here! While the public is worrying about their online privacy and their digital footprint, we are modelling the societal impact of full-immersion virtual realities! What happens to property, to identity, when a person can spend ninety percent of their life in a digital world? *Niemand denkt darüber nach!* Nobody is thinking about it!"

Crispin listened, calm and reserved, a small, amused smile on his face, his posture the very definition of the unflappable Englishman—a perfect foil to Hendrik's Teutonic fervour.

"And this!" Hendrik said, flipping a page. "Neuralink! Human-AI integration! We are no longer just using the machines; we are *becoming* the machines! Forget the 'evil microchip' conspiracies; this is a willing upgrade! And the AGI—the true Artificial General Intelligence—it is not a matter of *if*, but *when*. The political ramifications of decentralised autonomous organisations replacing corporate structures alone will cause chaos!"

He leaned in, his voice dropping to a low whisper, though his excitement was still palpable. "We are giving them stories about lizard-men and devils so they do not see the real storm that is gathering. We are throwing them a bone to keep them busy. As we say here in Germany, *man muss dem Affen Zucker geben.*"

I looked blank.

"You must give the monkey sugar," Crispin translated, very matter-of-factly. "Keep the masses entertained with sweet little nothings."

Hendrik didn't miss a beat, "We are talking about designer babies and radical lifespan extension! We are arguing about pronouns while the very definition of 'human' is being rewritten in a laboratory in California! It is happening now!"

He finally paused, taking a deep breath and straightening his rumpled jacket. He looked from me to Crispin, a look of weary conviction on his face.

"It is a complex problem," he finished, with a shrug of finality. "*Auch ein blindes Huhn findet mal ein Korn.*"

Crispin leaned over with a dry smirk. "Even a blind chicken sometimes finds a grain of corn." I wasn't entirely sure what he meant by it, but it seemed to satisfy Hendrik immensely.

I left them to themselves and wandered over to a small coffee area, where I found Beth sitting back in an armchair, her feet up, a notebook resting on her lap. "Will," she said, her smile warm and genuine. "Good to see you. Coffee?"

We chatted for a few minutes before I asked her what she was working on. "Ah," she said. "A new piece for the collection. Take a look."

She slid the notebook over. The title on the page was *The Tunnel Queen,* and for a moment I thought it was a poem. But it was something else. Something ancient in its bones, disguised in modern clothes:

"Long ago—though not in the age of swords and scrolls, but of modems and motorways—there lived a princess. She was beautiful, not just in face, but in truth..."

I read the whole thing, my coffee growing cold in my hand. The story was familiar, of course. The beautiful princess, the cruel Queen Mother-in-law, the riders in black, the strange ray-gun, the car, the tunnel. I'd been pushing the component parts of this narrative on the forums for years, framing it as a political assassination, a classic conspiracy. As far as I was concerned, it was just another piece of the ongoing anti-establishment rhetoric, but I had never seen it written down like this—not as a conspiracy theory, but as a fairy tale. I was stunned.

"God, Beth," I said, looking up from the page. "It's a fairy tale! I've been peddling it all this time and I never realised. It's one of your stories!"

"It's mythology, Will," she corrected me gently. "One for future generations, like all the others we're forming right now. All myths have a grain of truth, a historical event at their core. But over time, other elements are added. Magical elements. Symbolic layers." She leaned forward and started to deconstruct her own work for me.

"The *Princess* is an archetype," she explained. "She embodies truth, beauty, and vulnerability. She is beloved by the people but destroyed by the palace because she threatens the old order simply by being a better person. The *Queen* is the classic symbol of entrenched, dynastic power. The *Riders* are modern-day Furies, the faceless dogs of power. The *Ray-Gun* is the fear of secret, unaccountable state technology. And the *Tunnel,* as always, is a trip to the underworld, a place where truth disappears."

"And the car?" I asked. "The white Mercedes?"

"Yes," she said. "The chariot. The vehicle of the hero. A white Mercedes convertible—another enhancement, of course, for added symbolism. It represents timeless elegance, reliability, a kind of graceful freedom. It's the perfect contrast to the snarling, aggressive motorcycles of the riders. And Diana's *cassette player*? That's the most important part. In those days, a cassette was personal, curated. It was your voice, your choices. The idea that her voice might still whisper through the static is the soul of the myth. It says that even when truth is suppressed, it finds a way to return."

Just then, Crispin wandered over, a cup of tea in his hand. "What a decent sort, that Hendrik," he remarked. "A bit excitable, of course. But then, he *is* German." He left the comment hanging there with a self-satisfied smirk.

Beth showed him the story. He scanned it quickly. "Ah yes," he said, nodding. "The evil stepmother archetype. Ino, Juno, Medea. Plenty to choose from in the classics."

"Cinderella? Snow White?" I offered. Beth nodded.

"He's a nice young man," Beth said to me later, after Crispin had wandered off. "Rather charming, actually." I'd never once considered Crispin to be charming. I put it down to Beth being Canadian and therefore susceptible to his upper-class English accent and effortless air of superiority.

I made a mental note as I walked back towards the main room. I had to start thinking differently. I had to look past the surface-level conspiracy and see the deeper story, the mythological architecture hidden in plain sight. I had been a storyteller for years, but only now was I beginning to understand the true power of the stories I was telling.

Later that evening, after we had all returned to our usual hotel, I couldn't settle. My mind was buzzing with myths and archetypes, with Hendrik's manic energy and Crispin's relentless wit. I needed some air. I left the hotel and took a walk into the centre of town.

It was a normal, quiet evening. The shops were closed, the streets were clean, and couples were sitting outside cafés, their faces illuminated by the warm glow of candlelight. And yet, for the first time, I felt like I was seeing it all through Hendrik's eyes. The signs of the great disruption were everywhere, quiet but insistent.

I walked past a group of teenagers huddled around a small, glowing display. They weren't just making a call; they were jabbing and swiping at the screen of a phone. They were navigating a new world that existed on top of our own. I thought about the *App Store* I'd read about. It wasn't just a feature; it was a floodgate. It was the delivery mechanism for a thousand new services that would dismantle entire industries. Banking, transport, dating, fitness—all of it was being rewritten, not by governments or committees, but by unseen coders in California.

I saw a young woman filming herself, probably for one of those new *video blogs* on YouTube. The old gatekeepers of media—the BBC, the Hollywood studios—were being made irrelevant. Why wait for them to tell you a story when you could tell your own, and broadcast it to the world from a street corner in a small town near Frankfurt?

I stopped at a bakery to buy a pastry. The person in front of me didn't pay with cash or a card. They just tapped their watch against a small reader on the counter. A seamless, frictionless transaction—silent, automatic, and managed entirely by systems no one could quite see. I saw a man jogging past, a strange-looking band on his wrist, his body's data—his heart rate, his steps—being monitored, collected, and sent into the digital ether. The beginning of the end for traditional healthcare, replaced by preventive, data-driven wellness managed by a tech company.

Each of these things, on its own, seemed like a small convenience, a cool new gadget. But seen all at once, they formed a pattern. I finally, truly understood what Lord Harrington meant when he said, "It's a long game." I remembered the old saying: *whoever controls the basic resources, controls the world.* For centuries, that had meant land, gold, oil. But the fundamental resource now was technological know-how. And the people who owned that—the ones who wrote the code, who owned the platforms, who controlled the data—were quietly building the infrastructure of the new empire, right under our noses.

Jez had been right—standing there in that cemetery, when he'd first spelled it out to me. We were living through the start of the Technological Revolution. And most people, like the happy couple in the café enjoying their coffee, had absolutely no idea. They were just enjoying the new, easier way of doing things, unaware that the very ground beneath their feet was being systematically replaced—one line of code at a time.

Chapter Twenty-One

From Punchline to Pride

THE SUPERMARKET CAMPAIGN WAS a roaring success. The documentary, *Shopping for Secrets*, had been a ratings hit, and sales of our clients' own-brand products had soared. Signalroom was solvent, respected, and turning a tidy profit. For a while, life felt almost normal. We were just a growing, successful PR agency, doing what PR agencies do. Then Dave called.

He didn't want to talk about the Ministry. He wanted to meet for a drink. He was in London, he said, for a "sociological symposium", which I knew was his code for a week-long pub crawl with some old university mates. I met him in a quiet, wood-panelled pub in Bloomsbury. He was already there, a pint of ale in his hand, looking totally at home.

"Alright, Will?" he said, his gravelly voice a familiar comfort. "I've got something for you. A bit of private work. Not for the Ministry, but... adjacent to it."

"Go on," I said, intrigued.

"Word of your work on the teenage pregnancy project has reached the right ears," he said. "They've got something else for you, along the same lines."

"It's a consortium," he explained. "Progressive think tanks, a few human rights charities, with some quiet backing from forward-thinking factions in Whitehall. They have a problem they want to solve. A social problem."

He leaned forward, his voice dropping slightly. "Homophobia, Will. They want to make it... go away."

I stared at him. This wasn't entirely new territory, but it was a hell of a step up. We'd sold biscuits, we'd sold festival tickets, we'd nudged teenage behaviour. But this was different. This wasn't about changing what people do in private; this was about fundamentally rewriting the rules of society and of how people treated each other in public.

"It's a social engineering project, pure and simple," Dave continued, seeing the look on my face. "And it's long overdue. Look, when I was a lad, it was completely normal to be casually racist, sexist, homophobic. It was just the background noise. It's how it was. You'd hear jokes on the telly that would get a comedian cancelled today. That was the normal world we lived in. Our job..." he said with a glint in his eye, "is to create the 'new normal'."

He was pitching me a job. A legitimate, socially progressive, world-bettering job.

"So," I said, "how do we sell tolerance?"

"The same way we sell anything," Dave grinned. "You don't lecture people. You don't tell them they're bigots. That just makes them defensive. You make the alternative so appealing, so normal, so *mundane*, that the old prejudice starts to look weird and embarrassing. We're going to make tolerance fashionable."

And so began *Project Horizon*. Dave, the sociologist and demolition expert from The Long Blue Wall, was now the chief architect of a campaign for social cohesion. Signalroom was hired as the primary contractor.

Our first and most powerful tool was the humble television soap opera. "The soaps are the most influential medium in the country," Dave explained, scribbling on a beer mat. "More powerful than the news. People don't just watch them; they live with the characters.

We'll work with the writers on *EastEnders* and *Corrie*. We'll help them introduce a new gay character."

"But," he stressed, "the crucial thing is that his storylines won't all be about him being gay. He'll have arguments with his mum. He'll struggle to pay his bills. His boiler will break. We'll normalise him through mundanity. We'll make him boring, just like everyone else."

Next came the *Just Like You* print campaign. "Remember the hair transplant stories?" Dave asked. "Same principle. We find a lovely, stable, long-term gay couple—maybe they run a successful B&B in Devon—and we get a feature written about them in a Sunday supplement. The story is about their love, their success, their contribution to the village fête. It's heart-warming. It's aspirational. It says, *Their love is just as valid as yours.* And again—just as boring."

We also needed to shift the language itself. We worked with our contacts at the BBC and the commercial channels to influence their editorial guidelines. The goal was to make casual homophobic jokes socially unacceptable. Not through censorship, but by making them seem old-fashioned, uncool, and deeply embarrassing. We wanted to get to a point where someone telling one of those jokes at a dinner party would be met with a cold, awkward silence.

And then came the most insidious part of the plan: the framing of the enemy. "We need to find the most extreme, cartoonish, fire-and-brimstone protestors we can," Dave said. "The ones with the placards saying 'God Hates Queers'. The cruder and more extreme the better. And we give them oxygen. We make sure they're on the news. We make them the public face of all opposition. By association, anyone who disagrees with our position gets lumped in with the nutters. It's a classic tactic: define your enemy by their most unappealing fringe."

Over the next few years, we executed the plan. Crispin, with his sociopathic talent for media manipulation, was brilliant at it. He'd work with publicists to carefully manage the "coming out" of a minor celebrity, framing it as an act of immense bravery. He'd feed stories to the tabloids, and arrange for big burly male celebrities to become vocal allies—giving the heterosexual majority the green light to do the same.

Slowly, imperceptibly, the cultural tide began to turn. You could see it happening in real time. Jokes that were standard fare a few years ago now seemed jarring and cruel. The gay characters in the soaps became part of the furniture, just the same as everyone else. The public conversation shifted from a debate about morality to a discussion about rights.

It became clear to me that this was the most powerful proof of concept for The Long Blue Wall I could ever imagine. This campaign, this deliberate, behind-the-scenes rewriting of our shared social values, was, in its own way, a force for good. It was making the country a more tolerant, less oppressive place for a significant portion of its population.

But the methodology—the subtle manipulation, the framing of enemies, the creation of narratives, the co-opting of the media—was identical to the work we were doing for the Ministry. We were using the exact same tools to sell tolerance as we were to sell lies about the Queen of England and the Illuminati.

The whole campaign served as a powerful reminder of a fascinating professional paradox. Our tools are amoral. A hammer can be used to build a house or to break a window, and the hammer doesn't care which. And I also had to admit, working on something positive with Dave and Project Horizon was making a refreshing change from the doom and gloom negativity of the Conspiracy Movement. It felt good to be building a nice house for once.

***

New York City, 1928

The air in the private suite at the St Regis Hotel was thick with the scent of expensive cigars and quiet desperation. George Hill, the formidable president of the American Tobacco Company, stared out the window at the bustling streets below.

"It is a problem of perception, Mr. Bernays," he said, his voice a low growl. "A problem of morality. We are not selling a product. We are fighting a societal taboo."

Edward Bernays, a young man with old, watchful eyes, simply nodded, letting the industrialist voice his frustration.

"A woman smoking in public?" Hill continued, turning from the window. "She's not just breaking a rule; she's signalling something about her character. She's seen as a harlot, a degenerate, a loose woman. It's not a matter of taste, Mr. Bernays. In the public mind, it is a moral failing."

Bernays waited a beat, then spoke. "Then we must stop talking about taste, and start talking about something else." He gestured towards the window, at the new, energetic city buzzing below.

"The modern woman is breaking down barriers," he said, his voice now filled with a quiet, strategic passion. "She is fighting for the vote, for equality, for a place in the world that is not defined by her husband. What she needs are symbols of her new power."

Hill looked at him, intrigued. "Go on."

"We must use every tool at our disposal," Bernays explained. "A coordinated media campaign. We will work with journalists, with photographers, with influential figures in society. We will not sell cigarettes. We will sell the *idea* of the cigarette as a symbol of female independence. A 'torch of freedom'. We will take their moral taboo and reframe it as a political statement."

He let the idea hang in the air, simple and audacious.

"We will deliberately and systematically change the public's perception," Bernays concluded, his voice calm and certain. "We will make them change their way of thinking, not by force, but by giving them a new, more compelling narrative to believe in."

Hill stared at him for a long moment, a slow, dawning look of awe on his face. He wasn't just a salesman. He was an architect of belief.

"My God, Bernays," he said finally. "I believe it will work."

Chapter Twenty-Two

The Architecture
of Fear

THE CALL FROM HENDRIK came on a Monday morning, a digital
cattle prod to the start of the week. Since our trip to Germany, he'd
been in touch more frequently. He was our Head of Future Studies,
our Ghostwriter of the Apocalypse, and his job was to monitor the
data streams, to take the temperature of the collective consciousness.
And according to his models, the patient was far too calm.

"William! The projections are unacceptable!" he barked down the
phone, his German accent making it sound like a military command.
"The public complacency index is dangerously high! They are sleepwalking! They are watching the cooking shows and the celebrity gossip
while the freight train of technological disruption is less than a mile
down the track! They are not prepared! The *Future Shock* vectors are
flat! You must amplify the fear! It is your primary directive!"

He was right. Crispin and I had been focusing on the grand mythological work—the Alien Origins story, the Tunnel Queen myth, the
slow burn of the 2012 End-of-the-World narrative. But we had somewhat neglected our other two key roles: stoking the fires of the anti-establishment protest movement and, crucially, preparing people for the
coming turmoil. We were the support staff for Michael Wright, and

our job was to build the architecture of fear that his sermons would inhabit.

Fear. It's the oldest and most effective tool of persuasion. It bypasses logic and speaks directly to the brain's primal survival system—the part responsible for instinct, reaction, and self-preservation, the part that is hard-wired for survival, the part that's often called the 'lizard brain' by pop psychologists—a term Michael Wright had adopted with relish. It's the currency of power. Religions have used it for millennia: *"obey the doctrine, or face eternal damnation."* Politicians use it every election year: *"vote for us, or the barbarians will be at the gates, ready to destroy your way of life."* And now, we were using it too.

But there's a crucial second step. Fear alone leads to paralysis. You have to provide a solution, a path to safety. That's the real trick. "*Be afraid,*" the priest says, "*but the church will save you.*" "*Be afraid,*" the politician says, "*but I will protect you.*" "*Be afraid,*" Michael Wright says, "*but I have the secret knowledge that will set you free.*" It wasn't panic for panic's sake. It was engineered dread—fear with blueprints. Our job was to help create the fear. His job was to offer the salvation.

"Right, Crispin," I said, putting the phone down. "The boss says we're not scaring people enough. Time to get back to basics. Martial Law, civil unrest, FEMA camps. Let's start building the case."

Crispin rubbed his hands together with a ghoulish delight. "Excellent. A bit of good old-fashioned panic-mongering. It's so much more stimulating than flogging vegan burgers."

We both laughed, but as I logged into my various personas, I felt that familiar, unwelcome twinge of shame. I don't like drama. Yet here I was, about to deliberately inject a dose of pure, undiluted anxiety into the digital bloodstream. I took a deep breath, put my trust in the experts at The Wall, and went to work.

We needed new narratives, new angles to make the Illuminati feel less like a distant conspiracy and more like a present, almost supernatural threat—a modern Devil for a modern age. We moved away from the complex financial stuff, and moved towards more simple, primal fears. I logged in as *Veritas_2012* and started a thread about strange weather patterns.

PROFESSIONAL CONSPIRACY THEORIST

Title: It's Not Climate Change. It's Weather Warfare.

Post by Veritas_2012:

Friends, have you noticed the weather lately? The 'freak' storms, the droughts, the floods? The media tells us it's 'climate change'. Another convenient lie. I know they have the technology—HAARP, chemtrails, call it what you will—to control the weather. These aren't natural disasters. They are targeted attacks. They're using the weather to control the food supply, to create chaos, to justify more control. They can turn the sky itself into a weapon.

And to hammer home the 'modern bogeyman' angle, we started seeding stories that went beyond simple corruption and into the realm of the truly monstrous.

Post by TruthSeeker77:

Has anyone heard the whispers about what they're doing with the blood? I know someone who works in private medical logistics. He says there's a huge, undeclared market for one specific blood type: O-negative. The universal donor. And it's being bought up, quietly, in massive quantities, by private clients linked to the elite banking dynasties. They're not using it for transfusions. He says the whispers are about... 'youth therapy'. About harvesting something from it. Adrenochrome. They believe it extends their lives. They are literally feeding on the vitality of the young to stave off their own decay.

Crispin's main attack persona, *Patrician_Gaze*, was a thing of beauty—a distillation of his own innate snobbery and intellectual contempt. But for this new, overtly fear-mongering character, he needed a different voice.

"The *Patrician* is perfect for dismantling an argument," he explained to me, staring thoughtfully at his screen. "But he's not the right tool for this particular job. One needs a more common touch. The voice of the man on the street."

"And how will you do that?" I asked, a little sceptically.

"William," he said, turning to me with a look of faint pity. "Before I went up to Oxford, my father insisted I get some 'real-world experience'. He had me work for six months in one of the family's less glamorous holdings. A call centre. In Romford."

I stared at him, trying to picture it. Crispin, in a cheap headset, dealing with angry customers, sitting alongside Tyler and Chantelle from Essex. It was like trying to picture a swan working in a chip shop. He must have read the look on my face, because he let out a short, dismissive laugh.

"Oh, good heavens, no," he said, as if the thought were physically painful. "I wasn't actually *on the floor* with the hoi polloi. That would have been absurd. Father had them set me up in a small, private office, away from the main... din. My job was ostensibly to 'analyse customer satisfaction data.' In reality, I just spent six months with a headset on, listening in on the calls."

"It was an anthropological goldmine," he continued, a nostalgic smile playing on his lips. "An absolute masterclass in the vernacular of the common man. The slang, the syntax, the specific rhythms of genuine grievance."

He turned back to his keyboard and created a new profile. The username was a work of genius: *Gaz_From_The_Pub*. I watched, fascinated, as he began to type. The transformation was instantaneous. The precise, aristocratic intellectual disappeared, replaced by a completely different person.

Title: MATE, CHECK OUT THE LAMPPOSTS!!!

Post by Gaz_From_The_Pub:
I swear, you lot need to listen. You seen those new lampposts they're putting up? The chunky ones with the weird boxes stuck on 'em? Council reckons they're 'traffic sensors'. Yeah, right. What a load of old balls. Was watching that Michael Wright geezer last night—proper switched on he is. Says they're tooled up. Got signal jammers and microwave kit inside. All turned off for now, just sitting there ready.

So when it kicks off, like when the banks go belly-up and people really get the 'ump, they won't need to roll out the boys in black straight away. All they'll do is flick a switch. Bang. Phones dead. Internet gone. You won't even be able to text the missus to say you're running late for your tea. Full blackout, just like that.

And if it really goes Pete Tong, they can power up the emitters. It won't kill you—too obvious. Nah, it's worse. Makes your skin feel like it's burning, so you've got no choice but to leg it. It's a weapon, mate. Dressed up as a lamppost, right outside your house. We're getting boxed in, and we're just standing here like right mugs.

It was a stunning piece of method acting, a demonstration of his many, and slightly unnerving, talents.

We were the architects of anxiety. We built the prison of fear in people's minds, and Michael Wright stood at the gate, holding the only key. It was a perfect, self-perpetuating system. And as I sat there, typing out another post designed to make some poor sod in a bedsit in Birmingham feel a little bit more scared of the world, that twinge of shame began to feel less like a twinge and more like a dull, persistent ache.

***

Laguna Beach, California. The Oasis Hotel, Wellness Lounge.

The room was bathed in a soft, white light. The air smelled faintly of eucalyptus and expensive green tea. Two hundred people, dressed in expensive, high-performance 'athleisure' wear, sat on brightly coloured yoga mats, looking up at the stage with an expression of captivated, hopeful adoration.

On the stage stood Julian. He was in his late forties, tanned, with perfect teeth and a head of artfully tousled silver hair. He wore a simple, elegant, dark grey technical T-shirt that clung to a perfectly toned physique. He wasn't a preacher; he was a *lifestyle architect*.

He paced the stage slowly, a microphone headset curving along his sharp jawline. His voice was a calm, reassuring balm, but the words he spoke were of a silent, invisible war being waged on their bodies.

He spoke of the "toxins" in their water, the "inflammation" caused by gluten, the "adrenal fatigue" from the relentless stress of the modern world.

"And who benefits?" he asked, his voice swelling with a quiet, controlled anger. "The establishment. *Big Food* with its processed, nutrient-dead products. *Big Pharma* with its pills that mask the symptoms but never cure the disease. They don't want you to be healthy. They want you to be a customer. A patient. A dependent."

He paused, letting the implication settle over the silent, nodding room.

Then, after two hours, his tone softened. A warm, benevolent smile appeared on his face. "But you..." he said, "...you can choose a different path. You can choose to be pure. You can choose to be vibrant. You can choose to be *clean*."

He gestured to a sleek, beautifully designed display at the side of the stage. On it were rows of elegantly packaged bottles and boxes.

"There is a way forward," he said, his voice now a gentle promise. "An incredible blend of adaptogenic herbs to support the adrenals. A 30-day detox protocol to help eliminate the toxins. A personalised supplement plan, based on unique vibrational frequencies, to help extinguish the inflammation."

He didn't need to do the hard sell. The room erupted in grateful, relieved applause.

Chapter
Twenty-Three

2012 : An Origin Story

Official Proclamation of the Scythian Monastery,
circa 525 Anno Domini

THE ABBOT, A MAN whose hands were stained with the ink of a dozen languages, unrolled the fresh parchment. The chamber was cold, the only light from a sputtering oil lamp, but the words he was about to dictate would reshape time itself.

"Let it be recorded," began the monk Dionysius Exiguus, his voice clear and steady in the quiet room. "For too long have we marked our years by the reign of the persecutor Diocletian, anchoring our history to an age of tyranny and darkness. But a new light has come into the world. A new age has dawned, though many did not see it at the time."

"We now understand that the true fulcrum upon which history turns was not a war, nor the crowning of an emperor, but the birth of a single child in a humble stable. With the Incarnation of our Lord, Jesus Christ, the old world of pagan gods and Roman law did not simply end; it was rendered obsolete. A new covenant was forged, a new understanding of Man's place in the cosmos was revealed."

"Therefore, let this be the year 525, not since Diocletian, but *Anno Domini*—in the Year of our Lord. We declare the beginning of a new epoch, a new calendar for a new world, so that all future generations will measure their lives not from the edicts of earthly kings, but from the moment that divinity itself walked among us and changed everything forever."

***

The summons came from Maks. The email that landed that morning was brief, formal, and had the unmistakable tone of a directive, not an invitation. It was stripped of all pleasantries, simply stating that a "significant breakthrough regarding the 2012 program" had been made and our presence was required.

We made our travel plans. Crispin had again invited himself along. "One must keep an eye on the continental operations," he'd said, as if he were a visiting field marshal.

We flew into the familiar German financial hub and made our way to the university campus. The team was assembled around the central table in the room of The Long Blue Wall, the mood one of focused, creative energy.

Jez stood at the head of the table, a cup of coffee in his hand. "Right, everyone," he began. "Let's get started. As you all know, our work over the past decade in building up the *2012* narrative has been a resounding success. The disaster movies, the books, the documentaries—we successfully created a global sense of anticipation. The world was told to expect something to happen."

He paused, a wry smile on his face. "And, of course, nothing *did* happen. It was never going to. The 2012 event was never about a real-time apocalypse. It was about creating a historical marker. Our job now is to lay the groundwork, the 'evidence', for future generations to stumble upon. We are creating a modern *Ancient Wisdom*."

Beth nodded in agreement. "In one hundred or so years," she explained, "a future prophet, another Michael Wright, will point back to our time and show them the cultural history: the Hollywood films, the media hype, the reported public belief. And this person will say, *You see? They had a sense that a great transformation was coming—it was in the air, in the conversations happening everywhere.*"

"But," Jez continued, "that's just the cultural evidence. We need something more. Something scientific. A piece of lost data, a forgotten anomaly, a hidden truth that a friendly researcher in the future can unearth in the archives. A *smoking gun* that 'proves' a physical event did actually take place." He turned and gestured towards Maks, who was standing by the board, his eyes alight with the look of a man who had just solved an impossible equation. "And that is why we are here today. Maks believes he has found a contender for our smoking gun."

Maks stepped forward, a look of quiet satisfaction on his face, a stack of printouts and charts in his hand. "My friends," he began, his accent heavy and precise. "Our objective, as we have discussed, is to engineer the historical record. The public was primed for an event in 2012—now, we must provide the scientific proof." He tapped the stack of printouts now on the table. "An apocalypse narrative is not logical. The data does not support such a clumsy story. But the data does suggest something far more elegant."

He paused, looking at each of us in turn.

"What if the event was not an actual catastrophe," he continued, his voice low and intense, "but instead... a recalibration? A subtle shift, hidden in the background noise of the data, waiting for a future researcher to discover? Not an explosion. An activation."

He laid out five charts on the table, each detailing a real cosmic event from 2012: the near-miss solar storm, the galactic alignment, a neutrino burst, and a silent radio signal.

"These events are facts," he stated, his voice flat and absolute. "Verifiable facts. They are the background radiation of our narrative. But they are not the catalyst."

He paused, letting his gaze settle on each of us. "The catalyst, my friends, did not come from space. It came from us, here on Earth. From a laboratory in Switzerland. That is the story I propose."

He pointed to the final chart, a complex diagram of the Large Hadron Collider at CERN. "July 2012," he said, "they announce the discovery of the Higgs boson. A triumph for public science. But my analysis of the raw data, the data that was dismissed as anomalous, as insignificant noise—it shows something else, something we can use." His voice was now a low, intense whisper. "Not just a discovery. *A creation*. A microscopic, fleeting instability in the quantum field. A bridge, perhaps only open for a nanosecond. It is the perfect hidden variable."

He looked up from the charts, a rare, sharp smile on his face. "When the whole world was looking to the heavens for a sign, the final, crucial move was made by human hands, right here on Earth. It is a beautiful irony, is it not?"

I stared at him. It was incredible. A grand cosmic conspiracy where humanity itself was the final, unwitting accomplice.

"So," Maks concluded, tapping the CERN chart with a single finger, "the world did not end in 2012. No. It was... recalibrated. The symptoms will take years to manifest, but they will be undeniable: the bursts of creativity, the sudden social awakenings, and, most importantly, the exponential acceleration of technology which is our primary concern. Humanity did not evolve. It was upgraded. And we," he gestured around the room, "are the ones who will write the official history of how it happened."

He finished, looking pleased with himself. The room was silent for a moment. Crispin was the first to speak.

"So, if I understand correctly," he said, his tone dry and analytical, "a series of cosmic flukes, culminating in a minor lab accident in Switzerland, has given the human race a kind of psychic upgrade? Is that the gist of it?" Maks nodded.

Crispin leaned back, steepling his fingers. "And the evidence for this re-tuning is... what, exactly? A vague feeling? A few people having the same dream? It's a bit thin, isn't it?"

I watched, fascinated. Crispin was doing exactly what Maks had asked: picking holes, testing the narrative for weaknesses. He was doing it with a natural, forensic skill that was both impressive and slightly unnerving. It made me think of Lord Harrington's belief that his class had an innate, instinctual wisdom for this sort of thing. Watching Crispin dissect Maks's theory with the cool precision of a barrister, I had to admit that he might have a point.

Dave let out a cynical chuckle. "So, let me get this straight. *2012* will be looked back on by future historians as the single greatest turning point in human history. But for us lot, who actually lived through it, absolutely sod all happened. We were all too busy watching the Olympics and worrying about the price of petrol."

"That's the beauty of it," Jez said. "A silent paradigm shift. The best kind."

Beth suggested that the first, early whispers of the story should be held back for now, that it was too big for Michael Wright. Instead, it should be passed, via one of their feeders, to his successor, to be used as their first disclosure of *secret inside information*—their first major revelation. It was the new, foundational text for our new future world-view.

That evening, after a long dinner, we decided to head into Frankfurt to a popular comedy club, housed in a basement venue off a side-street, and large enough to hold a couple of hundred. The air was thick with the smell of stale beer and anticipation. The headline act was a sharp, fast-talking Scottish comedian who, Jez assured us, was famous for his routines on the absurdity of modern life.

He came on stage to a roar of applause, a wiry bundle of nervous energy. He started with the usual fare, a brilliant, relatable takedown of the small, everyday frustrations of the new digital age.

"It's the passwords, isn't it?" he began, pacing the small stage. "My entire brain is now just a storage facility for passwords I'm not allowed to write down. You need a password to check your bank, a different one for your email, another one to prove to your toaster that you're qualified to operate it. I spent twenty minutes this morning in a password-recovery loop trying to remember the name of my first pet, and for a while there, I couldn't even remember that I'd even *had* a pet, never mind what its name might have been!"

The crowd howled with laughter. He continued, going off on one about the tyranny of software updates, the existential dread of the self-checkout machine, and the bizarre performance of trying to prove you weren't a robot for a CAPTCHA test. He was warming them up, building a shared sense of bewilderment at the world we were all living in.

Then, his tone shifted slightly, from simple frustration to a more philosophical bemusement.

"You know, there's a name for this feeling," he said, leaning on the mic stand. "I was reading this book about a thing called *Future Shock,* right? It's basically a polite way of sayin': WE'RE ALL HAVING A BLOODY MELTDOWN AND NOBODY'S NOTICED!"

The crowd roared again, but this time it was a laugh of deeper recognition. He had them. He had taken their small, everyday annoyances and connected them to a much bigger, more profound idea.

"It's like culture shock, but without the holiday!" he cracked. "Instead of you goin' to Thailand, it's like Thailand came to your house, set up a robot DJ, changed your gender pronouns, and replaced your job with an app that delivers artisanal toast!"

He paced the stage. "And the government's still runnin' on Windows 95! They're tryin' to regulate AI with a rubber stamp and a fax machine! We're runnin' a spaceship with the handbook for a horse and cart!"

The audience was in stitches. Dave was wiping tears from his eyes. Jez was howling with laughter. I looked over at Hendrik. He was not laughing. His face was a mask of thunderous fury. He was gripping the arms of his chair, his knuckles white.

The comedian moved on to his closing bit. "So we're all knackered, we're all flippin' out, we're all cryin' in Lidl because reality's movin' so fast it forgot to bring us with it. What's the answer, eh? Goat yoga?"

Hendrik shot to his feet.

"IT IS NOT A JOKE!" he bellowed, his German accent thick with outrage.

The comedian stopped, blinked into the spotlight. "Sorry, mate? Didn't catch that."

"THE SYSTEMIC COLLAPSE OF WESTERN INSTITU-TIONS IS NOT A PUNCHLINE FOR YOUR AMUSEMENT!" Hendrik screamed, pointing a trembling finger at the stage. "YOU SHOULD BE WARNING THESE PEOPLE, NOT MAKING JOKES ABOUT GOATS!"

The audience erupted in the biggest laugh of the night. They thought it was part of the act. A brilliant piece of audience interaction with a planted heckler.

The comedian, a pro, leaned into it. "Alright, calm down, professor! What do you suggest we do then?"

"WE MUST ACCELERATE THE MYTHOLOGICAL PRIM-ING!" Hendrik yelled, completely serious. "WE MUST REIN-FORCE THE NARRATIVE BUFFERS TO AVERT MASS PSY-CHOLOGICAL DISLOCATION!"

Two burly security guards started moving towards our table. The comedian held up his hands. "Give the man a round of applause, folks! My dad, everybody!"

The crowd cheered as the bouncers politely, but firmly, escorted a still-ranting Hendrik towards the exit. "BUT THE JOKE IS ON YOU! THEY ARE SELLING YOU THE SCRIPT FOR YOUR OWN OBSOLESCENCE!" were the last words we heard as the door swung shut behind him.

Dave was practically apoplectic with laughter, banging his fist on the table. "Oh, that's priceless," he wheezed. "Absolutely priceless."

Jez just shook his head, a wide grin on his face. "Never, ever, take Hendrik to a comedy club again. Lesson learned."

Official Address to the Global Governance Symposium, 100 TE Technological Era

The Stateswoman, her face calm and serene, flickered into existence on the holographic dais. The chamber was silent, the delegates from every global sector watching with rapt attention. Her words were being broadcast to the unified network, a message to define their age.

"Let it be formally recorded," she began, her voice clear and resonant. "For too long have we marked our years by the old, chaotic Gregorian system, anchoring our history to an age of division and nascent disruption. But a new consciousness has emerged in the world. A new age has dawned, though many did not see it at the time."

"We now understand that the true fulcrum upon which modern history turns was not a political election, nor the launch of a new device, but a series of quiet, interconnected events in the year previously known as 2012. With the Cosmic Realignment and the quantum breakthrough at CERN, the old world of nation-states and analogue systems did not simply end; it was rendered obsolete. A new symbiosis was forged, a new understanding of humanity's place in the network was revealed."

"Therefore, let this be the year 100 of the Technological Era. We declare the beginning of a new epoch, a new calendar for a new world, so that all future generations will measure their lives not from the borders of old countries, but from the moment that humanity connected to the global consciousness and changed everything forever."

Chapter Twenty-Four

Tears of a Clown

THE PHONE RANG ON a quiet Sunday morning. I was in the living room with Emma and Ellie, enjoying the rare, peaceful stillness of a weekend with no pressing deadlines. It was Jez.

"Are you in?" he asked, his voice sounding unusually close.

"No," I replied automatically, "I'm at home."

"Good," he said. "Look out of your window."

I walked over to the front window and pulled back the curtain. A pale blue, vintage Rolls Royce, the kind of car you only ever see in old films, was purring slowly along our suburban street, its quiet grandeur completely at odds with the rows of sensible family hatchbacks parked at the kerb. It pulled up directly outside our house.

Jez climbed out of the rear passenger seat, followed by another man. The man looked familiar, but out of context my brain struggled to place him. He wasn't wearing an indigo-coloured jacket, but an expensive-looking tweed one, together with cavalry twill trousers, the unofficial uniform of the country set. By the time I reached the front door, the penny had dropped. It was Michael Wright.

I tried to reconcile the man walking up my garden path with the one I remembered from the telly in the eighties. 'Mickey' Wright, the cheeky, cheerful comedian. Now, he was Michael Wright, the world-famous conspiracy theorist who believed the Moon was a spaceship and the world was run by lizard-men. And as he got closer, a question that had been nagging me for months now dominated my thoughts: *What does he actually believe?*

I knew, from Lord Harrington's dinner party admission, that it hadn't happened on its own. Michael had been to Ashcombe Hall. He had been given his brief. He had been told to "make them believe". So he wasn't an unwitting asset, a simple *signal booster* who had stumbled upon these ideas organically. He was on the payroll, spiritually speaking. He knew he was part of a larger project.

But the question that nagged at me, the one I couldn't answer, was how deep the deception went in his own mind.

Was he a complete charlatan? A brilliant, tragic actor who was just in it for the money, the fame, and the Rolls Royce, laughing at his followers behind their backs?

Or was he a true believer who had successfully compartmentalised the truth? Had he taken the briefing from Lord Harrington and the information from Brian the feeder and, through some impressive mental gymnastics, convinced himself that these other men were simply fellow travellers, helping him on his divine mission?

Or was it something else entirely? Something closer to home. Had they given him the same speech they'd given me? Had someone sat him down in a quiet place and explained the whole grand, terrifying theory—the coming Future Shock, the need for a psychological comfort blanket, the benign conspiracy to guide a panicked society through the dark? Was he, like me, a willing recruit? A professional who understood the mission, had agreed to play his part, and was simply enjoying the considerable perks of the job—the book sales, the sold-out tours, the adulation.

That was the most disquieting possibility of all—not that he was a fraud or a deluded prophet, but that he was simply a more successful, more visible version of me. Same motivation, same game—just played on a bigger stage. I was about to shake hands with either a cynical grifter, a self-deceived messiah, or a man who had made the exact same deal that I had.

"We're on our way to Ashcombe," Jez said cheerfully as they stepped inside, bringing the faint, expensive smell of leather and cologne with them. "Thought we'd stop by and say hello. My old banger is in the garage, so we're taking Michael's."

Michael Wright shook my hand warmly, a broad, practised smile on his face, as if we were old mates meeting for a pint. He then turned his gaze towards my family. He almost completely blanked Emma and Ellie, his eyes glazing over them with the briefest of looks, a curt nod that was more of a dismissal than a greeting. Then, without being asked, he strode over to our sofa and sat down, casually brushing our cat onto the floor with the back of his hand.

Ellie, now seventeen and in her final year at college, stared at him, her expression unreadable. "My dad said you used to be a comedian," she said, her voice a cool, simple statement of fact.

A flicker of something crossed Michael's face—weariness, maybe even pain—before the performer's mask snapped back into place. "I used to tell jokes, yes," he said, his voice smooth but hollow. "But I realised it's more important to tell the truth. Making people laugh is just a pleasant distraction. Waking them up—that's a real purpose."

"So you don't miss the old days, Michael?" Jez asked, jumping in to lighten the mood.

"Sometimes," he admitted, staring into the middle distance. "It was simpler. But the audience always wants the easy punchline, not the complex setup. It's the same now. They just want a simple story to explain what's going on."

"Tea?" Emma asked, her voice tight with a politeness that I knew was costing her a great deal of effort.

I nodded a yes to my wife. "I'd love one, Em. Thanks," Jez said with an easy smile. Nothing came from Michael.

She brought the tea in on a tray and put it down. Not even looking at her or waiting to be asked, Michael Wright instructed, "Two sugars, love."

I saw Emma flinch. She hated being called *love*. She saw it as out-dated and patronising, a verbal pat on the head. But she said nothing, not wanting to make a scene in front of my visitors.

Michael took the tea, and his eyes fell on the collection of crystals she kept on a bookcase.

"Oh, look at these," he said with a little chuckle, picking up a piece of rose quartz. "Still believe in all this old magic, do we?" He said it with a gentle, mocking tone, as if talking to a slightly dim-witted child. I caught Jez's eye. He gave me a wry, almost pained grimace.

Emma's jaw tightened. "They're about finding a quiet, inner peace," she said, her voice dangerously calm. "A bit different from finding enlightenment in the back of a Rolls Royce. I bought them after reading one of your books—*The Harmony Within.*"

Wright looked flustered for a second, a flicker of annoyance crossing his face. "Ah, yes," he said quickly, putting the crystal down. "That was... that was from a different time. Before I understood the bigger picture."

Ellie spoke again, "Is that your car?" she asked, motioning to the window, her voice laced with a cool, teenage scepticism.

"Well, duh?" Wright replied—his tone dripping with a sarcastic, dismissive humour that wasn't funny at all.

Ellie just raised an eyebrow and went outside to get a closer look. The driver, a large man in a dark suit who had been standing guard by the car, immediately put a firm but silent hand out, stopping her from getting too close. A minder.

The conversation drifted to the work, and I found myself studying him, trying to fit the pieces together. But Michael kept his cards close to his chest. He spoke with the conviction of a true believer, yet he carried himself with the detached professionalism of a seasoned performer. He played the part so perfectly, it was impossible to see where the man ended and the myth began. He was the star of the show, and he was giving nothing away about his director.

He began talking about his work, about the crowd who came to his shows. "They're a lovely lot, bless them, but they'll believe anything, you know," he scoffed, talking to me as if we were co-conspirators, two sharp minds looking down on the gullible masses. "I could tell them the government was replacing pigeons with surveillance drones and they'd be looking for charging ports on the bird table by lunchtime. They're just lost souls, looking for direction." He spoke with the weary cynicism of a man trapped in his own success, forced to keep telling the same stories to an audience he had grown to disdain for needing them.

A little shiver went down my spine. I knew this type. I'd met them before in pubs and boardrooms. The opinionated middle-aged man, utterly convinced of his own correctness, who talks at you, not to you. It never crosses his mind that you might not agree with him, because in his world, his viewpoint is fact. He saw my job, my clothes, my presence here, and he assumed I was like him, that I was in his group, a member of his tribe. He assumed that I thought the people were idiots too. *I'm not in your group*, I thought. *I'm not one of you*.

I knew from Dave's lectures and my own work that this was classic group psychology. People seek validation from the crowd. We lean towards those who look and sound like us, and we use them as a social mirror to reinforce our own beliefs. Michael Wright saw me as his mirror. I resented it instantly.

The Final Act of Mickey Wright

"Right," I said, standing up abruptly. "We have to go. It's Emma's mum's birthday. We're all going out for a family lunch." I glanced at Ellie, who had just come back inside, praying she wouldn't contradict me. She didn't. She caught my eye and gave a tiny, knowing smirk, turning away to hide it from the room.

But Michael knew. He saw the lie. I could see it in his eyes. He detected the performance, the transparent excuse to get him off our sofa and out of our house—just as he had done with the cat. I knew, with absolute certainty, that someone like him, someone who had grown used to being the headline act, would not be able to handle being heckled, even quietly. He would remember this slight. I had not been subservient. I had not bent to his will. I had offered resistance to his fantasy of being the alpha male in every room he entered. From that moment on, I knew that Michael Wright would no longer see me as an ally. He would see me as an enemy.

As they left, climbing back into the opulent silence of the Rolls Royce, Ellie came and stood next to me at the door. We watched the car disappear down the street. "Well, he might have been a comedian," she said quietly, her voice sharp with teenage certainty. "But I think he's a joke."

I laughed. Her words hung in the air, and for a second, I wasn't standing in my own hallway in the 21st century. I was a young boy again, sitting cross-legged on the shag-pile carpet of my parents' living room. It was a Sunday night in the mid-eighties. The whole family was there, my dad with a can of lukewarm lager, my mum with a cup of tea, all of us gathered around the big wooden television set to watch the Royal Variety Performance.

And there he was. Mickey Wright. Young, energetic, wearing a slightly-too-tight tuxedo and a cheesy grin. He was a household name, a safe pair of hands for family entertainment.

"Evening, ladies and gentlemen!"

His voice echoed in my memory, tinny and distant.

"Great to be here! I took my mother-in-law to the zoo the other day. They thanked me and said they'd been looking for her."

A wave of gentle laughter.

"No, she's lovely really, but I hadn't spoken to her in two years. I don't like to interrupt."

It was simple, harmless stuff. The kind of joke you'd find in a Christmas cracker. It wasn't clever or subversive; it was comfortable. But just as Dave had pointed out about the homophobia and racism from the same era, it was the background noise of the nation, the shared, everyday talk of a different time.

I thought about how things had changed. That kind of comedy, the mother-in-law gag, the easy punchline—it was gone now. It hadn't been banned; it had just been retired. Gently nudged out of the mainstream and reframed as a 'dad joke,' or something your uncle would say after his third pint at a wedding. It had been made to feel old-fashioned, a part of the old world. It was another one of those slow, imperceptible shifts, another piece of quiet social engineering that you only notice when you look back.

Comedy had moved on. The world had moved on. And Mickey Wright, the cheerful man in the tuxedo had moved on too, transforming into Michael Wright, the self-important prophet in his Rolls Royce. And now, I realised, it was time for me to move on as well.

I knew in that moment that this was the end of the line for me. Seeing this man, this tragic clown, trapped in a theatre where the curtains never closed, I saw a vision of the person I could become if I stayed in the game. I didn't want to be that person. It was time to make my own exit.

Part 3

The Return Home

Chapter Twenty-Five

From Terraces to Tofu

THE ENCOUNTER WITH MICHAEL Wright at our house left a nasty taste in my mouth that lingered for weeks. It wasn't just his arrogance, or the casual contempt he showed for my family. It was seeing the man behind the mask.

I'd seen him perform a few times by now, and I'd seen him adopt different personas. For the mind-body-soul crowd he radiated warmth, compassion, and inner peace, a benevolent prophet speaking of unity and spiritual awakening. And for the TV watchers, he was a fearless seeker with a flair for the dramatic, the hard-hitting investigative truth-teller, all drama and soap-opera confrontation. I'd admired his skill, the way he could tailor his performance for each audience. And it made me look back on that first talk in the Croydon community hall. I remembered being impressed by his raw sincerity, his passionate conviction. But now, seeing the different masks he could wear, I was no longer sure what was real. Was the sincerity just another part of the act, another perfectly tailored performance? Or was the genuine man still in there somewhere, buried beneath the robes? I didn't know, and the uncertainty of it was more unsettling than a simple lie.

But in my living room, with no stage and no audience, the performance had dropped. I'd seen the man underneath it all and I simply didn't like him. He was petty, self-important, and had a cruel streak that had nothing to do with his grand mission.

Had we created this monster, or was it already there and we'd simply given him a bigger stage? I wasn't sure it mattered. All I knew was that the game had stopped being fun. The line had been crossed. I wanted out.

And so, I threw myself into the legitimate work of Signalroom. The world might have been a stage, but I was tired of playing my part in the tragedy. I wanted to go back to the comedies.

I found myself pulling back from the work of The Long Blue Wall. The late nights spent online stirring up paranoia on conspiracy forums started to feel less like a clever game and more like a grubby, thankless chore. That dull, persistent throb of shame was now becoming a cold, heavy weight in the pit of my stomach. Besides, I had a legitimate excuse to be busy now. Signalroom was thriving.

Crucially, the jobs were no longer just gifts from Lord Harrington's network. Our work on the supermarket campaign and the Glastonbury repositioning had been so successful that our reputation had grown organically. We were getting calls based on merit, not connections.

One such call came from a major sportswear brand. Our Cool Dad campaign had caught their eye. They were about to re-release a range of their classic '90s trainers and wanted an agency that understood how to sell nostalgia to men of a certain age.

"Right, Crispin," I said, putting the phone down. "New client. They want us to make Gazelles and Sambas fashionable again."

"Ah, *Blokecore*," Crispin said, his eyes lighting up like a scientist who's just found a new specimen for his collection. "Of course. Masculine nostalgia. Football-inspired cool. Vintage kits. Pub culture. It's a perfect storm of arrested development and brand loyalty. The emotional levers are so wonderfully simple, so gloriously primal. This won't be work, William. This will be an exercise in anthropology."

"That's the business we're in, Crispin. We don't live in a world of free will; we live in a world of carefully managed choice. Our job is to play on people's emotions—their memories, their sense of belonging, their fear of being left out—to steer them towards the choice our client is paying for. It doesn't matter if it's a pair of trainers, a political party, or a belief in lizard people. The mechanism is the same."

This, I had to admit, was the kind of campaign I loved. It was classic, old-school PR, straight from the playbook of the masters. It was *Bernays 101*.

***

The Blueprint Meeting—Mercer & Lock, New York

Thomas Mercer stood at the head of the table, hands clasped behind his back, eyes scanning the faces in front of him. Five of them. Four men in jackets too warm for the weather, and Helen Renner, her sleeves rolled to the elbow, a pencil tucked behind her ear like a weapon. Mercer cleared his throat.

"We're not selling jackets," he said quietly. "We're selling permission."

"Permission to do what?" asked Sidney Lock from halfway down the table, his voice dry as a ledger.

"Permission to belong," Mercer replied. "To wear something that says, 'I understand the new world, and I didn't have to ask how it works.'"

Helen leaned forward. "This is about style as story."

"Correct," Mercer confirmed. "The client makes the clothes. We make the narratives."

The sketches on the wall behind him showed a new menswear line from *Maison Deveraux*: simple jackets, tapered wool trousers, heavy canvas bags. All of it crisp, modest, clean—and expensive. It looked like a dockworker's kit ironed by a valet.

Lock clicked his pen. "You're calling this a narrative?"

"I'm calling it a condition," Mercer said. "A man walks into a room in one of these jackets and says, 'This is who I am.' But it's the six people here, in this room, who gets to decide who that is."

Helen flipped open her notepad. "We build the man first. Then we build the clothes around him."

"What kind of man?" Lock asked, with only half a smirk.

"The kind who's up early. Drinks his coffee black. Doesn't say much, but reads everything. Useful. Unshakable. A little mysterious."

"So, fictional?" Lock muttered.

"Yes," Helen replied, without looking up.

Mercer moved to the head of the table and tapped the board with the back of his knuckle.

"We're going to call it *Trueform*."

There was a pause.

"As in: True to Form," he continued. "A man in Trueform is not fashionable. He is correct. Not modern. Not trendy. Just...composed. Like he stepped out of a photograph and into your life."

"And the trick is that nothing about it is spontaneous. Every detail will be planned. But it will look like he didn't think about it at all. That's the power. We'll perfect the look of not trying."

Helen looked intrigued. She nodded, slowly. "That'll land."

Lock glanced toward the window. "And how do we sell it?"

"Social proof," said Helen. "We place five young women—dancers, models—in restaurants, rail stations, hotel lobbies. Each one with a man in Trueform. Paid, of course. But it won't look like it."

Lock raised an eyebrow. "We're selling the women?"

"No," Mercer said. "We're selling the fact that they chose him."

Helen stood and added, "He doesn't boast. He doesn't pose. He just is. And *she* wants to be seen beside that."

The room was quiet for a moment.

"We print a story in *Collier's*," said Lock. "A short piece. Something like: 'Barber Reports Uptick in Tapered Cuts, Modest Jackets.' Neutral tone. Implied movement."

"And make it look like it's already happening," Mercer said. "Imply scarcity. Murmur demand."

They started tossing out slogans, shorthand, copy phrases. Some stuck. Some didn't. The ones that did were written quietly into Helen's notes:

You've seen it before. That's the point.
Cut for the quiet man.
For those who arrive on time, speak with purpose, and dress accordingly.

By the end of the hour, the energy had changed. The campaign had a pulse now. It was breathing. Everyone in the room knew it would work—not because it was true, but because it would feel true.

Helen closed her folder and looked at Mercer. "And when everyone copies it?"

He smiled faintly. "They can take the jacket. They won't understand the shape of the idea."

***

Our first move was a piece of beautiful, indirect manipulation. I dug out the number for our very first client, the head of the *Field & Flame* catering collective from all those years ago. It was disguised as a friendly courtesy call, a nostalgic catch-up to see how business was. But my real intention was to plant a new seed. I talked about our original Glastonbury campaign, and in passing, I mentioned the rising appetite for Britpop-era nostalgia—a genuine longing to revisit those days. I suggested, ever so casually, that they should approach the festival organisers with a proposal for a new, stand-alone event: a full-blown Britpop revival festival.

"Think of it," I'd said. "Oasis, Blur, Pulp, all back in a field. The original line-ups. They'd go mad for it. And they're all grown up now,

191

with careers and good salaries, so they'll happily spend a fortune on your posh burgers."

She loved it. I knew that if the festival went ahead, sales of our new client's vintage trainers and '90s tracksuit tops would go through the roof. We weren't just marketing a product; we were creating the cultural event that would make the product indispensable.

The next phase was hitting the socials, which by now had become the primary battlefield. The upcoming World Cup was the perfect platform. We used our contacts to get ex-footballers and indie musicians from the '90s to start posting pictures of themselves in the old gear, reminiscing about the 'good old days'.

Just as the Blokecore campaign reached its peak, another, very different clothing company approached us. A high-end, famously 'ethical' fashion brand. Let's call them *Terra*. They'd seen our success and wanted us to do the same for their new range of guilt-free clothing, a whole new initiative they were calling the '*Our Planet Pledge*'.

And just like that, the wind changed. We were pivoting from one form of identity marketing to its polar opposite.

"So," Crispin said, looking at the Terra brief with an air of resigned amusement. "We go from selling football hooligan chic to selling outfits for people who apologise to their houseplants. Marvellous."

I remember the radio in the corner of the office was playing a classic from the '80s. The unmistakable, pounding bassline of "Two Tribes" by Frankie Goes to Hollywood filled the room.

"Well, there's our soundtrack," I said with a laugh. "One tribe in vintage trackies, the other in organic linen. And we're being paid to arm them both."

The playbook was entirely different. The language of Blokecore was about tribalism, retro-cool, and a kind of masculine swagger. The language of Ecowear was soft, virtuous, and communal. This was a "Fake Nice" campaign. It wasn't about being cool; it was about being a good person.

The tactics shifted. Instead of ex-footballers, we were now dealing with *Greenfluencers*—beautiful, healthy-looking people who posted pictures of themselves doing yoga on a mountaintop, clad in our client's organic, beige-coloured linen. Instead of stoking FOMO, we were alleviating guilt. Big retailers were already doing it with their "Conscious Collections", a brilliant piece of guilt-washing that allowed people to buy fast fashion and still feel like they were saving the planet.

Our job was to create the feeling that buying Terra's clothes wasn't a consumer choice; it was a moral statement. It was a uniform for the new secular church of environmentalism. This was Edward Bernays and his colleague Ivy Lee at their most subtle. They understood that you could sell anything if you linked it to a person's core belief about themselves. You didn't sell soap; you sold cleanliness and purity. You didn't sell cigarettes; you sold freedom and rebellion. And we weren't selling beige jumpers; we were selling virtue. We were selling our customers the opportunity to feel good about themselves.

I stood in the Signalroom, looking at the two campaign boards side-by-side. On one, a poster of a snarling rock star in a red tracksuit top. On the other, a serene-looking model meditating in a field. Two completely contradictory versions of modern identity, both being sold out of the same dusty old building.

It took me back to that conference in Stockholm, all those years ago, when we first discussed the potential of the internet. The 'online diaries,' the 'third-party influencers', the ability to build entire movements from scratch. This was it. This was the world we had planned. The tactics had changed, the platforms had evolved—but the formula was the same. A few well-placed stories, a few good-looking messengers, and people would follow along with the script without ever realising there was one.

Chapter Twenty-Six

Meat for Good People

Scientists Achieve Breakthrough in Lab-Grown Meat Development

By Staff Science Correspondent

In a quiet but historic moment at CellAg Innovations, a team of scientists has made a fundamental breakthrough in the development of lab-grown meat...Researchers confirmed yesterday that they have successfully cultivated structured muscle tissue without relying on animal-derived serums..."This is more than proof of concept—it's proof of possibility," said lead researcher Dr. Amara Reyes. "We've taken a step toward meat without slaughter, farming, or environmental degradation."

I read the article on my laptop in the Signalroom. It wasn't a front-page headline, just a small piece tucked away in the science section. But to me, it felt like a starting gun. The great disruption

Hendrik was always ranting about wasn't a future prophecy anymore. It was here.

A week later, as if on cue, the new client came to us. They were a slick, incredibly well-funded food-tech start-up, the kind with a minimalist logo and a headquarters full of beanbags, exposed brickwork, and BMX bikes hanging on the walls instead of paintings. They were about to launch the first mainstream, high-end plant-based meat alternatives—burgers that 'bled' beetroot juice, sausages made from pea protein.

Their brief was simple. "The world isn't yet ready for lab-grown meat," their young CEO told us over a video call. "It sounds weird, unnatural, so our job is to be the bridge. We need you to make the idea of *not eating farm-grown meat* seem normal, aspirational, and cool. Prepare the ground for the transition."

The company itself was selling vegan burgers, but that wasn't the whole story; I knew what they were really selling. They weren't the main event; they were the opening act. Their job was to wean an entire generation off the idea of traditional meat, and to create a ready-made customer base for the in vitro meat companies like CellAg Innovations that would follow. They were the Trojan Horse for the entire biotech food revolution.

Crispin was delighted. "Ah, splendid," he said, after taking the call. "Mother has a significant interest in one of these synthetic biology start-ups. A holding company, you understand. It's terribly forward-thinking of her."

I got started. "The brief is to prepare the market. We will be making plant-based the new normal. So, how do we do it? We can't use fear. This isn't about the Illuminati. This has to be positive. Aspirational."

Crispin nodded, already sketching in his notebook. "It's a *Fake Nice* campaign, but on a much grander scale than the Ecowear thing. We're not just selling virtue; we're selling a whole new way of life."

Our strategy had three main pillars. I laid them out on the board:

"Pillar One: The Health Angle → Clean Eating"

"We need to frame this as 'clean eating'. It's about vitality, energy, purity. We'll work with our network of nutrition influencers—the ones with the perfect white teeth and the sun-drenched Instagram kitchens. We'll have them push the narrative that a plant-based diet is the secret to their flawless skin and boundless energy."

"And we'll seed articles in the Sunday supplements," Crispin added, "written by friendly journalists. '*The Ten Foods That Will Change Your Life (And They're All Plants!)*' or '*Why I Gave Up Meat and Never Felt Better*'. It's not science; it's testimony."

"Pillar Two: The Celebrity Angle → Aspirational"

"This is crucial. It's something to aspire to. We'll target A-list actors, musicians, and especially athletes. We'll work with their publicists to get stories placed describing how they are 'thriving' on a plant-based diet. How it's the secret to their success."

Crispin laughed. "I can write those *What's In My Fridge* articles in my sleep. '*A shelf of fusion-style tofu, a bottle of cold-pressed kale juice, and a single, ethically-sourced tear from a happy Peruvian farmer*.' They'll happily believe that a well-stocked fridge might transfer the celebrity's entire personality—and possibly even their bone structure—simply through the process of osmosis."

"Pillar Three: The Cool Angle → VIP Members' Club"

"This cannot feel like a sacrifice," I stated clearly. "It has to feel like an upgrade. An exclusive invite." This was Crispin's world. We worked with trendy, high-end restaurants in London and Manchester—places we knew the food critics and magazine editors liked to go—to create "secret" gourmet vegan tasting menus. It wasn't about nut roasts and sad-looking salads. It was about culinary innovation. We positioned plant-based food not as something you *have to eat* for ethical reasons, but as something you *get to eat* because you're sophisticated, cosmopolitan, and in-the-know. We'll turn veganism from a dietary restriction into a status symbol.

The campaign was a masterclass in the art of identity creation, and a textbook example of choice architecture. We didn't just promote vegetarianism; we created and popularised an entire menu of dietary identities for people to adopt. Our job was to make giving up meat feel less like a sacrifice and more like joining a cool, exclusive, forward-thinking tribe.

We had the hardcore options: the straightforward *Vegan*, the slightly more virtuous *Whole Food Plant-Based Vegan*, and the truly devout *Raw Vegan*.

But the real work was in creating the 'soft' entry points for the persuadable majority. We branded and promoted the *Reducetarian*, for people who wanted to feel good about eating less meat without actually giving it up. We created the *Climatarian*, for those who framed their choices around carbon footprints, allowing them to eat a chicken but feel morally superior to a beef-eater. And we pushed the *Flexitarian*, a ridiculous term for a normal everyday person who eats whatever they want, whenever they want—but now reframed as a conscious, modern lifestyle choice.

Crispin, naturally, was in his element. "We're not selling them a diet, William, we're selling them a personality. It's almost unsporting how easy it will be."

While all this was happening, Ellie had started university. It came as no surprise to anyone that she'd chosen to study something at the intersection of technology and the real world. The course had a typically modern, jargon-heavy title: *BSc Information Technology Management for Business*. I was just glad about the *Business* part. It showed a practical streak. She'd always been a digital native, totally at ease in a world of screens and code that still felt slightly alien to me. But for her, the tech wasn't just for fun, it was a normal, integrated part of her practical life.

I'd always harboured a quiet, secret ambition of one day rebranding Signalroom as *'Camden & Daughter'*. But watching her map out her own future, I knew it was unlikely to happen. She was on a different path, one being paved by the very forces our work at the Ministry was designed to manage.

There was another, more immediate dilemma, too. Ellie had recently announced she was going fully vegan. It wasn't a huge leap. Emma had been a vegetarian for as long as I'd known her—a simple, personal choice made years ago because she loved animals, and didn't fancy eating them. I was happy to eat whatever Emma cooked, though I still loved the primal satisfaction of a good steak or a chicken curry. It was never a source of conflict. I just had to be mindful of cross-contamination, and to clean up properly afterwards. I was a flexitarian before we'd even invented the term.

For Ellie, influenced by her mum, the shift to veganism was a natural progression. But for many of her new friends at university, the ones who had grown up in meat-and-two-veg households, the decision had come from somewhere else entirely. That influence had come from me.

They had chosen their new lifestyle as a direct result of the sprawling, multifaceted PR campaign that I, and others like me, had been running for the last few years. It was a massive astroturf campaign, designed to gently nudge an entire generation towards a plant-based diet, in preparation for the upcoming lab-grown meat revolution. But what if Ellie ever found out? What if she knew that her friends' deeply-held ethical convictions were, in fact, the carefully engineered outcome of a marketing strategy? Would she resent me for it? Would it even matter how they got there?

Meanwhile, our brainstorming sessions at the Signalroom had become wonderfully, horribly surreal. "You do realise," Crispin said one afternoon, "there are far wider ramifications to the introduction of in vitro meat. Once we start consuming cultured tissue, grown from stem cells in a sterile dish, we'll no longer be constrained by social taboos."

"In what way?" I asked.

"Well..." he continued, a wicked glint in his eye, "we won't be limited to only cows and sheep. We could culture anything. Elephant. Giraffe. Dolphin. We won't actually be killing them, so why not?" He paused for effect. "The supermarkets will likely have an *Exotic Meats* aisle, and we'll go on *Edible zoo experience weekends.*"

"Urgh, I'm not sure about that," I said. "And imagine the arguments..."

"Precisely!" he crowed. "And think of the ultimate taboo—human meat," he said, raising an eyebrow. "Ethically harvested, of course. No harm done. So...?" He let the silence sit. "Imagine the backlash. Imagine the headlines. It's irresistible."

But as our campaign rolled out, one thing puzzled me. We were pushing our narratives online, but an equally powerful push was happening in the real world. Schools, all across the country, had started adopting a policy of *Meat Free Mondays*. It was a classic, brilliantly simple PR slogan. But how had our clients, the new-money tech firms, managed to get their message into the heart of the state education system? Schools were the responsibility of the Establishment, whose friends and colleagues in the powerful farming unions and agricultural industries stood to lose everything from this. I posed the question to Crispin.

He looked at me with a sly, knowing smile. "It's very fortunate," he said, "that Mother also happens to be the Chair of the Committee for Educational Futures and Policy."

He let the statement hang in the air. "The tech companies have the innovation, Will," he continued, enjoying my stunned silence. "But we still have the influence. We have the committees, the boards, the institutions. We write the policies."

I thought of Lord Harrington at Ashcombe Hall. They hadn't been defeated by the technological revolution. They'd done what they had always done. They'd adapted. They'd realised they couldn't stop the freight train, so they'd calmly walked up to the driver's cabin and offered to help steer.

***

I was on the train home from the office, the early evening sun casting a golden, hazy light over the urban sprawl of South London. The carriage rattled along, past endless rows of terraced houses, industrial estates, and scrubby patches of green. It was the usual, familiar journey.

The train then broke out into a more open stretch, running alongside a major arterial road. There was a huge billboard, one of those massive ones you can see for miles. It was an advert for butter. The picture was a masterpiece of pastoral fantasy: a single, handsome-looking Friesian cow, standing alone in a lush, impossibly green meadow under a perfect blue sky. The tagline was something simple and wholesome, like "Pure, Natural, British."

A few years ago, I would have admired it for the clever piece of marketing it was—selling a highly processed block of fat by linking it to a romantic, idealised vision of the English countryside. But now, I saw something else. I saw an endangered species. Not just the cow, but the entire world that cow represented.

I looked out the window as the train gathered speed. The billboard was replaced by the real thing: a scrappy, muddy field squeezed between a motorway and a new housing development, a few bored-looking sheep huddled by a fence. It wasn't a Constable painting; it was a sad, forgotten corner of a world that was being paved over. I resigned myself to a smile. I saw clearly that I was looking at a living museum. An exhibit on the verge of extinction. In just a few short years, this entire scene—the billboard fantasy, the grubby reality, the very concept of animals grazing on grass—would be a thing of the past. A quaint memory for future generations to look at in old pictures.

I thought about the huge, tectonic shift of the coming change. For millennia, humanity had been a hunter, chasing our meat across open land and through dense woodland, our survival dependent on our skill and speed. Then came the first great disruption, the Agricultural Revolution. We stopped chasing the animals and put them in a field enclosed with a fence, making life significantly easier. We thought it was the pinnacle of progress.

Now, we were on the cusp of the next leap. We were about to make it easier still. We were taking the animal out of the equation entirely, moving the whole process from the field into a sterile, stainless-steel laboratory. We were going from hunting on the savanna, to farming in a field, to programming in a factory.

It was the clearest, most palpable example yet of the Technological Revolution that Hendrik was always screaming about. This wasn't just a new product; it was a fundamental rewriting of how humans produced their food, a complete dismantling of a system that had sustained us since the dawn of civilisation.

And if this could happen to something as ancient and fundamental as farming, it could happen to anything. Transfer this change to our other institutions. Money—it's value no longer controlled by governments, but by code. Our legal system—criminal trials, no longer decided by juries, but by neural scanning. Government—no longer a system of representative democracy, but instead an AI or an interconnected global brain.

I looked out at the peaceful, timeless English countryside rolling by my train window. And I could see, clearly, that they had all been right. Lord Harrington, Hendrik, Dave, Beth... the world was catching up with their forecasts. I wasn't just selling vegan burgers. I was writing the epitaph for the world I was riding through.

Chapter Twenty-Seven

The Happy Rant

THE PHONE RANG. IT was Hendrik. I instinctively braced myself for a tirade, a high-speed blast of existential dread and Germanic fury. But the voice that came down the line was different. It was...happy.

"William! It is wonderful!" he boomed, his voice effervescent with a joy I'd not heard from him before. "The data is beautiful! The models are responding. Your campaign, the *Meat for Good People* as you call it, it is a magnificent piece of pre-emptive psychological conditioning! You are preparing them properly!"

I was so taken aback I was momentarily speechless. "Uh, thanks Hendrik."

"No, thank *you*!" he chirped. "I am coming to London! I have an invitation to visit the Google DeepMind headquarters—to see the new gods in their Olympus—and I must see you while I am here. David will collect me from the airport. We will have a beer, yes?"

We met in a pub in Soho. A proper, slightly grubby London boozer. Dave and Hendrik were already there. A pint of ale in front of Dave, and a gin and tonic for Hendrik, who was radiating a manic, joyful energy that I found slightly more unsettling than his usual apocalyptic gloom.

"This is much better, Will," he said, sipping the gin straight through a slice of lemon. "You are preparing them properly now. But you must do more of this! You must realise, not everyone can be prepared by selling them stories about the Illuminati. You are shooting at sparrows with cannons. People react to different things. We must use all channels!"

He leaned forward, his eyes shining. "There are the movies about zombies, yes? The ones Beth is working on? And we have so many? They are preparing us for a world where humans no longer die in the traditional sense—the convergence of regenerative biology and cybernetic augmentation! We are entering the age of synthetic permanence, where bioengineered longevity platforms and neural-integrated prosthetics render the old idea of death... quaint. You see? The zombies—they are just the transitional archetype. Half-dead, half-alive—exactly like the early adopters of these techno-biological upgrades!"

"And the superhero movies? They prepare us for a world of medical implants that will enhance our natural abilities! Yes—no more glasses or insulin pumps. No! I'm talking about subdermal exo-boosters, optic augmentation arrays, neuroplastic enhancers that rewrite what it means to be human! We will not only *heal* anymore—we will *upgrade*!"

"Captain America? Iron Man? These are prototypes in narrative form. Predictive myths for a society hurtling toward selective evolution via biomechanical enhancement. It's not science fiction—it's early-stage clinical trials!"

"And the cultural normalisation of the existence of aliens! The UFOs, the TV shows, the celebrity scientists, you see? It is all part of the same project. There is a matching screwdriver for every screw—yes?"

He was happy. Genuinely, frighteningly happy. He was seeing his grand, terrifying theories being validated, and it filled him with a kind of intellectual ecstasy.

Over the course of the afternoon, and more drinks than any of us had planned, the conversation inevitably drifted into a classic pub session of putting the world to rights. Dave, the sociologist, led the way, focusing on the ramifications of the very campaign I was running.

"You have to look at the current structure, Will," he began, drawing an imaginary map on the beer-soaked table. "The meat industry isn't just about burgers. It's a global ecosystem. Yes, you've got the farmers, but you've also got the feed suppliers growing billions of tons of soy and corn, the animal pharma companies selling antibiotics by the lorryload, the slaughterhouses, the logistics, the leather and gelatin industries—it's a web that holds up entire economies."

"And lab-grown meat?" he said, taking a long drink. "It doesn't just disrupt that map. It burns it. It makes it obsolete." He started ticking off the consequences on his fingers. "Farmers get displaced. The animal feed industry collapses, rural economies in America and Brazil are devastated. The big pharma companies lose seventy percent of their antibiotic market. Slaughterhouses become monuments to a forgotten age. It's a domino effect of catastrophic proportions."

Hendrik, nodding eagerly, took over. "And the biggest risk?" he interjected. "If food is no longer grown, but *programmed*, it moves from a decentralised biological system to a centralised technological one! The power shifts from farmers to coders, to venture capitalists, to the lawyers who own the patents on the cell lines. We will no longer ask, 'How do we feed the world?' We will ask, 'Who owns the food code today?'"

Dave sighed, a weary but satisfied look on his face. "Yeah, it's going to be a right mess. And things are happening, Will. It's moving quicker now. You can see the Future Shock everywhere you look, if you know what to look for."

He leaned in, his voice becoming a checklist of modern anxieties. "It's the little things. The bloke in the office who refuses to learn another new app. The constant moaning about how *life is moving too fast*. The information fatigue, people so battered by the 24-hour news cycle that they just tune out completely. It's the social burnout, the feeling of alienation from the younger generation. It's the people turning to drink and drugs, sleeping on the streets, choosing to live outside of normal society because they can't or won't keep up. The system is starting to show the cracks. Society is becoming ill."

***

Reporter's Field Notes – Trent & Mersey towpath, Burton-upon-Trent.

The man shuffling out from under the iron ribs of St. Peter's Bridge is Mick Turner, 33. A rolled sleeping bag sits where a forklift truck might once have been. I ask if he'll talk. He shrugs: "Aye, go on then."

Q: *What brought you out here, Mick?*
Mick: *"Truth? Weren't one big thing—just little screens shutting doors in me face. I'd been at the bottlin' plant since I left school. Good job, steady coin. Finish shift, pint at the Dog & Barrel, last bus home. Never touched a computer; never had to. Paid me rent in notes, kept the receipts in a Fox's biscuit tin. Life was simple, y'know?"*

Q: *When did it start to slip?*
Mick: *"Plant got new robots last year—boss said we needed to 're-skill online.' They gave us a link, no paper forms. I said, 'Mate, I haven't even got an email.' He laughed like that were the punch line."*

"Job centre was the same—'Log in, upload your CV.' I told 'em my CV's what I been doin' every day for fifteen years. They printed me off a URL—cheers for that—then sent me on me way."

Q: *And at home?*
Mick: *"Landlord stopped knockin' for rent. 'It's all on a portal now, Mick—check your inbox.' What inbox?"*

"Then the leccy company switched to online bills. Paper statement used to drop through the letterbox; now it's hidden behind some password. Missed two payments 'cause I never saw 'em. They cut me power in October—flat went dark same night the clocks did."

Q: *Did you try to get help?*
Mick: *"Phoned 'em. Got a robot sayin' 'Go to our website.' Went to the library—computers all booked by kids doin' homework. Asked the librarian; she says, 'Set up an email first.' It's gates inside gates, like them Russian dolls—only every doll wants a password you can't remember."*

Q: *What was the tipping point?*
Mick: *"Came home, fridge warm, arrears letter taped to the door—they still print that. No lights, no cash left. Thought, 'Why keep four walls I can't heat?' Packed a duffel, walked down here to the canal. Least the water don't send you an invoice."*

Q: *How's life on the towpath?*
Mick: *"Rough, but honest. Folk go by starin' at their phones, like little moons glowing on their faces. I watch 'em like you'd watch telly. Funny thing: work's still there somewhere, bills still need payin'. I just can't reach 'em 'cause the key's buried in a screen. Didn't know you could be locked out o' the world without breakin' a single law."*

Mick pulls his coat tighter, nods at the glow of passing handsets.
   "Reckon I'm an analogue lad stuck in a digital postcode," he says. *"And there's no postcode lottery when you're offline—everyone loses."*

***

The conversation circled back to the meat industry.
   "And people won't be happy, their world is about to crumble," Dave said with a grim chuckle. "The farmers won't be happy. The transport unions won't be happy. The religious folk will have a field day. What does 'halal' mean when the cow was never alive? Can lab-grown meat be classified as 'Kosher'? And what happens to rural heritage, land-based traditions, economic shifts?"

207

"They will all be furious!" Hendrik boomed, his good mood finally starting to fray at the edges, the familiar angry futurist returning. "The geopolitical implications—whole economies will collapse, Argentina, Australia, New Zealand. But the biggest danger is the fragility! A blackout in a bioreactor farm? You lose millions of tons of inventory. A single cyber-attack on a food-code patent holder? Starvation! It is madness!" He was back. The happy rant was over.

And as I listened to Hendrik's genuine and manic terror, and Dave's grimly satisfied sociological predictions, another voice echoed in my head. It was Michael Wright's. I pictured him on stage at the Brixton Academy, his voice laced with theatrical indignation telling his followers about the coming chaos.

He was talking about the same things of course, the same disruptions. I knew that by now. But his explanation was so much simpler. So much easier to swallow.

He wouldn't talk about the geopolitical implications of a collapsing Argentinian beef market. He'd talk about the *Illuminati buying up all the farmland to starve us into submission.* He wouldn't talk about the fragility of a centralised, tech-based food system. He'd talk about the *globalist cabal planning a fake cyber-attack to trigger a food crisis and declare martial law.* He wouldn't mention the complex tragedy of people choosing to live on the streets, left behind by a world that had moved on without them. He would lump them all together as victims of a deliberate plot, their personal struggles reframed as battles in a great cosmic war. He was taking real, complex, and terrifying problems and giving them a simple, cartoonish villain. He was offering an easy target for their fear and anger.

It was brilliant. It was effective. And sitting there, listening to the real, messy, and complicated truth, I felt a real sense of disgust at the simple, elegant lie we were pushing him to tell. We weren't preparing people. We were patronising them.

As they talked, or rather, as Hendrik began to properly rant, I pondered his earlier words. The idea that all these different cultural products—zombie movies, superhero films, TV scientists—were all part of the same soft-conditioning program. It was a new seed, a new way of looking at what was all around us, right there in plain sight.

"Right," Dave said eventually, draining his glass. "I think we've sorted everything out now. Shall we go to a club and watch a comedian try to do the same?"

We both turned to look at Hendrik. His face was thunderous again, his good mood completely evaporated. The mere mention of a comedian had clearly transported him back to the humiliation of the club in Frankfurt, to the frustration of having his urgent warnings met with laughter. He was consumed once more by his vision of a technological apocalypse that the rest of the world was treating like a joke. We laughed. It was good to have him back again.

Chapter Twenty-Eight

The Telly is Talking About Us

IT WAS A QUIET Sunday evening, one of those rare, precious pockets of domestic tranquillity. Emma was curled up on the sofa, half-watching *Open Minds TV*. Ellie was away at university. I was at the kitchen table with my laptop, not working, not doom-scrolling through the forums, just aimlessly drifting through the internet, skimming articles about football, music, tech. A headline caught my eye:

"*Estonia Opens Its e-Borders to the World*".

Curious, I clicked. I started reading about *e-Estonia*. After the collapse of the Soviet Union, the country had a clean slate. Instead of trying to patch up old, analogue systems, they'd built a new society from the ground up, one for the digital age—*e-Tax, e-Business, e-Banking, e-School, i-Voting*. The article was focused on their new *e-Residency* scheme. Anyone at all could become an e-Resident of Estonia. You didn't have to live there—or even be Estonian—to become a virtual resident and use their advanced, borderless digital infrastructure to set up a company, to open bank accounts, and to process payments.

211

A few years ago, this would have been a mildly interesting story about a small Baltic nation. But now, with the knowledge I had, it felt like reading a dispatch from the future. The conspiracy narrative I'd been pushing for years was one of a deliberate, hostile collapse of national borders by the evil Illuminati, but I remembered Jez all those years ago at the airport, predicting that national borders would become obsolete. And though it had sounded a bit far-fetched back then, it now just sounded inevitable.

Countries once existed based on a geographical patch of land and a monopoly on the services provided within it. You paid your taxes, and the state fixed the roads and emptied the bins. But here was Estonia, a country decoupling its services from its geography. It seemed such an obvious thing to do now, I wondered why Google hadn't done it already? They could become the service provider for an entire city. They could collect *G-Taxes* from their *G-Citizens* and subcontract the bin collection to the local council. In time, they could provide the services themselves.

We think of our countries as permanent, ancient, almost sacred things. But they're not. They're a relatively modern invention. For most of human history, our territories were defined by the tribe—how far you could walk, what you could see from the highest hill. Then came the empires, like the Romans, who drew lines on a map with a sword and called them provinces, vast administrative zones held together by legions and straight roads. After they collapsed, Europe fractured into a thousand feudal fiefdoms, little patches of land ruled by a local lord whose power extended only as far as his men could ride in a day.

It was only a few hundred years ago, after centuries of wars and treaties and royal marriages, that these little kingdoms and territories started to coalesce into the modern nation-states we know today. Germany, Italy—they're barely 150 years old. These things we hold so dear, these national identities, they are brand new, built on shifting sands.

And now, I could see the next stage of the evolution happening right in front of my eyes, in the very same way as our food production system and our monetary system. The territories were moving online.

212

The new empires weren't being built with armies, but with fibre-optic cables. The new borders weren't rivers and mountains; they were account passwords and terms of service. The power was shifting again.

I kept reading. A tech journal was debating the future of the FBI, arguing that modern crime was now a digital problem that old-school law enforcement was unequipped to handle. Another article quoted a futurist: "*We are morphing so fast that our ability to invent new things outpaces the rate we can civilise them.*" Another quoted *Amara's Law*: "*We tend to overestimate the effect of a technology in the short run and underestimate the effect in the long run.*" It was all happening, all around us, just as Dave and Hendrik had been saying. We were living through the first, chaotic moments of the Technological Revolution, and most people had no idea.

On Open Minds TV, one program ended and another began. As if on cue, a familiar face filled the screen.

"Oh look Will, it's your friend Michael Wright again," Emma said. "I wonder if he's driven there in his Roller?"

I went over and sat next to her, watching as Wright did the same with the avuncular Theo. But my perspective on him had shifted. I wasn't just seeing a performer anymore. I was seeing a *Content Creator*, a man perfectly adapted to the new media landscape. His job wasn't to deliver a single, coherent lecture. His job was to generate outrage, to feed the algorithm. The love-and-light guru from the festival was gone, replaced by the hard-hitting harbinger of doom, because confrontation and fear generated more views, more clicks, more engagement. He wasn't a prophet; he was just a very successful brand manager for his own paranoid ecosystem.

He was talking about the 'sleepers', the people who refused to "wake up" to the Truth. His voice was laced with a new kind of contempt, a weary frustration with the ignorant masses.

"You see, Theo," Wright was saying, leaning forward with a pained, earnest expression. "There are people out there, good people... probably. Middle-class wannabes. They have their nice little house, their cat on the sofa, a few crystals on the bookshelf as a sign of their supposed spirituality... and they are sleepwalking, *absolutely sleepwalking*, into a fascist takeover of the entire human race."

Emma and I looked at each other. We looked at our cat, asleep on the sofa. We looked at the amethyst crystal sitting on our bookshelf.

"What?!" Emma exclaimed, a bubble of laughter escaping her lips. "Is he talking about *us*?"

It certainly sounded like it. We both turned our full attention to the screen, a shared, surreal amusement passing between us. He was in full flow now.

"They are gearing up to take your money! They are planting God-knows-what in your food! And they are preparing for a complete societal shutdown with troops on the streets when the shit really hits the fan! Make no mistake, their final plan is to introduce a one-world government, a one-world currency, and a one-world global religion! And while they're doing that..." he turned slightly, staring directly into the camera, directly at *us*, "...we're busy wondering where to take Nan for her Sunday lunch! Wake up, people! It's happening!"

We roared with laughter. We were famous. Michael Wright, the prophet of doom, was attacking us personally on national television.

But as the laughter subsided, a different feeling washed over me. The surreal humour of the moment gave way to a heavy sense of weariness. And in that quiet moment, a memory surfaced, sharp and clear, from over twenty years ago.

It was a scruffy pub in Holborn, just around the corner from the PR agency where Jez and I had done our work placement. Our time there was over. I had just accepted a job with a decent little commercial agency run by Jeff. It felt like a proper step up, a real career. Jez and I were having a final, celebratory beer before our paths diverged.

I was buzzing, talking about the campaigns I'd be working on—launching a new brand of trainers, creating a buzz for a new chocolate bar. I saw PR as a creative trade, a game of words and ideas, a slightly grubby but endlessly entertaining business.

Jez listened patiently, a familiar, fond but slightly condescending smile on his face. His own future was already mapped out. His father had arranged a junior position for him at a discreet, powerful political lobbying firm in Westminster.

"I'm glad you're happy, Will," he said, taking a sip of his lager. "But fizzy drinks and trainers? It's all a bit small-time, isn't it?"

"It's a living," I'd said defensively.

"Oh, it's a living," he agreed. "But it's not the real game. The real game isn't changing what people buy. It's changing what they believe. That's where the real power is."

At the time, I'd laughed it off as typical posh-boy arrogance, the grand pronouncements of a man who had never had to worry about paying his own rent. But sitting there now, on my own sofa, decades later, I realised he'd been right all along. I had been drawn into the real game. I'd played a part in changing what people believe, in shaping reality itself. And for a while, it had been the most exciting, intoxicating experience of my life.

But I knew, with a certainty that settled deep in my bones, that I wasn't cut out for it. I wasn't Jez. I wasn't Lord Harrington. I didn't have their stomach for the long, morally ambiguous game of power. My heart, I realised, had always been with the smaller, more creative ideas. The fizzy drinks and the trainers. The clever slogans and the funny campaigns.

The memory faded, and I was back in my living room. The decision, which had been a vague, nagging feeling for months, now felt simple and solid. I knew what I had to do. I was going to talk to Jez. I wanted out.

On the television, Theo's gentle voice spoke again. "Next up on Open Minds TV, we talk to David Doyle about the Big Bang, the history of the Egyptian pyramids, and his theory that angels were, in fact, extra-terrestrial alien beings..."

The machine, I realised, would keep on running, with or without me.

Chapter Twenty-Nine

Standing in a Future Memory

THE CONVERSATION WITH JEZ was surprisingly, almost thankfully, easy. I'd been rehearsing it in my head for days, trying to find the right words, the right tone. I felt a quiet, nagging guilt, the kind you get when you know you're about to let a good friend down. I was preparing for a long, awkward conversation, perhaps a bit of gentle persuasion to stay on. I got none of it.

I called him on the landline. "Jez," I said, getting straight to it. "I'm out. The work at the Ministry, it's not for me anymore." There was a pause on the other end of the line, but it wasn't a tense one. It sounded more like he was taking a sip of tea.

"No problem, mate," he said, his voice as breezy as ever. "To be honest, I'm surprised you lasted this long. I thought you'd get fed up with the doom-mongering after a couple of years."

"So, you're okay with me moving on?" I asked, thrown off balance by his nonchalance. "And you have my word, obviously, I won't be telling anyone about the operation."

He laughed, a genuine, warm laugh. "Of course I'm okay with it. It's not a cult, Will. It's a project. You can leave whenever you want. And mate..." he added, "tell whoever you want. Write a book about

217

it. It doesn't matter. No one will believe you. They'll just say it's all fiction, or dismiss it as disinfo. That's the beauty of it all. We've muddied the waters so much that the truth itself has become just another conspiracy theory. I might even ask Crispin to put it around that you're working for the Illuminati. Just for a laugh, for old time's sake."

He wished me well, said he'd see me soon at a party they were throwing for Maks, and that was that. Years of my life, a secret that had reshaped my entire worldview—dismissed with the casual ease of someone cancelling a magazine subscription. Crispin, however, was rather more disappointed.

"You're giving it up?" he said, looking at me with an expression of genuine dismay. "But the fun is just getting started, William! Sparring with the terminally dim-witted on those forums is the only intellectual sport I get before luncheon. It's dreadfully stimulating."

He sighed dramatically. "Well, I shall carry on, of course. But purely for my own amusement now. I shall become the most pedantic, infuriating, and witty internet troll in existence. A digital gadfly, tormenting the intellectually inadequate for sport." He smiled. "It's the closest thing our generation has to fox hunting. I shall call myself *Doctor Strangeglow*."

A few days later I received an email from a prospective new client. It was from an organisation I'd never heard of: the *World Forum on Emerging Systems (WFES)*. The subject line was intriguing:

Subject: Opportunity: Public Engagement Brief for a Low-Visibility Futures Project

Dear Signalroom,

We're reaching out to explore your potential involvement in a quiet, design-led engagement project being developed by the World Forum on Emerging Systems (WFES).

The campaign—titled *The Civic Imagination Project*—is a non-digital, analogue public awareness framework intended to help communities:

- Reflect on long-term social and environmental transitions
- Develop emotional confidence in the face of uncertainty
- Engage in low-key, participatory future-thinking activities

Rather than broadcasting messages, the campaign uses cultural planting methods:

- Poster series with poetic prompts
- Conversation kits distributed through schools and cafés
- Curiosity installations in community spaces
- Micro-workshops that feel more like creative evenings than programs

We are seeking an agency to:

- Co-develop rollout language, visual identity, and tone
- Oversee soft local placement (libraries, festivals, councils, campuses)
- Manage discreet amplification without visible campaign framing
- Engage trusted micro-channels (book clubs, artists, teachers)

The style should avoid anything overtly didactic, futuristic, or institutional.

If this aligns with your practice, we would love to speak further and share the internal concept deck.

Warm regards,
Emily Packham
Programme Lead, Civic Engagement
World Forum on Emerging Systems

The *World Forum on Emerging Systems*. I'd never heard of them, but the name alone had the weighty, self-important ring of the global establishment. Before replying, I did a bit of digging. I clicked the link at the bottom of the email and was transported to a world of clean lines, muted colour palettes, and stock photos of diverse people looking thoughtfully at transparent whiteboards.

Their website was a masterpiece of respectable, high-minded corporate waffle.

Our Mission:

The WFES is an independent international organisation committed to improving the state of the world by engaging business, political, academic, and other leaders of society to shape global, regional, and industry agendas. We believe in building a more resilient, equitable, and sustainable future by fostering public-private cooperation and preparing global citizens for the profound transitions ahead.

It was beautiful. "*Preparing global citizens for the profound transitions ahead.*" It was the exact mission statement of The Long Blue Wall, just laundered through a PR-friendly Swiss address and stripped of all the scary bits about aliens and lizard people.

I clicked on their 'Publications' tab. It was an endless library of white papers and policy documents with titles like *"Navigating the Polycrisis: A Framework for Systemic Resilience," "The Fourth Industrial Revolution: Governance in the Age of AI,"* and *"Stakeholder Capitalism: Redefining the Social Contract."* It was Hendrik's apocalyptic rants, but translated into the calm, reassuring, and utterly impenetrable language of the globalist elite.

Then I clicked on 'Leadership and Governance'. A gallery of distinguished, serious-looking faces stared back at me. Board members from major tech corporations, former prime ministers, heads of NGOs, presidents of prestigious universities. And then I saw a name on the Board of Trustees that made me smile. *The Honourable Marmaduke de Vere.* It was Crispin's uncle.

Of course. It was all connected. This wasn't just a job offer from a stranger. It was a message from the heart of the network. A transfer from the black-ops division to the public-facing one. A reward for services rendered.

I stared at the screen, quietly awestruck at the elegant audacity of it all. Jez really did have the connections. Or rather, his family did. This *Civic Imagination Project* was fantastic. It was a bit different from what I had been doing, but it still allowed me to play my part in preparing people for the shock of the future. But this time, I'd be doing it in the light.

Plus, there was a big bonus. This was a proper, bona fide contract that paid proper, bona fide money. This time, I would be getting paid to be one of the good guys.

I immediately replied to Emily Packham and, after a brief, pleasant video call where it was clear that the decision had already been made, we agreed there and then that the contract was ours.

I went back to the main office, where Crispin was meticulously polishing his already-gleaming loafers. "Right, Crispy," I said, a new energy in my voice. "Clear the decks. We've got a new client. And I think you'll find they're very much our sort of people."

He looked up, a flicker of interest in his eyes as I explained the project. We quickly put our own initiatives to one side and got to work. The project was a world away from the aggressive, manipulative campaigns we were used to. It was gentle, subtle, and surprisingly creative. We developed a series of imaginative, community-driven initiatives.

There was the *What If Wednesday* Pop-Up Series: simple, table-top prompt cards to be left in cafés and libraries. "*What if money expired after a year?*" one read. "*What if school ended at age 10—then began again at 60?*"

We designed *The Community Curiosity Cabinet*, a portable wooden cabinet filled with strange objects and postcards from fictional futures, which could be hosted in community spaces to spark imagination.

We created printed packs for Micro-Workshops called "*Tools for Uncertain Times*," simple, one-hour sessions with titles like "*How to stay grounded when the future feels weird,"* designed to be run by teachers or librarians—not experts.

And finally, my favourite, a cryptic visual campaign called *"The Future Leaves Clues:"* a series of beautiful, thought-provoking posters and stencils. *"This bench is waiting for someone from 2040."* And, *"You are standing in a future memory."*

The *WFES* were delighted. They had a sizeable, ongoing budget that never seemed to run dry. Our work was professional, creative, and making a real, positive impact. We were helping people. We were the good guys. And I had to admit, after a few months... I was bored out of my mind.

The buzz was gone. The thrill of the double life, the dark humour of the digital puppet theatre, the adrenaline rush of seeing one of our narratives catch fire online. It was all replaced by a quiet, worthy, and deeply dull sense of professional competence.

I missed the excitement. I missed the arguments with Crispin over how far to take our attacks when we were dealing with a particularly knowledgeable poster. I missed the late-night calls from a manic Hendrik. I missed the fun of promoting conspiracy theories.

My new role was to be a responsible midwife for the future. But deep down, a part of me missed being one of its most mischievous and effective horsemen of the apocalypse.

Chapter Thirty

The Future Has Arrived

I HAD FOUND MY new purpose. It was worthy, quiet... but a little bit dull. The Civic Imagination Project was making a positive impact, but it lacked the thrill of the fight. Hendrik's words from our last pub summit kept echoing in my head: '*You must use all the channels...the movies, the games...*'

The solution, when it came, wasn't from a secret briefing paper or a clandestine meeting. It was from my own daughter. Ellie was home from university for the weekend. I was showing her the Civic Imagination Project materials—the prompt cards, the workshop plans. She listened patiently, a thoughtful frown on her face.

"It's good, Dad," she said finally. "But it's all a bit analogue. A bit slow. Have you thought about turning it into an app?"

I blinked at her, momentarily thrown. *An app?* The thought hadn't even crossed my mind.

"Look," she said, pulling up a chair and suddenly switching to the articulate, confident language of her IT Management for Business degree. "The core concept is about cognitive flexibility, right? Getting people to think sideways. That's a game mechanic. You could create a series of fast, fun, creative challenges. No right or wrong answers, just points for originality. You could disguise a serious psychological tool as a silly party game."

And just like that, a lightbulb didn't just go on in my head; it exploded.

The idea, which we instantly started calling 'MindMorph', took over our entire weekend. Ellie was in her element, sketching out user flows and talking about development sprints. I was buzzing with the PR potential. We were a team.

The core concept was simple and deeply subversive: a fast-paced, surreal puzzle game where you were forced to think sideways. It was a party game designed by a confused philosopher and a stand-up comic, where players earned points not for being right, but for being weird, original, and creative. "We'll have different modes," Ellie said, scribbling on a tablet. "*Morph Match*: you get two wildly unrelated things and have to connect them in under 30 seconds."

"Give me an example," I asked.

"Okay," she grinned. "How is a Tuesday morning like a disappointed badger? Explain quantum physics using only lyrics from '80s power ballads. Connect the concept of *ennui* to a single, forgotten teabag."

It was brilliant. Utterly absurd and deeply intelligent.

"Then there's *Brain Swap*", she continued. "You have to solve a real-world problem, but as someone, or something, else. Like, 'Fix the national debt as a flock of sarcastic pigeons,' or 'Negotiate a peace treaty as a Viking who has just discovered coffee'."

The best part was the scoring. A global leaderboard wouldn't rank you on points, but on originality. We'd have weekly winners in categories like *Most Unexpected Logic*, *Deepest Nonsense*, and my personal favourite, *Best Use of a Duck in Political Theory*.

"We need a catchphrase," I said, my PR instincts kicking in. "Something simple, sticky, and slightly odd. Something people can say at the end of a sentence. A verbal signature."

We brainstormed for an hour before Ellie hit on it. "*Morph On!*" she announced.

It was perfect. Positive, slightly strange, and memorable. I immediately started mapping out the launch campaign in my head. This wasn't a product for the conspiracy forums. This was mainstream.

***

"Right, Crispin," I said on Monday morning, buzzing with a new energy I hadn't felt in years. "New project. We're launching an app. And we're going to make 'Morph On' the most ubiquitous sign-off in the country."

Crispin listened to the concept, a rare, genuine smile spreading across his face. "An app that rewards people for being ridiculous? Oh, I love it. It's a public service."

"We need to get it onto the telly," I said. "Daytime. We need the trusted faces."

"The Loose Women panel," Crispin said instantly. "It's perfect. We find the one most likely to enjoy it—likely Carol McGiffin or Denise Welch. We get the app to her publicist. A week later, she's on the show."

He adopted a perfect impression of a daytime TV host: "'So, Carol, what have you been up to?' *Oh, you know, same old. Though I have been playing this mad new game on my phone, MindMorph. Yesterday's challenge was to design a new form of government based on the principles of a garden shed. Kept me up all night! Anyway, must dash. Morph On!*"

"Yes, that's it!" I said. "And for the blokes, we go to *Talksport*. We get an ex-footballer, someone like Ian Wright. We get him talking about how the young players are all hooked on it in the dressing room." I slipped into a bad Ian Wright impression: "*Yeah, it's mad, keeps the brain sharp, you know? The lads love it. Right, gotta go. Morph On.*"

The plan was simple. We wouldn't run a single traditional advert. We would just get our catchphrase into the mouths of trusted, likeable people, over and over again, until it became part of the national conversation. It was the oldest trick in the book, retooled for a new age.

And this time, I thought, we were using our powers for good. Or at least, for something fun.

That evening, the three of us were at home, a rare night with no deadlines and nothing to do but relax. It was supposed to be a normal evening off, but as I looked around, I realised that 'normal' wasn't what it used to be. Our home had become a living exhibit of the very future we'd been discussing for years.

"Fancy a takeaway?" Ellie asked, already on her laptop, deep in planning for the MindMorph launch. "My treat."

"Sounds good," I said. "I'll grab the menu from the drawer."

Ellie laughed. "Dad, no one uses paper menus anymore." She spun her laptop around. On the screen was a single app, a global delivery platform. A hundred local restaurants, all their menus digitised, all their businesses now paying a commission to a single tech company in California.

As she scrolled, I was struck by something else. On every single menu—the Indian, the Italian, the burger joint—the plant-based section was no longer a sad little after-thought at the bottom. It was huge. Prominent. *Vegan Korma, Plant-Based Pepperoni, The Impossible Burger.* There were almost as many vegan options as meat options. I was looking at the direct, real-world result of my own campaigns, a cultural shift I had helped to engineer, now being sold back to me as a dinner choice.

"I'll have a Thai, thanks daughter," Emma said. "Tofu with basil."

Ellie clicked a few buttons. "Okay," she said. "Paid."

"With my card?" I asked.

"Nope," she said, not looking up. "With Bitcoin. Just transferred it from my digital wallet."

A few minutes later, her phone buzzed. "Right," she said, grabbing her coat. "The rider's just picked it up. I've messaged him, I'll meet him half-way. Need to get my steps in." She tapped the fitness tracker on her wrist.

While she was gone, Emma and I sat in the living room. "Computer," Emma said to the small, cylindrical speaker on the bookshelf, "play something chilled."

A soft, algorithmically curated playlist of ambient synth music began to drift from the speaker. A moment later, the main lights in the room subtly dimmed, replaced by a warmer, softer glow from the lamps. The *Evening Wind-Down* routine had kicked in. Our house was now gently managing our mood for us.

Ellie returned with the food, delivered not by a restaurant employee, but by a gig-economy worker on an electric scooter she'd tracked in real-time on her phone. We ate, and then settled down to watch a film.

"What's on?" I asked.

"Let's see what it recommends," Ellie said, flicking through the menus of a streaming service. The screen was a mosaic of personalised suggestions. She landed on one. "*Ex Machina*," she said. "Heard this is good."

I knew the film. It was a sharp, unsettling thriller about a tech billionaire who creates a sentient AI, but I was now seeing things differently, I was watching movies and videos and TV not through the eyes of a viewer but instead through the eyes of Beth and the members of The Long Blue Wall. I watched as Emma and Ellie were drawn into the story, into the complex, almost romantic relationship between the human protagonist and the beautiful, intelligent machine.

But the film I saw wasn't just telling a story; it was teaching us something. It was carefully blurring the lines between artificial and organic consciousness, making the idea of having a deep, emotional relationship with a machine feel not just possible, but plausible and natural. It was making us comfortable with the idea.

I could almost hear Hendrik's gleeful voice in my head. *"Soon, your therapist or doctor will be an algorithm—and you'll embrace it, because Hollywood has already trained you to!"*

The film was brilliant, of course. It was also a perfect piece of social priming, a beautifully shot and intelligently written advert for a future we hadn't even realised was for sale yet. As the credits rolled, before we'd even had a chance to talk about it, the service automatically played a trailer for what the algorithm had decided we should watch next. A title card appeared on the screen: *Perfect Light*.

A gentle, thoughtful piano score began to play over beautifully shot, stark images of a pristine, glass-walled medical facility set against a rainy Nordic landscape, in a place called *New-Oslo*. A narrator's calm voice spoke:

> *"In a world where genetic engineering has become the norm for the wealthy, one couple's quest for the perfect child draws them into a quiet war of values."*

It continued,

> *"What begins as polite conversation, soon becomes a simmering confrontation over control, freedom, and the nature of love itself. A claustrophobic, slow-burning drama that asks: if you could design a flawless child, should you?"*

The screen faded to black, showing quotes from critics.

"Stark and philosophical... like My Dinner with Andre meets Gattaca." – *IndieWire*
"You don't watch this film. You sit in the room with it." – *The Guardian*

The trailer ended. It looked like a brilliant piece of intelligent, thought-provoking cinema. And I knew, as clearly as clear could be, that it was also a piece of propaganda. A beautifully crafted, high-end piece of social conditioning, designed by Beth's contacts to prepare the professional classes for the coming ethical dilemmas of genetic engineering.

I looked around my living room. The algorithmically chosen music, the automated lighting, the crypto-funded, gig-economy food, the AI-driven recommendations, the soft-peddled propaganda...

Hendrik's future hadn't just arrived. We were living in it. We were soaking in it. And it was all so convenient, so seamless, so nice, that we hadn't even noticed it was happening.

Chapter Thirty-One

The Last Signal

My time spreading conspiracy theories was over. For the better part of two decades, I had been a ghost in the machine, a digital puppet master helping to propagate the grand, sprawling myth of the Illuminati. I'd made people believe in aliens as our new origin story, I'd pointed them to the symbolism in movies and music videos as proof of a vast occult conspiracy, I'd laid the foundations for the future epoch myth of 2012, and I'd spent years carefully tending to our sprawling, anti-establishment astroturf campaign, creating fake outrage and nurturing genuine paranoia from my desk in a dusty signal box.

But the time had come for me to walk away. The encounter with Michael Wright had been the final, sour note in a symphony that was already grating on my nerves. Partly, I was just tired. Tired of the late nights, tired of the endless, circular arguments on forums, tired of living a triple life. But mostly, I was tired of the feeling it left in me. The anxiety our work deliberately caused in strangers, the cynical mockery of the very believers we were cultivating. I hadn't outgrown it. I had been worn down by it.

Do I think people are stupid for believing these things? No, I don't. That's the great misunderstanding of the rationalist, the thing that the professor signing autographs in the bookshop will never get, but the workman in the pub understood perfectly. That bloke in muddy boots knew that believing in the Illuminati was *exciting*. He knew it was a better story. People don't make their choices, or form their beliefs, based on a logical analysis of the evidence. They do it based on emotion, on a sense of belonging, on a need to validate their own identity.

Once a belief is accepted—*regardless of its truth*—it becomes embedded not just in a person's reasoning, but in their very sense of self. It's woven into their social connections, their trust in certain sources, their view of their own place in the world. Challenging that belief isn't just about presenting better facts. It's asking them to perform emotional and psychological surgery on themselves. As anyone in my trade knows, that's why repeating a simple, emotional story is always more powerful than a complex, boring truth. People aren't stupid for believing; they're simply doing what humans do.

Besides, my real life was going too well to ignore. Signalroom was now a well-established PR agency with a solid reputation. And we were branching out.

Using funding from the World Forum on Emerging Systems, Ellie and I opened an offshoot. We called it *Zignl-Box*, a mobile app studio born from the old signal box. Ellie, with her sharp mind and effortless grasp of the new world, ran the new business. Crispin, to his delight, was promoted to Head of Agency at Signalroom. And I divided my time between the old world of PR and the new world of "positive social engineering."

We used Beth, Dave, and Hendrik as consultants on our first suite of apps. Beth helped us shape the narrative for *MythCraft*, a collaborative storytelling game. Dave gave us the psychological framework for *Echo Chamber*, a social simulation that taught people to recognise online tribalism. And Hendrik's manic prophecies were the direct inspiration for *System Shock*, a game where players had to manage a modern city through a series of technological disruptions.

Life was good. The office was a joy. The three of us—myself, Crispin, and Ellie—had a wonderful time together, laughing and joking as if we were out socialising rather than being at work. The atmosphere got even better when Dave would pop down from London for a "sociological review," which was always just an excuse to drag us all down the pub for an extended lunch. My work for the Ministry was done. I was out.

But before I walked away entirely, there was one last piece of business. One final signal to send. A loose end I needed to tie up. Or rather, to unravel. I briefed Crispin on the plan. A wide, predatory grin spread across his face. He could hardly contain himself.

"Oh, this is deliciously petty, William," he said. "A character assassination. My absolute favourite."

I sought input from Charlotte, our genealogist, asking her to construct a carefully selected family tree—one that highlighted only the branches and connections needed to build our specific narrative. I picked the brains of Beth for her expertise on comparative religion and the history of secret societies. Everything was set.

One Saturday afternoon, Crispin and I sat side-by-side in the quiet of the Signalroom. For old time's sake. We logged into our old personas.

I opened a new thread on one of the biggest conspiracy forums:

Veritas_2012:
Is Michael Wright a Rockefeller? I've seen a suggestion online that his great-grandmother was an illegitimate child of the famous banking dynasty. Has anyone looked into this? The family resemblance is... interesting.

A few minutes later, on a different forum, Crispin posted.

Gaz_From_The_Pub:
Right, I'm just gonna say it. I like a lot of what Mickey Wright says, yeah? Wakes you up a bit. But am I the only one who thinks it's a bit rich him telling us the bankers are trying to nick our savings while he's driving around in a bloody Rolls Royce?

My mate Kev saw him the other week, getting out of one. A proper vintage one, cost more than my house. Says he had a driver and all. I mean, make your minds up. Is he one of us, or is he one of them, laughing all the way to the bank? Just seems a bit dodgy to me, that's all I'm saying.

I posted again, this time as *Skeptic_Sam*.

Skeptic_Sam:
Been having a look at Michael Wright's early teachings. It's almost a direct lift from Theosophy and the works of Madame Blavatsky. Is he a prophet, or just a very good plagiarist?

Crispin was now thoroughly enjoying himself, but he had one last trick up his perfectly tailored sleeve. It wasn't a forgery of his own making—something far more potent had come to light. Jez had unearthed it from the digital undergrowth and delivered it with a smirk, refusing to say exactly how he'd known about it.

The image was a long-forgotten, badly photoshopped picture of Michael Wright dressed in full Masonic regalia, originally posted years ago on some obscure *Angelfire* conspiracy page.

The brilliance of the move lay in its inversion: a perfect piece of psychological jujitsu. We weren't presenting the image as truth—we were presenting it as planted disinformation, a clumsy smear supposedly orchestrated by the *Powers That Be* to discredit Michael Wright. But in doing so, we were giving the old fake a new life, feeding suspicion and fanning the flames of paranoia, all while posing as defenders. It was cynical, elegant, and ruthlessly effective.

Crispin adopted his most aggressive and intellectually contemptuous persona, *Patrician_Gaze*, and went on the attack.

Patrician_Gaze:
Oh Dear. It seems the establishment has finally exhausted its limited intellectual reserves and resorted to creating crude forgeries. One has to assume this sort of thing is designed for an audience that struggles with joined-up thinking.

The logic, I suppose, is this: let us take a photograph of our fiercest critic and crudely paste his head onto the regalia of one of our most notorious

sub-sects. The simpletons will surely fall for it. It is an insult not to Mr.
Wright, but to the very concept of intelligence. I post it here as a lesson.
Observe the sheer, clumsy desperation of a dying elite. They are not just
liars; they are becoming profoundly untalented ones. And that, I'm sure
you'll agree, is the most unforgivable sin of all.

And finally, I delivered the killing blow, a long, detailed post under a
new persona, *Just The Facts*, titled: **Michael Wright Debunked.**

It was a masterpiece of innuendo and carefully selected 'evidence,'
weaving together all the threads we had just created, complete with
Charlotte's lopsided family tree. It didn't make any definitive claims;
it just asked questions, planting seeds of doubt, a thousand tiny cuts
designed to bleed his credibility dry. We were using the exact same
tactics we had used to build him up, but now, to tear him down. We
were turning the machine on one of its own.

Was it a betrayal of the project? No. I had everyone's blessing. I
reminded Jez of my last encounter with Wright. He just laughed. "The
man's a dick, Will. Always has been. And that flash car? Utterly tragic.
Doesn't suit him at all. Do what you need to do."

Beth had been even more clinical. "All heroes eventually fall, Will,"
she'd told me over the phone. "It's a crucial part of the mythic cycle.
The tragic end, the martyrdom—it can be even more powerful than
the initial rise. We can weave his demise into the grand narrative. Don't
worry, his story isn't over."

Michael Wright was on his way down, his successor already identified. This wasn't betrayal. This was housekeeping. And was I being
petty? No, it wasn't that either. This was about something else. It was
about him sitting on my sofa, in my house, and insulting my wife. It
was about him dismissing my daughter with a sarcastic sneer. This was
for them. It was the only way I knew how to get him out of our lives, to
symbolically fumigate the room he had sat in. It was the last, necessary,
and deeply satisfying task of a man who had spent two decades telling
stories for other people, and had finally decided to take control of his
own.

Sometime in The Future

Michael of The Light

A Bedtime Story (104 TE)

THE LIGHT FROM THE holo-projector cast soft, shifting constellations on the ceiling of the small bedroom. The child, tucked under a self-warming cellular blanket, looked up at her father, her eyes wide with sleepy anticipation.

"Just one more story, Papa?" she whispered.

"Just one more." He smiled, settling into the chair beside her bed. "Which one will it be tonight?"

"The First Prophet," she said instantly. "The story of Michael of the Light."

Her father nodded. It was her favourite. He took a deep breath, his voice dropping into the familiar, gentle cadence of a storyteller.

"In the old time," he began, "in the Age of Sleep, the world was not as it is now. It was a place of quiet desperation, where humanity was unknowingly enslaved by the Shadow Weavers, the Men of the Unseen Hand. They used the flickering screens and the endless noise of their media to keep the people in a state of perpetual slumber, unable to see the truth of their own divine nature."

"In this world lived a man known as Mickey the Jester. He stood in the bright lights of the palace stages, and his gift was to make the people laugh. He was beloved. But in his heart, he felt a great emptiness, for he knew that laughter was not enough. He could make the people laugh in their prison, but he could not show them the key to the door."

"He felt a strange pull, a guidance he could not name. And the call, when it came, was a whisper. At a gathering of seekers, a wise woman, a keeper of forgotten lore, placed a sacred scroll in his hands. *'The spirits have chosen you,'* she told him, *'a man with a troubled spirit, to receive this knowledge.'* Michael—for that was his true name—was torn. The cynic in him, the Jester, wanted to laugh. But the seeker in him could not ignore the call."

"In a moment of doubt, he cried out to the heavens for a true sign. And the sign was given. He was led to a hidden city sanctuary, to an oracle who channelled the voices of the Guardians of the Light. They spoke to him directly. *'You asked for a sign. Here I am.'* They told him he was The One, chosen to break the chains of the Shadow Weavers. They told him he must write down what he learns, to begin the Great Awakening."

"And so Michael, now filled with purpose, wrote his first book of truth. But the Shadow Weavers would not allow the light to spread so easily. They sent their army—the scribes of falsehood, the media—to ambush him. They mocked his sacred indigo robes, they twisted his words, and they cast him out into the wilderness of public scorn. This was his first great test."

"Though cast out, he was not broken. He was guided by the Guardians on a great pilgrimage. He journeyed across continents to the high, sacred waters of Lake Titicaca in Bolivia, the place the ancients called the *Navel of the World*. There, he climbed the holy hill of Palla Khasa, *the place where the sun was born.*"

The child's eyes were heavy now, but she listened intently as her father continued.

"At the summit, within a circle of ancient stones, the sky opened. A pillar of pure, cosmic light descended and struck him. His old self, Mickey the Jester, was burned away in an ordeal of divine energy. The Voice of the Cosmos spoke to him, not with words, but with pure knowing. It reprogrammed his very being. It bestowed upon him the Elixir: the gift of true sight, the ability to see the hidden architecture of the world."

"With his new sight, he could see clearly the lost history of humanity. He saw how the Shadow Weavers—the cold-blooded, reptilian masters—had hidden the truth of our divine, extra-terrestrial origins. He understood that they had suppressed wondrous technologies—free energy, vibrational healing—to keep humanity dependent and weak."

"Michael returned from the mountain, no longer a seeker, but a vessel of truth. He took to the great gatherings of the people. And this time, they did not mock him. Thousands who had heard his whispers in the digital wilderness greeted him not with ridicule, but with a roar of loving acceptance. The jester was dead; the Prophet was risen."

"He shared his gift with them all. He told them of their true, cosmic heritage. He revealed the existence of the Shadow Weavers. And he told them that the great change they felt, the chaos of the old world dying, was not an ending, but the painful birth of a new, freer age. He gave them not just knowledge, but hope. He was the first hero of our new time, the man who dared to speak the truth and, in doing so, began the process of setting humanity free."

The father finished the story. The child was quiet for a long moment, her eyes almost closed.

"Papa?" she whispered.

"Yes, my love?"

"The Shadow Weavers... the lizards... are they all gone now?"

The father looked up at the constellations swirling on the ceiling. He smiled, a gentle, slightly sad smile.

"Mostly," he said. "Now, go to sleep."

An Unfinished Story...

The story you have just read is not the end.

Back in the quiet of the library at Ashcombe Hall, the conversation wasn't truly over. After the talk of myths and history, Lord Harrington leaned forward, a different, more serious expression in his eyes.

He had one last thing to ask of me. Not another story for the public. A different kind of task. A quiet job, far from the noise of the forums, in a world where the stakes were infinitely higher.

One more game—a big one.